CHEEKY
SPANKING STORIES

CHEEKY
SPANKING STORIES

EDITED BY
RACHEL KRAMER BUSSEL

CLEiS
PRESS

Published in the United States by Cleis Press, Inc., 2246 Sixth Street, Berkeley, California 94710.

Printed in the United States.
Cover design: Scott Idleman/Blink
Cover photograph: Fotosearch Premium
Text design: Frank Wiedemann

First Edition.
10 9 8 7 6 5 4 3 2 1

Trade paper ISBN: 978-1-57344-818-5
E-book ISBN: 978-57344-818-5

Contents

INTRODUCTION: THE VERY VARIED WORLD OF SPANKING DELIGHTS

Spanking fans, sometimes called spankos, come in many types, just as spankings do. Some people love the role-playing aspect, the way engaging in spanking allows them to enter another persona, become a heightened, kinkier version of themselves. All these and more are represented in this varied collection of spanking stories.

In some of these tales, spanking is simply a given, an innate part of a couple's (or single's) life, a way of communicating, connecting and loving. It's the ultimate give-and-take for the partners who engage in it, and they are able to read each other's verbal and physical cues. These are the characters who come prepared—or at least think they do—like the narrator in Shanna Germain's "Shine," who lays out a round leather paddle, a rawhide flogger with suede tails ("a mean little toy") and a metal zester. Germain delivers a before, during and after that is the type of story I know I will reread again and again. In my story "Marks," a couple embarks on a vacation to a nudist resort armed with spanking implements as well, but they get used in a way Emma, at first fearful of what her fellow vacationers will think of her kink desires, wasn't expecting.

"A Timely Correction," by Dorothy Freed, looks at a Master and sub where spanking is part and parcel of their relationship. Vincent is a stickler for punctuality; Lucy, not so much, and when her lateness finally makes him take her to task, she claims, "If I'd known what Vincent had planned for me, I might have stayed on the plane." One can't help but think she's a bit of an unreliable narrator at that moment, or rather, that she captures the way many who want spankings also want to act like they don't. Perhaps it's even more complex than that: Lucy wants to get spanked, but by entering into an agreement where Vincent determines how hard and how long, she has forfeited her agency, which, protest though she might, turns her on very, very much.

For other characters, spanking unfolds as part of a burgeoning relationship, or there's a shift in who's doing the spanking and who's getting spanked. In "Proxy," by Lucy Hughes, when a man's lover isn't available, a stranger is sent to his home to do the deed, while his lover watches by webcam. There, the actions may be the same, but the intent behind them, and the reason lonely Zach submits, are different and arousing anew. Hughes draws out the tension between all three characters to its maximum effect. She writes, "Zach loved the fact that both of them were enjoying themselves at his expense," capturing the thrill of pure submission.

Then there are the curious characters, including writer Ms. Patterson, in Donna George Storey's "The Assignment," who goes to investigate a professional spank daddy and winds up getting a very personal, gonzo journalism look at how he's become so successful. In Elizabeth Coldwell's "The Spanking Salon," a woman sneaks into the famed Salon to slake her curiosity and becomes the centerpiece of the action, much to her delight. Other surprises include the woman vacationing in Giselle Renarde's "Butch Girls Don't Cry" and the titular "Bad Boy" in Isabelle Gray's story, who expresses his shock outright, while the woman spanking him calmly continues delivering her blows, making him see not only the error of his ways, but that being "punished," with his own belt no less, is something he didn't know he would enjoy quite so much.

Other stories simply revel in the art of spanking, in the way it affects so many senses at once, in how lost the spanker and spankee can get in their actions. In "Echo," by J. Sinclaire, the semipublic setting adds to the naughtiness of a very thorough, loud and glorious encounter.

As Shanna Germain writes after the spanking scene in "Shine," "Somewhere, the pinpricks of pain become a flush, a burn, a test that I have endured and won. My ass radiates heat as though I have a fever. And the rest of me moves into a space that is beyond anything else, beyond pain, beyond the soft brush of Rob's fingers along my clit, beyond the soft mews that come from my mouth." That sense of victory, of pain turned into something so much more, of communion with a partner through the act of spanking, is what makes these stories come alive and what makes them so powerful.

Rachel Kramer Bussel
New York City

THE PERFECT DOM

Lucy Felthouse

*S*pank *me.* Is that an invitation?"

Shit. Mia had completely forgotten about him. Her flat-mate, Katy, had asked if it was okay if her brother stayed on their sofa for a couple of nights. His own place was being fitted with a new bathroom and conditions over there weren't exactly hygienic. Mia had been rushing around in order to get to work and hadn't really been paying attention, so she'd just agreed and then promptly forgotten.

Now, however, she was being treated to a huge and incredibly embarrassing reminder. Katy was on a night shift at the hospital so when Mia had woken up at nine in the evening—her own body clock being on that of working in the club, though tonight was her night off—she'd deemed it safe to wander to the kitchen to get a drink in what she was wearing.

Big mistake. Alex was sitting on the sofa, an eyebrow quirked and a leering grin on his face. He held his iPad, and earphones hung around his neck. He'd obviously been watching a film or playing some ridiculous game before Mia had flipped the light on and sauntered through the living room in nothing but a skimpy vest and hot pants. The hot pants were, of course, what he was referring to. The fuchsia garment had SPANK ME emblazoned across the ass in large black lettering.

Mia gave Alex a look that would have turned a lesser man to stone. He, however, simply grinned even more widely, then said, "Well? Do you need a firm hand to that luscious butt of yours? Like a spanking, do you?"

Mia sighed. "Shut up, Alex. It's none of your business. I'm just getting a drink. Get back to your damn gadget and leave me alone."

"Oooh, someone's defensive. I'm just saying, you must have those on for a reason. A statement like that printed on your back-side would definitely be construed as an invitation in my book."

"Well, maybe it *is* an invitation, Alex. But it's certainly not directed at you. Now if you'd kindly stop passing judgment on my nonexistent sex life I'll get my drink and get out of your way."

Without giving him a chance to reply, Mia flounced off into the kitchen and made herself a drink. As she stood at the sink, Alex's voice came from right behind her, startling her and making her drop the glass. Luckily, it fell a mere couple of inches into the sink, but it didn't stop Mia from turning furiously to Alex to give him a piece of her mind.

"What?" Alex said, his hands spread wide in supplication as he received yet another cool stare. "All I said was that if the invitation *was* directed at me, I'd definitely take you up on it. And I'd do it right, too."

Mia felt a mixture of embarrassment and anger color and heat her face as Alex's gaze assessed her from top to bottom. Much to her surprise, a further jolt of heat hit her groin and her nipples stiffened against the thin material of her vest top.

She put it down to the fact that she was going through a dry patch. After all, if you go long enough without a good seeing-to, people you wouldn't normally consider start to look more and more attractive. Any port in a storm and all that. And as for Alex's boast that he'd do it right, well...

"Really? I'd like to see you try."

Fuck. Where had that come from? The look on Alex's face told Mia that she had in fact said the words out loud. He was totally taken aback. He obviously hadn't expected his blatant flirting to get him anywhere, and now she was challenging him.

Now that Mia had said the words, had laid down the challenge, she actually wanted to go through with it. She'd never looked at Alex that way—she'd always thought he was an arrogant ass—but that arrogance had to come from somewhere. Perhaps, despite the personality she'd always found so abrasive, he was exactly what she'd been looking for. The perfect Dom. Someone who could give her exactly what she wanted—and needed. He might not be, of course, but if Mia didn't at least find out she'd kick herself. One of her favorite philosophies was "I'd rather regret something I *did* do, than something I didn't." She just hoped that Alex wasn't all mouth and no trousers.

"Seriously?" he said, not managing to keep the shock out of his voice.

Mia gave a curt nod. It was now or never.

"Well," said Alex, his surprised expression melting into a somewhat predatory one, "I don't have to be asked twice."

With that, he hoisted Mia into a fireman's lift and strode to her bedroom. Pulling the door closed behind them, he deposited her unceremoniously onto the bed and uttered a single word that made a gush of cream soak the offending hot pants.

"Toys?" It was a question and a command at the same time.

Mia felt a delicious heat curl throughout her entire body at

Alex's tone. He'd slipped into the role so effortlessly it was clear to Mia that he was experienced at this. Much more so than she was, Mia suspected. She'd never played with an actual Dom before. Sure, she'd been tied up and spanked, but it had all been just play and experimentation with previous partners. Nobody had ever given her a really good, hard spanking. They'd always been too frightened of hurting her. And Mia had never been able to say that she wanted it harder—much harder.

She yearned to be spanked so hard that she cried and came at the same time, but she'd never felt able to express that need before. Until Alex. She'd obviously never been in the presence of a true Dominant before. And now that she was, she intended to take full advantage. Whether it would go any farther than one night, Mia had no idea. But even one night was better than none, and it would at least satisfy the craving that had been building up inside her for so long, threatening to drive her crazy.

Yes, Mia thought, *a temporary respite is definitely better than none.*

"Under the bed," she said. Then, without thinking, she added, "Sir."

Alex had bent to reach under her bed, and he paused momentarily at the word "Sir." Then, a devious expression appeared on his face and he continued in his quest to retrieve her toy box. Somehow, Mia knew there was no going back now. It was Game On.

What's more, she didn't care. She'd never been so ready to play.

Alex swiftly brought the large black box out from its hiding place and lifted it onto the bed. Flipping open the lid, he examined the contents. Mia saw a glint in his eye—he was obviously pleased. She sat still and silent, watching and awaiting his instructions.

Alex reached into the box and pulled out a black leather paddle, adorned with metal studs. Mia's pussy clenched with anticipation. Holding the handle in one hand, Alex held out the other and applied a swift blow to the palm. A loud crack rang out, and Mia watched as a smug grin spread across Alex's face. He'd chosen his weapon. With a flick of his wrist, Alex whacked his palm again.

"I like it," he said, his grin widening. "It delivers a good hard blow for a minimum of effort. And I will *make* the effort."

The obvious ramifications of this remained unspoken. Then, before Mia could give it too much thought, Alex moved around to the other side of the bed and sat on the edge of the mattress, his feet still touching the floor. His next words made Mia's stomach lurch.

"Come here." His position made it clear which one he expected Mia to adopt. Quickly, eagerly, she scrambled off the bed and then closed the space between her and Alex. Then she draped herself over his lap and waited.

She thought about the view Alex had—her ass high, ready and covered with those provocative words. That blatant invitation. SPANK ME. Mia could hardly believe that the hot pants she'd grabbed out of her drawer and pulled on for bed without a second thought had resulted in this.

Seconds later, all thoughts were driven out of her head except for one—*ouch*. Without warning, Alex had begun his assault on her ass. She'd been expecting him to pull the hot pants down, so the blow had caught her completely unawares. The noise fell from her lips before she could stop it.

"Owwww!" She managed to stop herself from moving a hand up to cover herself. Somehow, she knew just making the noise had already made things worse. She tensed, awaiting her punishment.

"Oh, Mia," Alex said in a bored voice. "You're not a moaner, are you? I can't abide moaners."

He paused. "Okay," he continued. "I'm feeling generous, so you get that one for free. But from now on I expect you to take everything I give with the minimum of fuss. All right?"

Mia nodded frantically. After all, she'd wanted this. She *did* want this. Even if her brain hadn't quite caught up, her body was certainly making its feelings known. With just one smack her nipples were rock hard and straining against her top, and her clit throbbed.

And that was just the warm-up.

"Sorry, what did you say, Mia? I didn't hear you."

Shit. She wasn't doing very well here. She needed to shape up or she'd be in serious trouble. Opening her mouth, she practically gasped, "Minimum of fuss. Yes, Sir."

"Very good, Mia. Now, before I proceed, I'd like to know your safeword. I don't expect you'll want to use it, but I am nothing if not thorough."

A shiver ran down Mia's spine at his words. *Thorough. He was going to be thorough.* Her pussy squeezed at nothing and Mia closed her eyes and sucked in a breath.

"Mango, Sir. My safeword is mango."

"Very well. Thank you, Mia."

With that, Alex began his *thorough* campaign. Mia felt him move and squeezed her eyes more tightly closed, anticipating the first blow. It came immediately, followed by another, and another. Alex was clearly the master of the paddle because he kept the spanks coming in rapid succession, yet he never hit the same place twice in a row.

As Mia had expected, Alex spanked her much harder than anyone had ever done before. Soon, her bottom and the backs of her thighs felt like one big hot glowing...thing. Mia couldn't work out exactly what it felt like. Except for fucking *good*. Alex brought the metal-studded paddle down again and again on each millimeter of her ass and thighs. Then when he was done, he started again. He was doing it much harder now, having worked out that Mia wasn't as delicate as she looked.

Before long, Mia couldn't think of anything except how she *felt*. The pain had long ago morphed into pure pleasure, and she was sure her pussy was so slick and open that even her thickest dildo would slide right in without any resistance. Her clit felt like an over-inflated balloon, like the merest touch would make it burst. She *wanted* to burst. Oh, god, did she want to burst.

She wriggled slightly on Alex's lap, hoping that she could get some friction from somewhere, *anywhere*. Just enough to tip her over the edge and give her the orgasm she was so desperate for.

Alex froze. *Fuck*. She'd been rumbled.

"What are you doing, Mia?" he said coldly.

There was no point in lying. He'd know. "I'm s-sorry, Sir. It's just that—" she tailed off, unsure now what exactly it was that she wanted. Did she just want to come, or did she want more than that? Did she want Alex to fuck her? Did he want to fuck *her*? She'd been so lost in her own pleasure that she hadn't noticed if he had an erection or not. A twitch beneath her hip indicated that the answer to that question was a definite *yes*.

"Just what, Mia?"

"I'm just so horny, Sir. I'm desperate to come." She cringed. What would he do next? Would he make her take more strikes for being so bold? Or would he leave her high and dry? She had no idea how these things worked. Did Doms and subs always fuck? Or did some of them just give and receive pain? Mia had no idea. The only thing she knew for sure was that by the time the evening was out she would have to come, one way or another. She was almost dizzy with desperation. Or that could have just been the blood rushing to her head as she dangled over Alex's lap.

"Well," said Alex, "you're in luck." Pushing Mia unceremoniously off his lap, he waited until she picked herself up off the carpet, then tossed the leather paddle behind him. She'd barely scrambled to her feet when he continued. "Luckily for you, I'm desperate to come, too. Get those off."

He indicated her clothes. She immediately undressed. Alex stood up and did the same. As he'd only been lounging around on the sofa, he was only wearing a T-shirt and jeans. He pulled them off to reveal a tight pair of gray boxer shorts, which were straining against his erection. They also did nothing to hide the wet patch of precome, the sign that he was every bit as aroused by what they'd been doing as she was. She squeezed her thighs together, enjoying the slight relief it gave her and hoping against hope that she'd get full relief, and soon.

Hooking his thumbs into the waistband, Alex pulled the boxers down and dropped them to the floor. Mia risked a glance at his cock, hoping his male pride would allow her to look without getting into too much trouble. It did. Alex's cock was delicious. Long and thick with a slight curve, it jutted proudly up toward his belly button.

Clearly deciding she'd had enough time to look, Alex moved onto the bed properly, positioning himself in the middle, with his head on the pillows. Then he issued his next order. "Condom."

Rushing to the other side of the bed, Mia quickly opened her bedside drawer and retrieved the contraception, holding it out to him.

"No. You do it."

With slightly trembling hands, Mia tore open the packet and dropped it on the floor. Then she clambered onto the bed and positioned herself between Alex's thighs. Grasping his hard, hot cock, she placed the condom on its tip then rolled it down, coating the thick shaft in latex. Then she waited. But not for long.

"Hop on, Mia. Sink that hot pussy down on my cock and ride me."

As she willingly obliged, her nether lips parting around his meaty bell-end, Alex spoke again. "You get this one for free, baby. But only because I'm so desperate to fuck. Next time you're going to have to work much harder for it. *Much* harder."

As his words sunk into her brain, and his cock sunk into her cunt, Mia smiled. As much as she was about to enjoy her freebie, she knew it would be so much better when she'd earned it. *Really* earned it.

Alex really was the perfect Dom. He knew exactly what she needed, and how to give it. More so than she did, apparently.

Thank fuck for those stupid hot pants.

BIRTHDAY BOY

Cecilia Duvalle

Marta's fingers trembled. She dropped the black cord she had been struggling with and pushed her palms flat onto the counter in front of her, willing herself into a state of calmness. She met her reflection in the mirror and sucked in air until her lungs seemed ready to explode. She let the breath out in a long slow hiss before returning to the task of lacing up the leather corset she'd purchased just the week before.

The softness of the leather had surprised her. In the pictures of women wearing such things, the corsets seemed so stiff and unyielding, but in fact the fabric was pliable and comfortable against her skin. Just smelling the sweet muskiness of it sent shivers of expectation through her body. The stiff boning provided the structure without reducing the erotic suppleness of the leather against her bare skin. She tightened the strings to cinch in her waist for a bit more shape but left it loose enough that she could still breathe. She had no desire to pass out.

She turned to the floor-to-ceiling mirror behind her for the full effect. The short skirt, the matching corset and the knee-high boots were over the top, but that's what she had been aiming for. Something new. Something dramatic, transformative. She looked fucking hot. The outfit hid the flaws of her aging body and augmented her assets. No panties underneath left her with an airy and exotic buzzy feeling between her legs. Just seeing her reflection was enough to get her juices flowing. She clenched her thighs together in response to the growing warmth and to keep the liquid from flowing like a river into her boots.

She glanced at her iPhone on the counter. She had less than ten minutes before Carl was supposed to arrive. He'd sounded rather bemused by her directions but did not question them. He was going to be expecting sex. But did he have any idea what she really had in mind?

"Meet me at the Alexis Hotel at seven, Room Seven-Thirty-Five," she'd said when he asked about their plans for the evening. She'd assured him that his birthday would be fun. She had never actually asked him about what she had planned. It was just awkward. How do you talk to someone you've been married to for twenty years about sex? What hasn't been said? What possibly could be new? It turned out there was plenty on both counts, and Marta was beginning a new dialogue. She just hoped he would engage—and she hoped he would do it without laughing at her.

The seed for the evening had been planted a year before. She'd been reading a story from a dirty magazine as part of their foreplay. His reaction to the story had been dramatic. His cock had grown harder with every syllable as she read to him. Later, as she rode him cowgirl style, she grabbed his wrists, pushing them into the mattress, and pinned him in place. They had both come fast and hard before collapsing into breathless giggles of mutual contentment. Pretty simple play, but it was the start.

She began reading more stories to him and after a while, she put two and two together. Those that involved the woman taking charge made him harder faster and caused him to last longer than other stories. The sex that followed was hot, wet and more than satisfying. She'd begun to spend more time on top of him, and she had ventured into some dirty talk. After years together in what she had decided was "vanilla silence," that little bit had seemed daring and bold. She'd not, as yet, taken the chance to play out any of the kinkier scenarios she'd read to him, the things that made him groan aloud and had him raging hard and ready to be fucked. Those stories involved the man on his knees, tied up, or with a red and painful ass, and required the woman to be in command. She'd needed time to imagine herself in the role, to figure it out.

Google became her friend. She bought books, read articles and even went to a class at the local sex toy store. She was pretty sure living "the lifestyle," as it was called, was out of the question for them. But private play every now and again would fit into their life and busy schedules, or at least, she hoped it would.

That's why her fingers had been uncooperative. Nerves. There was some chance she could be wrong about Carl's true proclivities or her ability to bring life to the role for which she was now dressed. He could arrive at the hotel, take one look at her and burst out laughing. Of course, if he did, she might have a better reason to give his ass a very good spanking than just the birthday whacks she was planning. That thought sent a clear, sharp message straight to her pussy and got her juices flowing again.

She made one more quick tour of the room. The honeymoon suite at the Alexis was set up for sex. The bathroom sported a Jacuzzi soaking tub for two. The metal-framed, four-poster bed looked as if it had been designed for bondage. A movable folding mirror stood off to the side of the bed. The room came equipped with a lovers' package of massage oils, condoms and other accoutrements, though she had brought her own toys. She set these out on the table next to the bed, whose multiple pillows and covers she removed.

The knock on the door sent her stomach hurtling into a new dimension. The moment of truth had arrived. She gave herself a quick once-over in the mirror and still loved what she saw. As she opened the door, she stood back so that Carl could take in her entire presence.

He just stood there. His eyes went round and his mouth worked up and down like someone who might be talking with the volume on zero. He turned around to look behind him, and she thought he might just leave. Then he turned back toward her with the same confused expression.

"Carl, come inside. You look like an idiot," she said. Marta wasn't sure where that order or commanding tone of voice had come from. She'd not practiced it, and it had flown out of her mouth as if she'd rehearsed it just for him.

"Marta," he said on the exhalation of breath, both an affirmation and confirmation. His acquiescent body told her all she needed to know. Wonder mixed with acceptance, desire and relief crossed his face. After twenty years with the same man, sometimes words weren't necessary. And sometimes, they were just impossible.

Better yet, there was no laughing. The unspoken moment had turned her stomach upright and given her that little oomph out of insecurity and worry into an abrupt state of clarity and control. No more shaking hands. Certainty flooded through her. It was better than any high she'd ever experienced.

"Of course it's me," she said, as if it could have been anyone else. She spun on the toes of her shiny boots and motioned for him to follow her into the room. She didn't look over her shoulder. She didn't need to. It was a powerful moment to know that he would step inside, shut the door and be right behind her.

"Get naked, Carl," she said.

His eyes hadn't left her, and he hadn't said anything but her name. His hands flew to the paisley tie that set off the navy blue of his Van Heusen shirt. Marta watched his every move, willing her intense scrutiny to unnerve him just a little bit. By the time he'd reached the last button of his shirt, his hands were trembling more than hers had been just minutes before.

Her pussy was burning with impatient wanting. She could almost be happy with just fucking him in that moment, making use of his ready hard-on, but such an impulsive taking would spoil her plans. She squeezed her thighs together again and reminded herself that it would just be that much better if she waited until she had completed the task at hand.

"So," he said, "I don't think I've seen that outfit before."

"I didn't say you could talk, Carl. Just get undressed."

His mouth opened and shut again, his lips making a sort of quiet smacking sound when they touched. Then, as if considering what she had said, he nodded while pulling at his belt buckle. When he was down to just his boxers he looked over at the bed and back at Marta. The look she gave him made him remove those as well, and then he stood there in his nakedness, cock erect and raring to go. With nothing on, and nothing else to do, his hands floated around for a moment, as if looking for a natural place for them, before landing on his cock, more out of habit than anything else.

"No," Marta commanded. "Don't touch yourself. Get on the bed, facing the mirror, on your hands and knees."

"Yes, Ma'am," he said, his hands flying off his cock and

onto his hips. He made a beeline for the bed and scrambled into position.

"I don't think I've ever given you a proper birthday spanking," she said, as if it was a wistful thought that had just come to her. She moved in against the bed, pressing her upper thighs and pussy against the tall mattress, her face near his.

Carl's cheeks flushed, but he didn't say anything. He just lifted his head enough so he could look at her in the reflection of the mirror.

"You turned forty-five today. Do you think you can handle it?" she asked, her words a hot and gentle buzzing against his ear. "Forty-five whacks plus one for good measure?"

"Yes, oh...yes, I think so," he said.

She pressed her ear against his and met his eyes in the mirror before he dropped his head. It was like reading his mind. The look he gave her in that split second conveyed such subtle nuance of desire that only someone who understood and knew him the way she did would have caught it.

"Oh, look at you blush," she teased. "You're going to be red on all your cheeks soon enough, sweetheart."

She reached over, pressed her hand against Carl's still-tight ass and caressed the firm round globes. She gave a silent prayer up to the powers that be that he hadn't become some old fat-assed couch potato.

Carl's soft groan at her touch was the final confirmation she needed to know her instincts had all been dead-on. She picked up the paddle and tapped it on her thigh, testing the pressure of her swing. The gentle sting had her suck in her breath. This could hurt. She held it up at a good distance from his face so he could see it.

"I special ordered this from Etsy," she said and laughed. The solid Koa wood paddle was beautiful, but the notion of ordering it off the arts and crafts website had been rather funny and deliciously naughty at the same time.

Carl swallowed hard as he looked at the paddle. He glanced at her in the mirror with serious eyes and bobbed his head just an inch in acknowledgment.

She placed the paddle on the center of his neck and drew an imaginary line down the center of his back, placing no pressure on his spine. She circled his buttocks with the cool wood, teasing and taunting him with the smooth edge and lack of any actual spanking. Then she ran the paddle down the outside of his thighs, across his bottom, up the inside of his thighs and cupped his balls with the large flat end of the wood.

Goose bumps coursed over his arms and legs, and he let out a slight whimper as she pushed his balls upward and toward his hard, erect cock. She touched his chin with the back of her free hand, scrubbing at his evening shadow.

"Look at how excited you are, Carl. Whimpering—and I haven't even hit you, yet," she said. She dropped the paddle from his balls and tapped it lightly between his thighs, back and forth several times. He squirmed under the movement in obvious desire. She'd never seen him so hungry with such want, such need.

She pressed the paddle against the roundest part of his left asscheek, pulled back her arm and hit him a little harder than she'd just hit her own thigh. The slapping sound of wood against skin was sharp and loud in the quiet of the room.

His head swiveled to look at her. His lower lip disappeared into his mouth for a second and then he said, "Um...that wasn't very hard, sweetheart."

"I'm just warming up, Carl. From this moment on, the only thing you are allowed to say is 'Yes, Ma'am,'" she said, hitting his other cheek with the exact same intensity she had just used.

He would be crying by the time she was done with him.

"Yes, Ma'am," Carl said. His shoulders sagged, and Marta sensed disappointment in the motion.

Marta's temper flared. She was ready to deliver on the promise, and there was no room for his attitude. She'd beat it out of him if she needed to. She wanted that whimper of his back, and she was going to have it.

She hit him much harder than the first two attempts, aiming for a spot just a bit lower on his left asscheek, and followed that hit with an identical one on the opposite side. Carl's head jerked up for a moment in surprise. She had his attention, and the newest marks were brighter.

She glanced at him in the mirror and saw the top of his head. Was he contemplating the stinging of his ass, was he bowing his head in submission or was he avoiding her gaze out of shame? She hoped it was all three. Her pussy throbbed at the thought.

She reached around, pulled at his hard cock and slapped it with her hand. Not very hard, just enough to remind him she was in charge. No need to add any words. The message was clear. Then she began to spank him in earnest. Each slap of the paddle sounded off in the room like a firecracker. The crispness of the slaps sent wave after wave of satisfaction through Marta. After she'd reached twenty strokes, she paused to look at the color of his ass and admire the even lines of red welling up along the round curve of his bottom.

Every time she hit him, he either stifled a whimper or a moan. He was putting forth an effort to remain silent.

His upper arms were shaking from exertion, and his head hung down to his elbows. Marta put the paddle down on the bed next to his knee and picked up one of the pillows she'd tossed aside earlier. She massaged his shoulders and helped him change his position so he was supported on the pillow and his upper body, giving his arms a much-needed break. His face was beet red, and he avoided her gaze.

"Not even halfway there," she said. "You think you can handle the rest, baby?"

"Yes, I don't want you to stop," he said. His voice was subdued and husky.

"Excuse me?"

"I meant, 'Yes, Ma'am.'"

"That's better."

She kissed his forehead and picked up the paddle again. She didn't know if this broke spanking protocol—it was her first time, after all. She didn't care. There was something different and hot about having Carl on his knees in front of her. The flush on his face nearly matched the bright pink of his ass, and it was an amazing, powerful feeling.

"No more stopping, Carl, but it's okay for you to whimper, or groan, or cry," she said.

And then she laid into him. She'd found what she thought was the upper limit of his pain threshold. Each swat elicited a small grunting sound from Carl, and his fingers grew white as they grasped the pillow he was holding onto. Marta found a rhythm and concentrated on the exact placement of the paddle. She moved up and down his ass, back and forth from left to right, to keep things even.

She spanked and teased. She made fun of his rigid cock, taunted him about getting off on being naked on his knees, and spanked again. By the time she hit forty-five, his ass was bright scarlet, and his body was shaking. Marta had never felt so alive. Her thighs were wet down to her knees, and her face glowed with the pleasure of finding a groove—and what a groove it was. His grunts transitioned into whimpers of pain.

"And one for good measure," she said. This final swat was

aimed right in the middle of his ass, at the most curved part of the crack.

Carl's sobs turned into a cry of relief. He had made it through the entire spanking without begging her to stop.

Marta placed the paddle on the table next to the bed before grabbing Carl's hips and rubbing his bright-red ass with her warm hands, soothing the sting. His flesh was hot to the touch, covered in long stripes of raw pain. She leaned over and kissed each cheek.

"You did it, baby," she said. She was proud of him. She'd spanked his ass good and hard, and it was clear that it hadn't been a walk in the park for him.

She guided him onto his back, baring his naked eagerness to her. He couldn't look away or hide his face any longer, but the redness from his humiliation remained.

"Thank you," he managed. "Did I do okay?" His wet eyes met hers for the first time since she'd started spanking him before flickering away again.

Marta climbed on top of him, trapping his cock in her pussy and his wrists in her hands above his head. She looked at her own reflection in the mirror as she took possession of him. What she saw was a woman filled with raw energy and power. She liked this new conversation with Carl.

"Yeah, you did great, sweetie. For the first round, anyway."

UNWRAPPING

Craig J. Sorensen

You stand, still as a startled rabbit measured by a circling cougar. You look so polished in your silver silk blouse, the antique silver pendant dangling down your chest. The monochrome of your light clothes and jewelry brings your warm cinnamon skin to life, accents the gold-brown hair brushing your shoulders. You look tactile, stylish, warm and so out of place here in my cold domain. So stunning, I almost forget why I brought you down.

Almost.

Your eyes follow me, questioning. I pause behind you and study the curve of your butt beneath your perfectly fitted white linen pants. I almost grip it. I circle and your eyes, big and brown, ascend until you tip your head back and meet my gaze. Your eyelids are painted soft silver but are wrapped in razor surprise. You bite your lip, and I think you may want to smile. You have to know what this is about.

I reach between your breasts and you hold your breath. I

release the top button of your blouse. You exhale just slightly
and I open the next button. The tiny strip of shiny fabric at the
center of your rib cage comes into view, joins the silver cups of
your bra. "You know why we're here, don't you?"

You shake your head ever so gently.

I trace up the inside of your blouse to the collar, then back to
the next button that remains clasped. You cannot deny it. Don't
even try.

You exhale fully and reach up, the silver rings on your fingers
and thumb sparkle like your long, manicured silver nails. You
circle the big ring on your right index finger and start to pull it
off.

I push your hand back down. "Leave it on, Erin." I stare at
your blouse.

You bite your lip. There is a hint of a smile, and you lift your
brow. You continue what I started and open each button down
your stomach, pause briefly to look in my eyes again before you
pull the tail of your blouse out from your pants. You unbutton
each of your cuffs. Your arms fall limp.

I reach up to your collar and open your blouse, ease it down
over your shoulders. Again your eyes tilt ever so slightly to look
at me. Don't give me that look. You have to know what this
is about. One close look at the boxes, carefully and precisely
stacked, was all it took for me to know. "You know what you
did."

You shake your head again.

When you're in the mood for such adventures, when you are
receptive, you send the signals, loud and clear. You parade in
your short black skirt and matching spaghetti strap top. You
strip your jewelry except for your wedding band. Maybe I have
given you a subtle cue, maybe you conjure words that push my
buttons and bring my anger to a soft boil. You get that defiant

look, jut your slim chin, purse your full lips. You cross your arms in front of you, tilt your hands backward to expose your wrists in surrender, begging my hand to consume them. It's been a long time since you did that.

But now you are in white and silver, your hands occasionally lift to your hips and flirt with your usual decisive stance. You reach for that ring again.

I shake my head, "I said, leave it on."

Your arms again fall haplessly. The confusion in your expression deepens. "What's this about?"

"Ah, you haven't lost your voice."

"I mean if you want to—"

"Quiet." I shake my head softly. I reach toward the top of your pants, and your butt arches away from me slightly. I let my hand hover just in front of the base of your stomach, rub my thumb against my fingers like a thief about to measure the tumblers in a safe. Your waist slowly returns to my grasp. I pull the tail of your silver belt from the side of its buckle and release it.

I unclasp the top of your pants. You look at the worktable, and your eyebrows lift in realization. Yes, I've taken the leather cuffs from the bedroom and affixed them to my workbench. You suck your lips inside your mouth and pull a deep breath thorough your nose. I've strapped you down many times before, but never for this. Do you still not get it?

You grin. Wait, Erin, this is not a game. I ensure my expression leaves no doubt as I circle you again. If you were in your short black skirt, right now you'd be obediently pulling your panties off and kicking them away. Now you remain eerily still. I pause again in front of you, and I take the tab of your zipper between my thumb and forefinger. I ease it down. You watch as it slowly descends.

I fold my arms and take a step back. "Do I need to say it?"

After a moment, your thumbs peel the sides of your pants over your hips. They fall into a snowy drift around your silver stilettos. "Jon, this isn't how we—"

"No, it's not. This isn't the place. This isn't the way. I'm glad this much is clear." That basement room is my domain. Tonight, it is all darkness except the bare bulb that illuminates us. You are like a delicate filament, as yet unlit. Flip a switch and you blaze like lightning, stretched taut, burning bright from the full charge. On your small bra, thin mercury ripples raise then smooth out with your deep, nervous, deliberate breaths. Your pubic hair forms a soft puffy mound at the southernmost point of your panties. "Step from your pants, Erin."

Your high heels clack like walnuts falling on the concrete floor. I hook my boots under your fallen blouse, toss it to the side from the sharp light into the shadows, then do the same to the pants. You scowl. You're mad I'm treating your good clothes like this, aren't you?

Good. Maybe you'll get this yet.

I stand at your side then take the elastic band at the top of your panties between thumb and forefinger. I circle again and pull the top elastic of your panties toward me. Your fair white tan line glows. "You know what you did."

"I—I really don't." Your voice is so soft I'm almost convinced.

I let the elastic top of your panties snap you, and you flinch. I pull one slim shoulder strap up. You are rigid, fixed. I like your consistency, your control, your assuredness, I always have. That's what vexed me so when I figured it out. Perhaps this is why I have not yet shown my hand. Will you surrender the truth with an air of mystery?

I set the strap carefully back down on your slender, carved shoulder. I place my thick middle finger behind your silver-studded ear, then trace your slim chin, elevate it slowly. Goose-flesh erupts at the base of every fine hair down your arm. I take your eyes in mine again. "So, what were you up to while I was away?"

Your brow crushes. "Nothing. I mean, you know, the usual." A composed shrug. Guilt?

"You know what I'm talking about."

"I don't, Jon. If you want to, you know, if you want to tie or spank—"

"Stop." I trace my rough thumb around your plump lips, bright and pink in the field of your moist tanned face. Your cheeks begin to blaze red, right through your meticulous makeup. "I don't want you to stumble, Erin. Step out of those shoes." You step down, so tiny now. Your silver toenails blaze against your dark feet. That floor is cold, isn't it? Your palms angle up from your forearms, parallel to the ground.

I kick your shoes away like a pair of .357 Magnums at the feet of a hardened criminal.

Should I give you a sample of what is to come? Will that render an admission? I smooth my palm over the triangle of slick fabric covering your butt and give the softest of taps. You gasp. There are times I've smacked it so hard you nearly fell over. You took all I could deliver, trusted me to stop, trusted me to know how much you needed. Would I even remember the safeword if you spoke it? Moot point, since you've never had to, have you, Erin? Trust.

Trust?

Your butt eases back into my hand. You close your eyes and stretch your throat back. It's the softest sigh I've ever heard. You smile again. You get it, but then you don't. I trace along your collarbone, up the ridges of your throat, then circle your chin. Thick hard nipples and buds poke from the thin bra. "Why do you think I used that delicate foil paper this year?"

You meet my eyes, inquisitive. You stiffen. "Foil paper?"

"The Christmas presents."

Your mouth goes slack, your eyes like a moon and its reflection over a still lake. Remember how we used to play strip poker until I had every last garment for the cost of maybe my socks and shirt? Remember how all you had to wager was a nice, nude, over-the-knee, bare-palm spanking, your hip pushing against my stretched zipper, then finally a long, at-my-will fuck, you stretched by leather cuffs across the bed?

Me fucking you and fucking you and fucking you for my pleasure alone? Oh, I love how you come when I take you like that.

I squeeze your dimpled chin between thumb and forefinger. "I had suspicions last year. But you're usually so controlled, so patient in every little thing, that I kind of didn't believe it. I still don't."

You let out a deep breath. You inhale the words, "Oh, shit." You really didn't think I'd be able to tell, did you?

"I knew that if you did it, you wouldn't be able to open the presents without marking that delicate foil paper. And I knew you couldn't rewrap them just the same as I did. I mean, you *are* good, but everyone does things a bit differently."

Your mouth gapes like an explanation is pending. You are utterly still.

"I bought each gift carefully. Some of them I made on this very workbench." I pat the top of the large table where I craft things, many of them for you, my treasure. I go from one side of the table to the other and position the cuffs up on the table. "I wrapped each one with love. It all took hours and hours and hours, Erin."

"I—oh, I know. I do, I..." Your voice is barely audible. Your eyes dance from cuff to cuff.

"Do you think I wanted to share in your surprise on Christmas morning? Have I ever surprised you with a present? And tell me, while I made things, were you coming down and 'sneaking a peek?'"

You lower your head. How many times have you said you honor the sanctity of my workspace? How many times have I said you can come in any time you like, unless I tie the ribbon to the doorknob, then please ask?

"The ribbon was on the door all of November, and you went right in, didn't you?"

Not a word.

"Didn't you, Erin?"

A shrug begets a gentle nod. "I—I didn't think—"

As mad as I've been, now I'm furious. I don't recall the last time I've been this pissed. "No, you didn't think. Step forward."

You do. You cross one foot in front of the other so your hips sway a bit, so your butt points out a bit more, the way you walk only when you're in black and stripped of jewelry. Those silver panties shimmer deep into the shadows of the basement like a black-light poster. You stop at the edge of the big table and look toward me only in your periphery.

"Bend over the workbench, Erin. Spread your hands wide."

Your favorite antique locket, four Christmases ago, clicks softly on the top of the simple gray table. Even in the dim glow I see the depth of your need, now that the true meaning of this consultation has been revealed. You did not marry me for my leather hands, large enough to cradle your butt easily when we make love, or punish it entirely, but you do like them so. Only once did you suggest that I make a paddle to your specific design. But I made it clear that I wanted to feel a measure of what I was distilling.

You accepted this, reluctantly.

Right now, I wish I had made that paddle. I'd love to use it. Hear the legs of the table dance on the cold concrete. Feel nothing in the palm of my hands but the vibrations of the handle, the same sensation in my hands I feel when I'm shaping with a hammer and chisel. That handmade jewelry box on your dresser, three Christmases ago. Remember?

I'd love to take you to that safeword. I guess my hand will have to get the job done.

I take one of the leather cuffs we've used so many times. You so love to be bound and helpless. You so love the tension of bindings or spankings. How will you feel about a cocktail composed of the two? Will that drive the point home? Will I smack you hard or soft? Maybe a teasing, gentle caress, the essence of a tickle, followed by a great, sudden swat, and you gasping. Will I finish you with a good, hard fuck over the workbench? No, right now it will be just hard, fast and to the point. The point. My fingers circle the fine silver Swiss watch I gave you last year. I pull it clear of the first cuff and bind. I ease the bracelet, with our names that I engraved on it right at this table two years ago, up to your hand and bind the other wrist. You pull a deep breath and look at me. You nod and bite your wet lower lip. You're ready. You want it.

You want it bad.

I take the top of your panties down to the base of your butt. You hold your breath audibly as I raise my right hand up, behind my head, so high that it touches the basement ceiling and you clam your eyes shut. I see that half smile, half grimace you get when you wear the black outfit. I can't wait to feel the snap of your tender flesh, hear how you echo in my workshop.

You want it?

Now a realization washes over me. My cock is so hard, and I want to spank you more than I ever have before, but I realize that this looks like just another coax. A big coax, but a coax just the same. Oh, Erin, I so want the pale surface of your untanned butt to glow so it'll look like Mars in the night sky. I want it so fucking bad. But what will you do next year, when I place my carefully selected and crafted presents under the tree and am away for more than an hour or two? I lean against the table. I ease your hair from your face over your ear and turn your chin so you are looking in my eyes.

Your eyes and mouth widen when I step back. "Jon?"

"I'm going to make one more present for you this year. And don't you dare open it."

You look puzzled, anticipating. A mischievous smile opens.

"No, it's not a game."

Your smile drains. "I understand." You push your butt up in the air a little bit.

"I'm not sure you do. One last gift, and I'll make it, wrap it carefully, lovingly. You will not open it."

"But—"

"You will not touch it. It will be the last gift you open on Christmas."

You remain flat across the top of the table. Your eyes probe with a question. You always ask for a hint on every present. Ironic, as you've opened every one when I am not around to share in the moment. Still, I oblige. "Wear black Christmas morning. Leave your jewelry in the chest. However, should you decide to open this last gift early, wear white. Wear anything but black all year round."

"Honey? Please?" You remain fixed to the table and your exposed butt arches as high as you can muster in this position.

I cover your tan line perfectly with the silver triangle of fabric, turn my hard cock to line up with my zipper. "Christmas is only two weeks away, Erin." I unbind your right wrist, and leave you to unbind the other. I walk up the stairs slowly. "Do I have to put a lock on this door, too?"

You peep, "No. No, Sir." You remain as if both hands are still cuffed. You even put your free hand back inside the open cuff like an offering to the widened mouth of a starved gator. You lift your butt again and I look at it. "Jon?" So very tempting. Oh, how I want to leave no doubt how I feel. Give you a spanking like never before. I take the doorknob in my hand and begin to close my fingers around it. I hear a soft sob. I've never heard that from you, and I want to run back down the stairs. I fight the door closed, find a ribbon in the junk drawer and tie it to the knob. I beg you not to open it after you come up. It will take me some time to make that last present just so.

I'll welcome you on my lap when you come up, hold you tight and tell you how much I adore you. If you apologize, I'll tell you I forgive you; I truly do. I'll fold you in my arms and carry you to our bed, my beautiful Erin. I'll massage and anoint you. I'll make love to you soft and sweet between fresh satin sheets. I'll cup your butt gently in my hands and curl it to gentle, long thrusts.

I know you will want more. When you need it, I know how you get. You don't stop wanting it. It sits in your mind, pokes at you like a long-held regret that you can't get past.

I've always been Johnny on the spot to quench that fire. Not tonight.

Perhaps you'll dare to dress in the black skirt and remove your jewelry before the twenty-fifth to tempt me. Parade that gorgeous butt in front of me, a few swirls of your hips. Oh, and I will be tempted. I'll be tempted to have you open your last gift first, and many days before the appointed time. I'll be tempted to take you back downstairs to where the cuffs shall remain, waiting, hungry to grip your naked wrists.

You will wait for it, Erin. We will wait for it.

Christmas. We will get it on Christmas morning, every last measure, but not a moment sooner.

I hear the door open. "Jon, I'm so sorry."

"Forgiven, Erin. I love you."

THE ASSIGNMENT

Donna George Storey

They say sex sells, and it does, but not for as much as you think. I'm a freelance writer, and recently I've begun to specialize in articles on sexuality, not because they pay better—they don't—but because I love to uncover secrets, tease out the bracing truth from convenient delusion. And when it comes to sex, there's no shortage of secrets and delusions.

So when an editor emailed to ask if I'd do a feature article on professional spank daddies, I jumped at the opportunity. A few years back I was in London browsing through a magazine and saw an ad in the personals inviting ladies who'd misbehaved to contact a certain Master Blake for a good spanking. At the time I thought, *Yeah right, what woman in her right mind would seek out and even pay some old guy to smack her ass?*

This was my chance to find out.

I immediately started checking around to line up some interviews. Thanks to my extensive network, I got the name of a guy who was the premier pay-for-play spank daddy in the city. His

name was Dr. Richard Armstrong, and he had an office in the
financial district. I rolled my eyes at the obvious pseudonym,
but sent off a quick email asking if he'd be willing to be inter-
viewed. Dr. Armstrong courteously replied within the day and
suggested we talk by phone.

Not surprisingly, Armstrong had a great phone voice—a
warm, smooth bass with a touch of crispness in the consonants.
I buttered him up a bit, told him that he'd come highly recom-
mended. He in turn expressed concern that he didn't want to
become the victim of sensationalist journalism. He explained
that he was a professional who helped clients with particular
needs, not unlike a physical or psychological therapist, or in his
case both. I promised I was committed to providing my readers
with a fair, intelligent report and told him I hoped we could
schedule an interview at his earliest convenience.

"Do we really need to meet in person?" he asked warily.

Now my curiosity was piqued. "I've found a face-to-face gives
me a more sensitive understanding of the key issues, Doctor."

There was a long silence.

My heart skipped a beat. Although I never put all my stock
in one source, I realized I would be genuinely disappointed if he
refused.

Finally he spoke. "Actually, I've done some research on
you myself, Ms. Patterson. You're an excellent journalist with
impressive credentials. Could you come to my office tomorrow
afternoon?"

I breathed a quiet sigh of victory. Once we'd settled on the
meeting time, the doctor bid me good night and said he was
very much looking forward to our appointment.

Given my racing pulse and decidedly damp panties, I had to
admit I was, too.

The good doctor's office suite was indeed located at a prime address, tucked away among investment banking offices and brokerage firms. The very proper older woman who was stationed at the receptionist's desk gave me a cool once-over.

"Ms. Patterson? You may go right in."

I pushed open the door to find the legendary spank doctor seated at a large desk framed by a gorgeous view of the city. I couldn't help noticing that he was pretty stunning himself— salt-and-pepper hair, strong Celtic features, and large, thick-fingered hands. The doctor was engrossed in a psychology journal, but he looked up as I entered. Our eyes locked. And I do mean "locked." His piercing blue gaze stopped me in my tracks, as if my shoes were riveted to the carpet.

As I stood there, frozen in place, my entire body began to pulse with a strange heat. Even my teeth tingled, as if the doctor's gaze alone had awakened a new sensitivity in every nerve.

At last he smiled. I exhaled, my body relaxing like a puppet on loosened strings.

"Thank you so much for taking the time to meet with me, Doctor Armstrong." To my relief, I sounded perfectly composed and professional.

"It's my pleasure, Ms. Patterson. Please sit down." He gestured to a comfortable leather armchair opposite his desk.

I slid into the chair, still somewhat rattled by those unsettling, sapphire eyes, and quickly pulled out my notebook and recorder.

"I'd like to begin the interview by asking how you got started..." My voice trailed off. The doctor clearly wasn't paying attention to me. On the contrary, he was busy attaching a sheet of paper to a clipboard, which he pushed across the desk at me.

"Take your time filling this out, Ms. Patterson. The more detailed your answers, the more helpful it will be to both of us."

Instinctively, I picked up the clipboard. The paper was a questionnaire, obviously for a client, requesting specific information: *preferred "play" name; religious upbringing; relationship status; if attached, does your partner know of your visit? Age of first orgasm, intercourse, and spanking, if any; describe your favorite spanking fantasy or fantasies (you may request additional paper, if necessary).*

I laughed. "This is fascinating. May I keep it as a reference for my article?"

Dr. Armstrong frowned. "I will be happy to provide you with another copy, but I expect you to complete this one in your own handwriting and with complete honesty. I always begin a client relationship with an in-depth consultation."

"But I'm not here as a client."

"Surely you agree that a deeper level of inquiry will make your article more *sensitive* to the issues?"

My jaw dropped. "Are you suggesting that I participate in a spanking session with you for the sake of my article?"

"Most certainly not. I'm suggesting that you experience a consultation, which involves no physical contact whatsoever. If you'll be satisfied with answers to the same tedious questions most journalists ask me, you'll find them on my website on the press page."

I winced. The doctor had a point about a good journalist delving deeper, but wasn't *I* the interviewer here?

"We do this my way, Ms. Patterson, or not at all," he insisted.

I'm not quite sure why I picked up the pen and started to fill out the form, but I did. I even answered each question truthfully. I was raised Catholic but no longer attended church; had my first orgasm at fifteen, first intercourse at eighteen; had no actual spanking experience, but had definitely fantasized about contacting Master Blake of London to see what he had on offer.

I also enjoyed imagining a kinky scene where my high school principal paddled me for doing it with my boyfriend behind the bleachers during a pep rally. Then the old goat was so overcome with lust at the sight of my naked bum that he took me from behind over his desk.

The assignment completed, I passed the clipboard back to Dr. Armstrong with a shrug.

He glanced over my responses, then flashed me a very warm smile. "Thank you for your cooperation. I've had some unfortunate dealings with interviewers, and this was my way of testing your sincerity. I'm at your service now, but I do hope it was valuable for you to get a sense of what it's like to be a new client."

I had to laugh. "Actually I did learn a lot. How do your real clients deal with such intimate questions?"

"The women who come to me are confident in their desires. They enjoy being dominated and appreciate my professional approach to establishing the parameters of my services."

"Indeed, while we're on that topic, Doctor, exactly what type of services do you provide?"

He leaned back in his chair, clearly relishing the chance to elaborate on his area of expertise. "That varies with the client and her level of experience. Many novices are satisfied with verbal chastisement culminating in a mild administration of the hand or paddle, just enough to keep them remembering the session for the rest of the day. The more seasoned veterans have built up a tolerance and seek variety in the implements— crops, canes, belts, hairbrushes. They appreciate my specialty— maximum sensation with minimal marking—especially if their partners are unaware of their sessions with me, although I'm confident my therapy has a positive effect beyond this office. A select group of special clients are permitted to request additional services. For example, I'll allow them to masturbate in my presence after their spanking or let them perform fellatio on me, if the request falls within the proper guidelines."

I immediately pictured a naked woman with a rosy bottom kneeling before the doctor to take his stiff cock in her mouth. Flustered by the obscene image, I spoke without thinking. "I see. Do you also have intercourse with these 'special clients,' Doctor?"

Armstrong's serene expression immediately darkened. "Ms. Patterson, you are showing your appalling ignorance of the type of eroticism I offer here. Spanking is an art, not a cover for male prostitution."

My face flamed with embarrassment at my faux pas, exactly the kind of cheap journalism he wanted to avoid. "I'm so sorry, Doctor Armstrong. That was terribly insensitive of me."

My hasty apology seemed to placate him. "Perhaps we can avoid such misunderstandings in the future if you look over some of the introductory materials I give to my first-time clients?"

I nodded vigorously. "I look forward to learning more."

"Then this is a good time to take a break. Can we follow up tomorrow afternoon at this same hour?"

"I appreciate the second chance, Doctor."

Escorting me to the reception area, the doctor told his assistant to "give Ms. Patterson the introductory reading and *An Education*." With a final nod to me, he disappeared into his office.

Smirking, the woman walked over to a well-stocked bookshelf in the corner of the room. The first book she handed over was a slim paperback with a plain blue cover entitled *Dr. Armstrong's Joy of Spanking*. It was the second, however, that made my eyes practically pop out of my head. The glossy cover was a photograph of a woman's bare buttocks, a plaid skirt hiked to her waist and white cotton panties pushed down her

thighs. The voluptuous asscheeks were marked by a red hand-
print, but most shocking of all were the exposed labia, pink and
pouting and glistening with arousal. The title was written in
neon pink: *An Education for Samantha* by Anonymous.

Blushing fiercely, I shoved the books into my briefcase and
rushed out the door.

When I got home, I flopped onto my bed to devour *An Education for Samantha*. A mischievous student at a posh all-female
academy somehow managed to hold on to her innocence until
her eighteenth birthday. Then a series of semipublic sexual
exploits with local boys brought her to the attention of the
headmaster of the school, who administered Samantha's first
spanking in an effort to deter her scandalous behavior.

By the end of the first chapter, I had to take a break to
masturbate. The descriptions of the headmaster's erotic
punishments made me so wet and squishy *down there*, I came
in record time and lay panting in surprise mixed with self-
disgust. The problem was that the orgasm had done nothing to
relieve the tingling ache in my belly. I marched to the kitchen
and grabbed a zucchini, the only dildo-like object in the place.
I plowed myself vigorously with the rounded end of the vege-
table while I diddled my clit, and again came to a quick, shattering climax.

And still my vagina prickled and drooled like a hungry
mouth.

Desperate for satisfaction, I called up my fuckbuddy, a fellow
journalist, even though I'd recently vowed to wean myself from
shallow, meaningless sex.

"Hey, Leo. You busy tonight?"

"I was going to go out for beers with a friend in a couple of
hours."

"Could you stop by my place first to have sex? I'm so horny, you can probably make me come with one flick of my clitoris."

"I'll be right over."

The moment he arrived, I dragged him into the bedroom and yanked off his clothes.

"My, my, you *are* eager tonight," he chuckled, somewhat hypocritically, for when I pulled down his boxer-briefs, he was already fully erect, his cock slit oozing precome.

"Fuck me from behind. Like a jackhammer. And I also want you to..." I faltered, the words wilting in my throat.

Leo laughed again. "What do you want, my horny friend?"

"If you want to, you can sort of spank my butt a little while we do it."

"'*Sort of* spank your butt *a little*'? I think I can do better than that. But hey, what's gotten into you tonight, Tamara? Not that I'm complaining, but you're usually pretty vanilla."

"No questions, Mr. Pulitzer Prize, just do as you're told."

Always obliging, Leo knelt behind me, pushed his cock in and began to thrust deep and hard. Unfortunately his awkward attempt at a spanking barely produced a mild sting. So I closed my eyes and imagined a true expert slipping into his place, a man with a sturdy, knowing hand that could play my ass like a conga drum. In no time I was coming, my pussy milking Leo's cock like a fist.

As soon he finished up, I tossed Leo out and snuggled under the covers to finish my reading assignment. *Dr. Armstrong's Joy of Spanking* actually was an informative treatise on the physiological foundations of an erotic spanking—adrenaline rushes, endorphin highs, the careful calibration of pain thresholds. But it was the saga of Samantha's education that ignited my lust once again. The initial similarities with my own principal's office fantasy were uncanny, but I'd never dared to dream of the

sweet humiliations Samantha enjoyed—spankings both before
and after she took the headmaster's cock in every hole; a decadent, candlelit induction into the academy's secret spanking
sorority; a formal exhibition of effective student disciplinary
measures for the salivating Board of Governors.

It was all sick and twisted and totally hot.

I raced through the entire book, pausing only to masturbate to four more rocketing orgasms before I finally fell into an
exhausted sleep.

"Did you get a chance to read the materials, Ms. Patterson?"

Seated primly in the leather armchair, I was intent on
keeping control of the interview this time. "I always finish my
assignments, Doctor. I found it particularly interesting that the
science discussed in your book was so vividly illustrated in the
novel. Did you write that as well?"

"You flatter me. In fact, *An Education for Samantha* was
written by a client, a published novelist. It was a sort of payment
for services rendered. The author posed for the cover, by the
way. Lovely, don't you think?"

I swallowed, wondering if that extremely revealing photograph was taken in this very room. "So you sometimes barter
your services?"

"On occasion." The doctor's eyes twinkled. "By the way,
Armstrong Press is always looking for talented writers. Might
Samantha's story have inspired you to consider writing a novel
of your own?"

I laughed nervously. The novel had certainly inspired me
to seven orgasms last night, but that was none of his business.
How was it that this man always managed to turn the tables
so that I was answering the questions? "Doctor, I can't help
but notice that you're always pushing the limits of propriety

with me. Please remember that I am here on assignment for an article, nothing more."

The doctor's eyebrows shot up. "Come now. Are you sure you're being completely honest about your motives for coming here, Ms. Patterson?"

My stomach clenched guiltily. "What do you mean?"

"I *mean* that every time I've suggested something 'improper,' you've been remarkably receptive. Not to mention you haven't stopped blushing and squirming since you stepped into this office. I propose that the real reason you insisted on seeing me in person is because deep down you know what you really need is a good, sound spanking."

I stiffened and let out a soft "oh," as if the words themselves were a slap. I would have protested, but the flutter in my pussy, the flush in my ass and thighs, suggested my body was in full agreement.

"Now, my dear," he continued in a soothing voice, "I have another client arriving in half an hour. If we dispense with the charade of an interview, we'll have just enough time for a little hands-on therapy."

My heart was thumping so fast I feared it might break through my ribs. Was I really going to let this arrogant man chastise me, spank me, be witness to my most shameful desires?

"Shall we begin? With your Catholic background, I'm sure you understand how liberating confession can be. So come kneel down before me. Put your trust in Doctor Armstrong and everything will be all right."

The elixir of fascination, fear and pure horniness pumping through my veins made his offer irresistible. I rose to my feet and walked to his side of the desk. As I knelt, I instinctively bowed my head and threaded my fingers together as if I were in a confessional.

"Why do you deserve a spanking today?" he asked in a voice as gentle as a June breeze.

The words poured out with surprising ease. "I was a bad girl, Doctor. I…I masturbated when I did your reading assignment last night. Five—no—six times. But I did something worse than that."

"You can tell me everything, my child."

"I made a man have sex with me because I was so turned on by the naughty things the headmaster did to Samantha. This person isn't even a boyfriend. I just used him."

As always, the doctor was right. After I spoke my misdeeds out loud, I did immediately feel better, lighter.

"Look at me," the doctor whispered.

I raised my eyes to his, so deep and blue.

"I see you now," he said. "I see that you are a young lady with a strong sexual appetite and a great deal of curiosity about the limits of her pleasure. Do you think a good spanking might help you with your urges in the future?"

Tears sprang to my eyes. "Yes, Doctor, yes, I do."

"Then I'd like you to join me on the spanking couch now. Penance is always more effective on a bare bottom, so please lift your skirt and take down your panties."

I arranged my clothing as he ordered, my hands shaking with excitement. Then I stretched out on the sofa, my naked ass humped up over the doctor's lap. His thighs were surprisingly warm and very firm. I secretly drank in the intoxicating scent of wool, male flesh, a hint of soap.

At the first touch of his palm on my skin, I gasped. But for the next few minutes, the doctor did nothing but leisurely caress and squeeze my fleshy demi-globes, as if taking their measure.

"You have a beautiful, *sensitive* backside," he said in a husky voice. "I'm sure it will look even lovelier when it's all pink and punished."

That's when the first loud smack landed on my bare cheeks. I cried out in surprise more than pain. In the next instant a diffuse wave of heat and pleasure rolled from my buttocks down my thighs and up over my hips. His palm found its target again. I sighed and arched my back.

He snorted softly. "Taking to this like a duck to water, aren't we? We're now ready for the official punishment. I've determined that you deserve to be spanked twice for each time you played with your insatiable little clit and ten times for being a cheap slut who fucked a man she didn't love. How many times is that altogether?"

In my erotic daze, it took a moment to do the calculation. "Twenty-two, Doctor. Sir."

"Correct. Count them out with me now."

And so I croaked out the number with each meeting of palm to bottom—*one, two, three, oh, god, yes.* Each successive stroke sent a rush of energy circulating from my skull to my toes, the sensation so engulfing that soon I was nothing but a pair of stinging buttocks, aching, squirming, flaming, pushing up for more. By the end, I was shameless in my lust, grinding my mons against his thigh, bellowing out my pleasure like the trollop that I was.

I didn't feel the bulge in the doctor's trousers until the spanking was over. I stifled a giggle in the sofa cushion. Maybe he'd let me suck him off if I asked nicely? My mouth began to water in anticipation.

But the doctor had other ideas. "That will be all for today," he said briskly.

"Don't I get to come?" I blurted out.

"What a presumptuous young lady. I told you I only permit

masturbation in special cases. Now please get yourself in order."

Get myself in order? I was so aroused, I doubted I'd be able to stand, much less walk out of here.

"Please, Doctor. If I promise to write a very hot, dirty novel for you with lots and lots of spankings, will you let me finish off? It won't take long."

His cock twitched against my hip.

I held my breath.

After an interminable moment, he said, "Very well. You have precisely five minutes to do your business."

Thank heaven for my journalistic instincts—I'd obviously touched *his* sensitive spot. Aware of my impending deadline, I shoved my hand between my legs and began to claw at my clit as if there was no tomorrow.

Just then a gentle hand began to stroke my hair.

"That's right, take your pleasure," the doctor murmured. "You've endured your punishment like a good girl and now you get your reward. Let the doctor watch you come on your own hand."

It was exactly the right thing to say. I whimpered and strummed faster, my smarting asscheeks fueling the fireball gathering in my clit. I was close now, so close, hovering just shy of the finish line.

As if he sensed my final need, the doctor's hand glided back down to my buttocks. His finger dipped into my crevice, circling my puckered back hole delicately. I'd never been touched there like that before. The sensation was so exquisite, I grunted like an animal. My thighs naturally eased open to give him full access to my secret place.

"Spread your legs nice and wide so the doctor can give you a special treat."

With that, he landed a slap directly on my anus. I yelped and bucked up. He spanked me there again. And again.

I came, my body jerking convulsively beneath his hands. It was, no contest, the most intense orgasm I'd ever had in my life.

When I finally recovered enough to sit up, the doctor gave me a quick, avuncular hug. "It was an excellent first session. I'm very proud of you, Tamara. May I call you that now? By the way, I intend to hold you to your promise to write that novel for me."

"I've never written a novel," I admitted with an embarrassed smile.

"No worries, my dear. With Armstrong Press, it's a collaborative process. Here in my office we will act out scenes involving your visits to the formidable Master Blake of London, and you will write up the highlights at home in explicit detail. It's sure to be an education for you."

I felt a new twist of lust between my legs. What well-spanked woman in her right mind would turn down an assignment like that?

On my way out, the receptionist raised her eyebrows at my disheveled appearance, but I only grinned at her and sauntered through the door.

Because I was a woman who was confident in her own desires. And I was very happy with the price.

A GAME
OF NUMBERS

Kiki DeLovely

You bring your hand to my mouth and I make the mistake of thinking you're about to do something sweet. You're not. After seventeen years together I ought to know better. You take the better part of my cheeks in your fist and squeeze, forcing my lips into an almost painful O formation. That unpredictable nature of yours definitely lends itself to keeping things hot between us. And always, always interesting. Take today, for example. Strolling through the botanical gardens, hand in hand, a sense of tranquility envelopes us. I occasionally point out some stunning color or a peculiarly shaped plant, and you nod, affirming its Latin name, as if these things are the most common of knowledge. (I've loved that about you since day one—your impressive, never boastful breadth of knowledge. The rest, well, that took a little longer to fall for.) Nothing about the ordinariness of this day, nor the low-key energy of it all, would suggest anything sexual in the slightest. But something at our feet caught your eye. So you slowly lower me to the ground to gather it for you, guiding me with just a glance and that one hand clenched tightly around my mouth.

Natural sciences were your first love. I came along second. For me, it was always math. Until you introduced a whole new numbers game into my world. None of my previous lovers had ever brought out this type of intense longing, this depth of passion in me. The kind that's rooted in something slightly darker. Always a little naughty. Or a lot, depending on the day. And on this day in particular, you've got me on pins and needles in anticipation of which one it'll be.

Your favorite numbers game to play with me is a simple one. One that such a mathematical genius would normally find quite dull and all too rudimentary. One that she should never, ever lose at. All that this game entails is counting. Counting. No fancy equations, no drawn-out formulas. Not the slightest hint of complexity. Yet, still, on a really good day, you are able to throw me off my game. My game—my other true love. Somehow you are able to rule supreme over me in this sadistic game of numbers. But only when you complicate matters. And that which you spotted on the ground is just such an implement to assist you in doing so. A gift from the universe too well suited, too ideal, to pass up.

I'll never know whether this is just another example of how your brilliant mind naturally sees cruelty in the everyday that others would simply pass by...or if you took me on a walk specifically in search of this perfectly paddle-shaped plant. Not that it really matters one way or another. Because, no matter what, this game is bound to play out in the exact same manner.

"*Opuntia ficus-indica,*" you whisper as I place it in your open palm. Turning it over and over, you regard the specimen as though you'd never seen one before in your life. Having been raised on a ranch in Mexico, however, I know this simply cannot be the case. Still, your fascination is endearing. Endearing, that is, until you utter your next words. Without bothering to look up from your newfound toy, you casually command, "Remove your panties and hike up your dress."

Normally I'm not one to question your demands, but it's not as if we're deep in some secluded wooded area. This is a public garden, and while it's a slow day, anyone could happen upon this particular path at any moment. "But..." I start. And then promptly stop. You give me that I-know-I'm-not-going-to-have-to-tell-you-again look. A look that is understated in its firmness, but quite daunting on the intimidation scale. A look that I know better than to question.

So you continue. "On all fours. And count for me, my little math whiz. We'll go with the Fibonacci sequence today—quite fitting, I believe, given our environment. Let's see how good you really are with numbers." You know that last bit of taunting will get me all kinds of riled up.

An integer sequence predictably named for a European despite being described in India years prior, Fibonacci numbers are simple enough: the next number in the series is the sum of the two prior. The pattern commonly appears in nature; from artichokes to sunflowers, seashells to honeycombs, it's a series beloved by botanicals, coiled within creation. Yes, quite appropriate for our surroundings indeed.

I struggle with my pride as I hand over my panties (you smugly tuck them into your rear left pocket) and I position myself, exposing both my ass and my dignity. You start in almost instantaneously. No warm-up, no messing around.

"Zero...one...one...two..." I call out the numbers precisely in accordance with each *thwack*. Playing the game perfectly. Perhaps I'll win a match for once.

Opuntia ficus-indica. I normally don't remember the Latin

names for anything, but this is one I won't be forgetting anytime soon. Some sort of smooth version of a cactus, it feels meaty and cool against my warm and somewhat sweaty flesh. Almost comforting. Almost.

"Three…five…eight…thirteen…"

As I continue counting for you, you chatter over me, delighting in the harmony of your treasured *Opuntia ficus-indica*-cum-paddle hitting my bare behind and thighs mixed with that of your own voice. It's only when you're in top mode that you so adore the sound of the latter, otherwise you are characteristically much more on the laconic end of the spectrum. "*Opuntia ficus-indica* traditionally has spines—you're quite fortunate we've stumbled upon a rare variety that doesn't. They bear beautiful yellow flowers and the most delicious red fruit your sweet little tongue hasn't ever tasted. We'll have to fix that, won't we?"

A question more rhetorical in nature than not and so I just continue my counting, "Twenty-one…thirty-four…fifty-five… eighty-nine…"

You spank me so lovingly, so evenly, oscillating between either cheek, knowing that this sense of balance delights me to no end. It's only when you're being really mean that you purposefully beat one side harder than the other. And that day is not today. Today the tingly then almost burning sensations match up perfectly as you work my sweetest spots over with this impromptu, eco-friendly sex toy. My breathing begins to catch with each stinging smack, but my counting continues with your rhythm.

"One hundred forty-four…two hundred thirty-three…"

I haven't lost count or skipped even one number, despite my nervousness around being so publicly exposed. Apparently I'm doing too good of a job at staying on my game and so you decide to switch it up a little. Grabbing a fistful of one asscheek in your free hand, you spread me open, revealing just how wet this little foray has made me. I can practically feel the slow grin inching across your face. The pause in action, as well as what I know is undoubtedly about to come, messes with my head.

My concentration foggy, I almost forget what number we were at when you start up again—this time taking aim at my pulsating and needy cunt. Luckily, I find the number, waiting patiently on the tip of my tongue, just in time.

"Th-three hundred seventy-seven..." The first one always catches me off guard. "...Six hundred ten...nine hundred eighty-seven...onethousandfivehundredninetyseven..."

You've become so thoroughly aroused at my excitement that you begin to spank my pussy faster and faster and I can feel an orgasm mounting quickly. If anything is sure to put me off my game, it's that. The broadside of the cactus drips with my juices. And each slap is coming so swiftly now that I've quickly lost count. I wouldn't be able to keep up—let alone differentiate one whack from the next—no matter how hard I try.

"It seems you're not so good with numbers after all," you tease me, your breath quite ragged at this point. Knowing it'll infuriate me. Knowing it just might push me over the edge.

"Seventeen thousand, seven hundred eleven!" I cry out in frustration, coming hard as you get in one last strike. My pussy quivering against the well-used organism, your hand cupping it, my come drizzles down to meet your skin. I know my math is off—we were far beyond 17,711 at that point, but it's my favorite number in the sequence. And by then I knew I had lost the game but didn't give a damn about those digits. As consolation you rest your fingertips on my clit just barely, just enough to make my whole body quake.

You drop your drawers, expecting to fuck me now. But

the sight of your gorgeous, honey-hued skin, a shade slightly lighter than mine, unveiled and vulnerable, sparks something unexpected in me. I spot the tiniest glimpse of my pink panties peeking out of the pocket now bunched up at your knees and dare to snatch them back. Shooting you a look that shocks you into a frozen stupor—you've never seen anything like it on my face before—I smirk as I pull them back on. Of all the innumerable scenarios we've played out in our years together, me getting to lay my hand on you has never been one of them, but loving you for so long means knowing your expressions better than my own. And your face reads of pure titillation. My heart races with such a bold attempt at role reversal—something that I had never even thought about before this very second, let alone voiced to you. I've always considered myself a bottom through and through. Not a dominant bone in my body. Until today. And apparently they're all in my left hand. I take the now limp bit of green from your hand and toss it aside.

Just before I land my very first delectable blow, I say, "Now I want to hear you count. And you better not screw up."

I'm about to take back my game.

MERMAID

Teresa Noelle Roberts

With many yards of sea-green rope and the help of a Two Knotty Boys video we'd found on the Internet, my girlfriend Mallory encased my lower body in a rope skirt that bound my legs together so I'd have to get around by hopping or wriggling like a snake. Not that I'd had much inclination to go anywhere. The wrap encased my legs, but left my butt and cunt exposed except for some strategically placed ropes with even more strategically placed knots. Why try to get away when I could writhe against the teasing strands and Mallory's wicked touch until I burst into shards of joy, held together only by the security of rope?

When she finished the tie, I said, "I feel like a beached mermaid: helpless but sexy."

"You look like one. I like it."

She pulled me close, my breasts against her rib cage, my face pressed against her breasts. She swatted my ass once, twice, three times, but before I could really get into the rhythm, she asked me,

"And what do you suppose I could do to a captive mermaid?"

"Spank her. Torment her. Love her. All kinds of things." It came out slowly, the words filtering into my head from far away. I was in an erotic fog, lost in Mallory's ropes on my body, Mallory's hands smacking my ass, Mallory's nipple temptingly close to my mouth.

I was just about to give in to the temptation presented by that alluring buff nipple when Mallory reminded me we were heading up to Maine that weekend for an off-season getaway. "The beach," she said with studied nonchalance, "should be empty at night."

I was in trouble. Really interesting trouble.

Maine is better known for rocky shoals than sandy beaches, but thanks to the foresight of some rich guy in the early twentieth century, Ogunquit Beach, which is about as close to a perfect beach as you'll find in New England, is free of amusement parks, clam shacks, or other development; just several miles of lovely sand, backed by dunes.

We parked at the beach entrance outside of town. Mallory had started the mermaid tie back at the hotel, teasing and laughing and smacking and caressing as she did, stopping just above the knees so I could hobble from the car onto the beach. I had to take tiny steps like a geisha. I suspect Mallory enjoyed it, even if some of the effect was lost under a long hippie skirt and Mallory's fleece jacket, huge on me.

I complained about the slow pace, but unconvincingly, since each mincing step, with my legs forced together, made me more aware of the ropes teasing my clit and labia, more eager to find out what further devious plans Mallory had for me. By the time I made it to the beach, I was wet as the ocean and pulsing like the waves, eager for more.

The tide was high, waves lapping sensuously to within a few yards of the dunes. The full moon lit a mysterious path on the waves. Earlier in the evening, closer to town, a few other romantics had wandered the night beach, but at midnight, we had those miles of beach to ourselves.

It was unseasonably warm for early October in Maine. It might not have stopped Mallory if it had been in the 50s—after all, she could stay fully dressed—but New England was enjoying a perfect Indian summer. It had hit the low 80s during the day and warmth still lingered in the air, even at midnight.

Still, I was grateful she allowed me to keep the jacket on once we had reached the beach and she knelt on a blanket to finish the elaborate binding on my legs. The hypnotic effect of waves and rope nearly lulled me to sleep, but when Mallory got me to remove the fleece, I jarred to full, aroused consciousness, focused on the soft but inescapable embrace of the ropes, my immobility, the salt breeze teasing my already hard nipples and discovering the trail of moisture at the juncture of my closed thighs.

I couldn't help wondering what would happen next. Mallory had brought a backpack with her, one she'd been careful to keep me from peeking inside back at the hotel. What did she have stowed there?

I soon found out. She had a net, not an actual coarse fishnet, but an approximation of one macraméd of fine rope. She dropped it over me. "Now you're properly caught," she whispered, running her hands over my taut nipples.

I could have shucked the net easily enough. Unlike a fish, I have opposable thumbs, and the movement of water wasn't conspiring to wrap the net around me and keep me thoroughly tangled. I couldn't possibly escape because I couldn't bring myself to do so. I was mesmerized by desire and curiosity, wanting to see how Mallory would take advantage of my predicament.

What Mallory did was scoop me up (she's a big girl who still plays rugby, long after college, and I'm five foot nothing, with the type of build described, depending on one's taste, as either elfin or scrawny) and carry me to the water's edge.

Was she going to dump me in? That was a little too much realism in October! If mermaids existed, I suppose they could be able to handle cold water like seals do; my skinny self was another story. "Don't you dare!" I shrieked, shattering the peace of the night.

She didn't dump me in. Instead, she set me down gently at the tide line, where the still-dry sand was threatened by waves that broke ever closer to the line of demarcation.

The sand was cooler on my butt and back than it had felt on my feet. I let out another muffled noise, but this one was more a gasp than a shriek.

My keyed-up nerve endings couldn't decide if the shock of cold was agony or ecstasy. Maybe both. As Mallory carried me, she'd managed to tangle me in the net, or maybe I'd tangled myself without realizing it. In any case I felt well and truly caught. The fact that I couldn't fight back, couldn't dart away from the waves, could at best struggle to sit up and then scoot on my ass, gave me a delicious feeling of helplessness. Pleasure washed over me, making me shudder, warming me from within. The sand was cool, and so was the breeze this close to the water, but molten lava filled my pussy, warming me.

Then a stray wave splashed me with water just slightly above the temperature of ice.

I yelped from the shock—couldn't help myself—but the contrast between the frigid water and my inner heat was oddly arousing. Sensual. Instead of trying to get away I wriggled, letting the rope play against my labia and tease my clit. The arousal crashed over me with more force than the small waves the ocean was giving us that night.

The next thing I knew I was scooped up onto Mallory's lap, safely out of wave range, and wrapped in a soft bath sheet. "Can't let you get chilled when you're out of your element, can I, mermaid?" she muttered. "Must keep my prize warm." She was certainly warming me internally, considering she was paying extra attention to my nipples and the juncture of my thighs. The wavelet hadn't actually reached there, but it was plenty wet. Her ministrations with the terry towel did nothing to make that part of me drier.

Desire flared into urgent need, powerful as fire and tsunami combined. I arched against her hand, squirming and mewling and begging, "Please, please..." I couldn't spread my legs, not tied as I was, and I couldn't make my brain work enough to articulate what I wanted, and I couldn't detangle myself enough to caress Mallory. I did my best to convey what I needed with moans and body language.

"Well, aren't you a naughty little mermaid?" Mallory purred. "Anyone would think you like being captured. Do you, mermaid? Do you like being my prisoner? Or should I put you back in the water?"

Oh, that bitch! That evil, wonderful bitch! She knows I hate admitting just how much I like to feel small and helpless when we play these games. I'd do almost anything to avoid admitting how much I like giving up the weight of responsibility and decision. We both know it's the truth, but saying it out loud is rough.

On the other hand, that water was fucking cold. Being splashed had been sexy in a playing-games-with-ice-cubes way, but being immersed would be awful. I wouldn't put it past her to carry out the threat, though. She'd whisk me back to the hot tub waiting in the hotel room, after she'd had her cruel amusement, but meanwhile I'd be damn uncomfortable. Sure, I could use a safeword—but what fun would that be? I didn't want to stop the game, just wanted to avoid that icy water. Admitting my need wouldn't hurt me. Would it?

I still couldn't get the words out. Maybe it was the roar of my own blood, drowning out the surf and my brain waves equally.

Mallory shifted, held me tighter, as if she was getting ready to muscle me back to the water's edge. "I guess you want to be set free, so I'll just put you back in the ocean."

That did it, as she knew it would. "No! I want to stay here. I like being your captive."

Even in the wavering moonlight, there was no missing Mallory's hot grin. "I knew you were a naughty mermaid. And you know what happens to naughty mermaids?"

"They get put into a nice warm hot tub so they can live on land with their sexy captor?" I suggested eagerly. I knew we'd get there in the end, but I was sure she had other plans, exciting plans, first. I knew that mischievous tone and now that I'd admitted I liked being a victim of said mischief, I was goading her along.

Mallory's slow smile lit up her face. "A naughty mermaid might end up in a hot tub, but first she gets spanked."

If I'd been awash with lust before, now I was drowning in it. I suppose a real captive mermaid would have struggled at that point, but I could only take my role-playing so far. Instead of fighting, I did my tangled, tied-up best to help Mallory arrange me over her lap, ass in the air.

The first smacks stung my chilled skin, though, stung enough to make me yelp and instinctively try to get away, even if I knew I didn't want to escape. "Oh, no you don't, you slippery minx," Mallory whispered, clamping her other hand on the back of my neck.

I went bonelessly limp at that proprietary touch. It made me feel relaxed and safe as a kitten carried by its mother. But there was nothing maternal in Mallory's grip on my neck or in the way she caressed my ass before spanking me again.

This time, the initial sensation was still a jolt of pain, but the sting transformed itself to heated arousal almost immediately, spreading out from my ass. The warmth didn't go straight to my pussy as it normally would. Instead, it played across the surface of my skin, traveling down my legs, up toward my breasts, but not quite reaching them.

Again, Mallory let her hand drift softly across my already sensitive butt before starting in with a slow but steady rain of blows. The warm pleasure-pain continued to swirl over my skin, embracing me as the ropes did, as the rumble of the surf and the moonlit velvet of the night did. My head swam in a good way, as if I was getting drunk on sensory input.

Mallory kept spanking, not hard, but inexorable as the waves, drowning me in sensation. From the surface of my skin, the sensation sank deeper, so my heart, my blood and especially my pussy were throbbing in time to Mallory's hand—which I realized was spanking in time to the waves.

That realization wove everything together: the ocean, the damp ropes, the cooling night air against my heated skin, the throbbing of my clit, the delicious way pleasure and pain blurred together. The night spun around me, holding me as close as the ropes, as close as Mallory.

When Mallory whispered, "Come for me, little mermaid," the pleasure broke over me like waves, warm as blood and bracing as the ocean.

BUTCH GIRLS DON'T CRY

Giselle Renarde

There are days when you just have to get out of the house. Or out of the apartment, in my case. I don't know what made *that* day one of *those* days. Call it cabin fever, or sexual frustration, or simply fate. That day, I just had to get out. One problem: the wind was howling, and channel three had predicted the storm would turn ugly. If I had to get out of the apartment without leaving the building, my only option was the penthouse pool.

I've never been much of a swimmer, but I knew the exercise would do me good. Too much built-up energy in my system. Kicking my legs and flailing my arms would take care of it, I hoped. Plus, I'd bought a lovely little bikini at the end of the summer and I had yet to premiere it. My building was full of hot young guys and gorgeous geek girls—no time like the present to strut my stuff in front of them! Hell, maybe I'd get lucky and some mysterious stranger would take me home like a lost little puppy.

When I stepped out of the changing room, the pool area was deserted but for one other person. If I'd seen her from behind, I would have thought for sure she was a man. From the front, it was only the big braless tits under a gray cotton tank top that gave her away. Her face and her middle were pudgy, but her tattooed arms surged with such strength my knees nearly gave out just looking at her. She had short hair, a dusty and indistinct color, and unshaven legs under big cargo shorts. Her face wore a focused expression as she worked out at the weight machine in the corner. The "gym" in our building got moved into the pool area when the residents' board decided to put saunas in both changing rooms. I still hadn't seen the inside of those steamy wooden caverns, just like I'd never seen this butch babe around the building before. The idea of both together made me hot.

As I unwrapped my towel from my nearly naked body, I felt a wicked smile bleed across my lips. Thank god I'd left the apartment today. Thank god I'd worn this bikini. You never know what you're going to find up here at the penthouse level. Could be boys and their toys or girls with their curls...or it could be this butch powerhouse at the weight machine. I knew I was staring, but I didn't care. I'd come up here to see and be seen, and I wouldn't be content until I'd achieved both goals.

From the far end of the pool, I watched my vigorous stranger's iron-pumping pace slow to a crawl. Those hulking arm muscles twitched as she set down her weights. Her gaze fixed on my flesh like a laser beam intent on burning off the white halter straps of my bikini top. If only her eyes could cut them loose! I wanted to expose my tits to her then and there, and watch her face harden with desire. There was an intensity to her that I could feel even across the expanse of chlorinated water.

Tossing my towel on a deck chair, I waded into the pool, flicking my long hair over my shoulders. I knew she was watching as my chilled nipples grew hard under my bikini top, but I didn't return her gaze. I didn't want to give her the satisfaction—not just yet. Everybody knows there's an art to this game of seduction.

I plunged my head beneath the cool water and tried to swim gracefully. It had been a while, but I wanted to showcase my lean figure with minimal splashing or thrashing of limbs. I did a damn fine job, I think.

When I'd finished a couple laps I glanced casually toward the weight machine in the corner, ready to tease that hot daddy some more...but she was gone. The weight machine had fallen to disuse. The whole pool area was empty. I couldn't believe my stinging eyes.

Well, she couldn't have gone far. I hopped from the pool, grabbed my towel and stomped on wet feet to the changing room. Empty. No signs of life or neighbors—granted, most of the people in my building worked during the day—but more importantly, no sign of the striking stranger from the weight machine. I couldn't help feeling insulted. What, I wasn't hot enough for her? Of course I was! How could she resist? No, how *dare* she resist? I tore out of my bathing suit and tossed it in the direction of my bag before slipping under a hot shower. Wringing out my wet hair, I wrapped the wet towel around my naked middle and figured I might as well cool my jets in the hot sauna.

It wasn't until I'd swung open the heavy wooden door that I realized there was somebody inside. And who do you think that somebody was? Yes, indeed, it was the big bad butch who'd caught my eye by the pool and then rejected me. She was still fully dressed, but her head hung low. Deep moaning sounds fell from her full lips. Between her feet in black flip-flops, tears sizzled against the hot wooden floor slats. My big strong butch was crying! Not whining like a girl, not whimpering like a puppy, but blubbering like a man. Like her father or her dog just died, as Leonard Cohen put it.

This mysterious stranger had suffered a loss for sure, but I was pretty sure it had nothing to do with a father or a dog. It was a loss in love, that much I could tell. I could feel it in my heart—my heart, which expanded to house her hurt with every breath. I knew just the type of dark-haired beauty who'd trampled her spirit with stiletto boots: deep red lips, bright red nails, short bangs and a vintage dress. A vixen. A tart. Oh, how many times had that beauty been me?

Tears streamed down her plump cheeks, barely distinguishable from the sweat gleaming on her skin. She didn't acknowledge me, except by sitting up a little straighter. Still, her chin swung down close to her chest. As she shook her head left and right, tears soaked the front of her sweat-dampened tank top. She mumbled indistinguishable words, but I got the sense she wasn't talking to me or even to herself. My guess? She was pleading with the woman now absent from her life, the pretty girl who'd hurt her so badly.

Everybody knows a breakup cry. You know it when you see it. Because we've all been there, everybody above the age of sixteen or so. We've all been hit by that bolt from the blue, or seen the end slowly creeping up on us like a creature of the night. And it hurts. God, it hurts like nothing else in the world and it leaves us weak as kittens. Time may heal the wound of this individual experience, but the next time a relationship comes to an end, we're torn open just as wide. There's no learning curve for emotion. We are subjected to it and rendered submissive in its hands.

I'm no mother, but I know what it is to care for another human being. My maternal instinct is strong enough to embrace anyone in need and open enough to realize the desire that care can generate. Open enough not to turn that desire away. Open enough to welcome it. So I walked across the sauna room. All it took was three small steps.

When I stood before her, she covered her face with both hands. She leaned so far forward her head nearly met my middle. She set her elbows against her knees, and her strong shoulders shook as she sobbed. Her whole body seemed to rattle, which gave her a skeletal appearance despite her bulk. I couldn't resist any longer. I had to touch her.

Easing forward, I set my hands gently against her heaving shoulders. Her bare skin was slick with sweat, and her muscles twinged under my touch. As I traced my palms down her big biceps and then up her straining neck, she leaned her head into my soft body. The moment I felt her face against my belly, a gush of warmth flooded my heart. Running my fingernails through the short hair at the back of her head, I whispered all the words of comfort my mother would have said to me. "*Shh shh shh*, now. This too shall pass, and all shall be well with the world."

In time, her sobbing subsided. When I felt in my heart she trusted me, I pried her hands from her face and wiped the tears from her cheek with my thumb. I even ran my hand underneath my towel and wiped her nose, because that's what a good mommy would do. And that's when she finally looked up at me. Her glistening hazel eyes were bloodshot from crying. The droplets clinging to her lower lashes sparkled, even in the sauna room's low light. Yes, her whole face was tearstained and red, but there was a masculine beauty to the sadness painted across her skin. She allowed me to see the wounded child behind the rough exterior, and nothing could have touched me more.

Unwrapping my towel, I held it end to end like a set of angel wings and revealed my nakedness to her. Her gaze descended my body, drizzling down my chest like hot fudge before settling on my bare tits. My towel slipped from my fingers and fell to the hot wooden floor. Taking her head in my hands, I offered myself to her in thought and in action.

As I stepped in close, she tipped her head upward. She set her face against my bare breast and my whole body burned to heal her pain. When she rubbed her wet cheek against my naked flesh, I traced my fingers down her neck. Like a babe at her mother's breast, she sought my nipple with her lips. Though her eyes were now closed, she found it with no trouble. Taking my tit inside her hot mouth, she suckled. She sucked rhythmically, as though my body were singing her a lullaby, and I felt my pussy grow slick as I soothed her.

Juice soaked my thighs, and she knew it as soon as I did. Wrapping one powerful arm around my waist, she pulled me into her broad lap. Her damp cargo shorts felt rough against my smooth ass, but her sudden movement no less enthralled me. She'd been such a predictable beast until now.

Switching sides to suck my other breast, she cast her hand between my legs. She plunged her fingers down the length of my pussy lips and hissed when she felt the wetness she'd inspired. For short hair, hers was so soft I couldn't keep my fingers out of it. I stroked the nape of her neck while she stroked my clit, and I honestly don't know who derived more enjoyment from the interplay of fingers and flesh.

Her touch made my stomach flutter. Every time she stroked my clit, my pelvis bucked up at her hand. She pushed me back down until my ass sat firmly on her thigh. With every rub, my pussy leaped forward a little higher and she pushed it back down a little harder, until my buck became a thrust and her stroke became a slap. The blood in my veins seemed to sizzle as her smacks landed against my engorged clit. My abdomen quaked every time she struck me with those firm, fat fingers.

The heat of the sauna was catching up with me, and my chest glistened with sweat. I prayed to the sauna gods this wounded stranger would never stop sucking my tits. The movements of her mouth corresponded perfectly to the actions of her hands, and she looked damn good doing it. She turned her head side to side, rolling it in cyclical motions as she drew my nipple into a bud between her lips. When she nibbled at my flesh, electricity coursed through my veins and my pussy surged toward the ceiling. She smacked it back down, and it sprang right up again.

She growled as she chewed on my tits and whacked my wet pussy with her hand. The sound was so fierce it should have scared me. Maybe it did scare me just a little. Certainly not enough that I would pick up my towel and flee. My pleasure far exceeded any pain she could inflict.

I'm not sure what compelled me to fall across her knee. It certainly wasn't a comfortable position. With my pelvis curved around her thigh, I had to bend to the side and hold on to the wooden ledge she was sitting on if I didn't want to topple headfirst onto the floor. Even so, I knew my awkward position didn't hold a candle to the terror she was about to rain down on my ass.

And, boy, did she ever! The first spanking didn't do much damage, but the first one never does. When her hand landed down again, I realized it was still wet with my pussy juice. The third smack rang in my ears while the burn set in. She didn't seem to hold back just because she was spanking a total stranger. That woman paddled my ass like it was a sport she'd set her sights on winning, and I bore the pain well.

In any other location I would have been screaming, but I didn't want to draw attention to our activities on the off chance there was anybody out in the changing room. The cries built up in my chest until my cheeks surely glowed as red as the butch stranger's. Her spankings were too measured to be taken for anger, but they fell so hard on my ass that I started to squirm. I couldn't help it. My flesh grew so raw and sensitive that every new smack saw me clawing at the wooden bench. She had to press her other hand down on the small of my back to keep me in place while she geared up for the next slap.

I found myself whimpering, "No more, no more," and crawling from her lap until my knees were up on the bench beside her. When I leaned on the hot wood of the upper row, my skin sizzled. The heat of the sauna scorched my sore spanked ass. As my butch neighbor stared at my poor red cheeks, I let my gaze wander the contours of her remarkable face. Her expression was hard to read. After bawling so relentlessly, she seemed strangely calm now. But that was always the way, wasn't it? I've endured those cries myself, sobbing until every semblance of emotion had drained from my body.

That's when I knew this was all a dream to her. I wasn't a person, a woman, an individual in my own right. I was only a body. I was catharsis. And, you know what? I was okay with that. She obviously needed the consolation that can only come from dirty, raw sex. I could be her slut/martyr/goddess. This wasn't about me.

When she stood, I looked away, but I felt her body behind me. I wanted to kiss her, but I knew better than to make any sudden movements. When I felt her hot palm against the sweat beading on my lower back, my whole body went rigid. She was close. I almost jumped when her tank top met my raw ass. Even simple cotton felt rough as burlap against my sorry flesh. But that harsh sensation fell away when her fingers reamed my slit. I was expecting *something*, but the sensation was still a shock.

She fucked me with her fingers. This was no pretty pawing.

No sentimental stroking. She just plain reamed me. I couldn't even say how many fingers she shoved up my cunt. Maybe it was three. There might have been a pinkie in there, too, I don't know. I didn't want to turn around. I didn't want to make eye contact. It's not that I was afraid of her or anything, I just thought it might be awkward at this point. Anyway, it felt incredible, so what did I care whether it was two or three or four? She pounded me with her fingers, and my body reacted. I banged back against her as she moved in me. Setting my forehead down on the hot wooden bench, I jerked my ass hard in her direction. She slid the hand from my back down my ass crack, and I just about jumped out of my skin.

When she spit on my asshole and shoved her thumb in there, I couldn't keep quiet any longer. Her fingers moved so impossibly fast inside of me that the friction baked my cunt. I bit down on my forearm and let the ridiculous orgasm noises vibrate against my skin. I couldn't recall ever coming so hard. I lunged back at her hands as they reamed my pussy and my ass simultaneously. My tits whacked the sauna seat and sizzled each time they touched the hot wood.

The stranger didn't say anything. Not that I heard, at least, though I was making enough noise for the both of us. I didn't even care if somebody walked in at this point. What would they do, spray us with a hose? Realistically, they'd take one look at the scene of hardcore butch/femme debauchery, close the door and walk away. Whether they'd go home and call security or masturbate in recollection really depended on the person. Either way, I wasn't afraid.

When I was spent and sore, my handsome stranger pulled her sopping fingers from my snatch and her brave thumb from my asshole. For a matter of moments, I didn't move. My chest heaved and I panted and moaned, but I didn't turn around until

I felt her body shift. When I looked into her face, she quickly escaped my gaze, like she was ashamed. Like she'd done a grave injustice to the girl who'd broken her heart.

It was the most innocuous thing I could possibly have said, but I said it anyway: "It'll be okay, you know. Give it time."

She met my gaze for a split second, and then looked to the door and nodded. As she moved her head up and down, her eyes filled with tears. Red splotches broke across her cheeks, and she quickly covered her quivering lips with the back of her hand. Before I could offer any more generic words of encouragement, she grabbed the handle, swung the door wide open and darted out. I might have followed her if my legs hadn't turned to jelly. Instead, I climbed up on the top bench fully naked, lay down on my blazing red ass, closed my eyes and smiled.

For weeks after the fact, every time I encountered a butch dyke on the subway or at the store or wherever, I felt my cheeks blush a little. *Everybody knows*, I kept thinking. *Everybody knows I screwed a total stranger in the sauna. One look at me, and they know what kind of girl I am.* It was like assuming the rest of the world had X-ray vision. Like every swaggering daddy on Church Street could see right through my clinging jersey dress. But maybe my coy embarrassment lent me a certain appeal, because I'd never been hit on by so many hot butch babes as I was in the weeks following that encounter. The whole sordid experience left a lasting impression. And could it happen again? Sure it could, if the opportunity arose. Everybody knows I'm a sucker for mysterious strangers and unquelled emotion.

ECHO

J. Sinclaire

There is a sound, a resonance, to a perfect spanking, a tone that can only be achieved by cupping a hand at exactly the right angle, pausing to confirm the intended area of impact and bringing that hand down sharply against a firm buttock. The subsequent gasp of pleasure is the punctuation confirming a flawlessly executed smack.

Certainly, other implements can be used in the attempt to achieve this sound, but there is a purity to hands on asses that is beyond compare.

To find someone who is willing and capable of achieving these intended results can be a blush-inducing ordeal, albeit less of one now than fifty years ago. However, that could be said of many things, so take that as you will.

Whether you are the recipient or the provocateur, the sweetest moment is in between. The moment after intention, but before impact. The delightful pause followed by exquisite pain-laced pleasure. This moment of tension, of anticipation, of promise of what is to come or what may be withheld if your excitement is deemed inappropriate, excessive or unfitting.

There are many variables to take into account, such as covered buttocks or uncovered? Even within these two options, there are endless possibilities: bare hand on silk panties; gloved hand on latex hot pants; bare hand on bare ass, but fully clothed participants otherwise. Each prospect offers a wealth of sensations otherwise unexplored, however minuscule the permutations of pleasure may be.

Will the latex cup the buttocks and present them neatly, ensuring the optimal visual guidelines for the spanker? Will the silk panties shift on contact, drifting over hypersensitive areas, prolonging the effects of impact? Will the bare skin and hands highlight the perversion about to occur on the otherwise mundanely adorned bodies involved?

Oh, there is much to consider but at this moment, in a deserted stairwell within a hectic, public government facility, all that concerns the two participants is, well, each other.

Them, and that perfect sound.

Madeline is bent over the steel railing at the top of the stairs in her black, high-waisted, pencil skirt, a red silk blouse and utterly impractical yet somehow work-appropriate heels. Her long black hair is in disarray, spilling over her shoulders and swaying softly in front of her face, limiting her view of the spiraling stairway below.

Smack.

The sound reverberates against the cement walls, echoing long past the moment the actual strike occurs. Madeline's body jolts forward momentarily, her hair swaying anew. She exhales, shuddering the air from her body and preparing for the next impact.

The culprit, a handsome yet dorky-looking gentleman named

Sean, from accounting, is preparing as well. In a black suit, white shirt and thin black tie, his appearance is professional, despite the circumstances. He glides his hand over Madeline's ass, soothing the affronted skin while plotting the location of his next strike. She has an ample bottom to work with, so he considers the possibilities carefully before tapping the crease of her cheek and thigh sharply. Once, twice, three times. Pausing only a heartbeat between them and increasing his pressure with each tap, he catches her off guard with the flurry of strikes, as he had been doling them out individually until that point.

Despite her attempts not to, Madeline lets out a breathy moan. It echoes in tandem with the sound of their spanking in an aural erotic assault. While the stairwell is rarely used in a facility stocked full of elevator-loving plebes, there is still a risk of an innocent stair-climber encountering their acoustic adventures.

That risk simply makes the excitement more palpable for the both of them.

Sean's hands move to the top of Madeline's hips as he presses his hard cock against her ass. It is straining against the fabric of his pants, ready to make its escape into whatever lovely moist place is available nearby. Not yet though. He takes a reluctant step back.

Smack.

Madeline no longer tries to stifle her cry. Her ass is on fire from the force of the hit, her pussy twitching in excitement around her increasingly sopping-wet panties. She ignores the echo of her outburst and steadies herself against the railing, her fingers starting to ache from holding on so tightly.

Smack.

Sean switches to her other cheek, an unexpected move as he'd been favoring the right side until now. This side is fresh, previously untouched and exceedingly sensitive to such a firm initial impact. The blossoming ache diminishes the blaze of his previous strikes, but only slightly.

He rubs her ass soothingly, relaxing her muscles before continuing the onslaught. Three sharp hits, increasing in force, the last making her cry out again.

As Madeline shifts her stance, thighs slick with her juices, Sean reaches down and tugs her skirt up over her hips to her waist. She's wearing a lacy black thong, her lips peeking out from beneath due to her wriggling. Her right cheek is slightly more inflamed looking, as it was the first to receive his attention, but the left is quickly catching up.

Her skin is soft and supple, her ass pleasingly firm. He revels in the feel of her, his hands running down her thighs to her calves, his breath drifting lightly over her cheeks as he dips his body down to touch her. She squirms; his lips are so close but he does not touch her with them, only his hands.

Sliding back up to her ass, he kneads it roughly before winding up for the next tap. She braces herself.

Smack.

It is light, barely registering. A shock of omission. She's in the middle of turning her head over her shoulder toward him to shoot him a questioning look when he strikes again.

Smack.

Flat palmed across both of her cheeks; no holds barred. Her cry reaches the level of scream, ringing in both of their ears. A jolt of pleasure shoots through her torso, radiating from her stinging skin. Her grip on the staircase has slipped and as she's recovering, chest heaving, legs fluttering, Sean quickly unzips his trousers and works his penis out of his pants.

Madeline is too focused on regaining her balance to notice his stealthy unsheathing, so when he puts his hand gently on her lower back, she trembles, expecting the lead-in for his next hit.

Instead, he presses gently on her back, arching her ass more before moving down to shift her thong to the side. Her pussy is soaked and her nerves are thrumming, already so close to the edge.

In one fluid motion, he slides his cock inside her.

Madeline's body jerks as if he'd hit her, her muscles contracting around his girth as the sudden orgasm takes her by surprise. One, two, three more times he thrusts inside her, the last one punctuated by a sharp slap on her ass, and she concedes to the waves of pleasure sweeping over her body.

Sean slows his movement inside her as she spasms around him, teasing her G-spot gently until she rides out the orgasm completely. He pulls out enough so that just the tip of his penis is resting against the entrance of her pussy and pauses there for a moment.

Smack.

He can feel her pussy flutter against his head as her body is again riddled with that powerful pain-laced pleasure. He slides inside her a bit more.

Smack.

Flutter. Madeline moans absentmindedly. He slides in even more, nudging her G-spot.

Smack.

She shudders around him and pushes back on his cock so he fills her completely.

Smack.

He begins thrusting into her methodically, punctuating his plunges with the occasional tap on her ass, hips or thigh. She can feel her honey dripping languidly down her thighs, her body oozing from his ministrations. He's penetrating her just far enough to bump her G-spot with each thrust and she quickly spills over into another orgasm within minutes. She gushes around him, a storm, a rolling thunder of release.

Sean pulls out completely, resting his cock between her lips as she recovers. Within moments she's sliding her pussy back and forth over him. He reaches down and shifts his penis up, so it is almost vertical between her asscheeks. He cups her buttocks with his hands, squeezing his dripping cock between them, leisurely thrusting against the firm, ruby-tinged flesh.

A trace of a grimace flashes across Madeline's face as he clutches at her tender muscles but it quickly fades after a few strokes. The feel of his hard penis is making her cunt ache with lustful demands and her patience wears thin.

"Sean, would you be so kind as to fuck me in the ass?"

Her words reverberate around them and he pauses in surprise; she's barely said a word since they arrived. He eagerly nods in agreement, then realizes she's not able to see him and instead spreads her cheeks and slides the head of his penis into her puckered asshole.

She's tight and her ass resists him initially, but she's lubricated him thoroughly enough with her juices that her anus relents to his advances. He sinks into her slowly, her moan growing louder the deeper he gets. She snakes her hand down between her thighs to begin rubbing her clit as he rewinds his motions, withdrawing just as slowly as he entered her.

Smack.

He slaps her ass sharply before thrusting back inside. She is so tight and her ass clenches more with each strike. He's having trouble focusing now, especially after the gorgeous display she's already put on for him thus far. Her fingers work at her clit, timing flurries of finger work to his thrusts.

Smack.

He keeps this rhythm, spanking her curtly as he plunges into her. As the tension builds, he unwittingly speeds up the tempo, fucking her harder as he feels his climax approaching. She's moaning loudly once more, indifferent to any innocent passersby who may overhear. She's far too gone in the moment to bother with useless emotions like shame or self-consciousness. If they were caught right now, she'd demand their discoverer just sit tight and rub one out until they finished.

Madeline's fingers flutter over her clit and her entire body clenches as the orgasm detonates within her. Her tremors prompt Sean's release, his hot come oozing out in spurts. Their bodies slump together as they come down, chests heaving from the exertion. His cock twitches, setting her pussy aflutter involuntarily. They chuckle absentmindedly at the sensation before he steps back and withdraws himself.

Wasting no time, they hastily tidy up, straighten their clothes and reestablish an acceptable level of professionalism in their appearance. It is flawed; Madeline's skirt is just a tad sideways and she can feel Sean's semen escaping from the barrier of her panties. Sean's dress shirt is damp in some places, though he catches it and does up his jacket casually. It covers the majority of telltale sweat.

They turn toward each other, Madeline meeting his gaze for the first time since their adventure began. She is wearing a satisfied smirk. He makes a move, almost as if to kiss her, but she speaks before he can complete it.

"Thanks, Sean. That was absolutely lovely. Now, can you be a dear and bring me a latte and the O'Doyle files when we get back to my office?"

He nods formally, but there is a smile in his eyes.

"Yes, ma'am."

BITCH

Elizabeth Silver

It's been a long week, and more than a small part of me would rather I just go home and waste this particular Friday night in my ugliest flannel pajamas, watching the week's worth of reality TV that I've got saved up on my DVR. I've spent the past hour fantasizing about a bag of Chinese takeout and a pint of non-politically-correct-named ice cream. A girl's got needs, I want to argue, but they're going to have to wait. I have obligations to meet, promises to keep.

The act of zipping up my PVC boots, ankle to thigh, is the same as pulling on my mantle. I stop being friend, sister, daughter; instead I become *Other*. I pull the laces of my bodice tight enough that the leather embraces me lovingly; the scrap of black satin panties covering my ass is like the kiss of a long-familiar lover. Crop in hand, the woman in my mirror is fierce and beautiful, a warrior who will tear your world to pieces if you dare defy her.

Yes. This will do.

I've met with him before, of course. Gone over all of my rules as well as his. And I listened to what he did and what he didn't say in between his stuttering requests and the laundry list of limits he gave me. It's what I do, what he's come to me to do: give him what he needs, even if he doesn't yet understand what that is. It's okay, though. I know.

That's what I always tell them. Not with words, because what we do needs something much more different than that. Speaking of...

I push into my playroom, the open door telling me he's ready. Once I close and flip the bolt, the game is on; that's how it goes with everyone. First, though, I check the room to make sure everything is in place; prayer bench on the dais in the middle of the room, ankle and wrist cuffs beside it; a table next to that, holding my favorite paddle and a paper bag; bitch standing in the corner, nose against the wall.

He flinches when I lock out the rest of the world, but says nothing. This might be our first time playing together, but he's done this enough to know how to behave. I take my time walking up to him, admiring the long, lean lines of his muscular back under the sheer material of his brand-new negligee, the way the bottom hem, flared out and edged in black lace so fashionably, trembles ever so slightly when he realizes how close I really am. Even with my boots, I'm still shorter than he is, but that doesn't matter here.

"Turn around, bitch." I snap off the words like I'm angry, and he twitches. But he does as he's told, like a good bitch, and gives me the full frontal I want.

The empty bra cups of the negligee are stretched wide and flat across his chest, his shoulders almost too broad for the size that fits that whipcord torso. He's got muscles defined from use and exercise, not bulk from hours of insecure weight lifting, and a light smattering of body hair that tells me he's confident enough in what he looks like that he doesn't need manscaping. So it's just the play that makes him uncomfortable, despite the obvious experience. I wonder if he had a lover reject him because of his obvious bend toward the not-so-conservative, but then shove the thought away. I'm not his lover, and I'm not here to push him away, so right now the point is pretty moot.

I look down and smile just a little when I see he's wearing the panties, too. Silk, cut with just enough room for a prick and held together with little bows on the sides. They're too small for him; he's spilling out all over the place. If I wasn't playing, I might be impressed.

"Didn't anyone ever teach you how to dress yourself, bitch?"

He hesitates, doesn't answer. Oh, he's a good one.

I tap his cheek with my crop. "Answer."

"Yes. I'm sorry."

"I didn't ask if you were sorry. Fix it."

He tries; long fingers tuck his balls back up into the small pouch in front, and then try to get his surprisingly long dick in alongside. It's sloppy work, and he's fighting a losing battle—there's just more of him than there is of the panties. Even when he stops, head hanging in shame, the soft tip of his cock is still peeking out of the right leg hole. Still, it looks better than it did.

"Good enough." He lets out a gust of air in relief, probably sure I was going to punish him because it wasn't perfect. He's going to get his punishment, but it'll be the one he needs, the one that'll give him what he really wants, not one because he's got too much pipe in his pants for the pretty undies I bought him.

I step back, give him a once-over. He's so pretty, flushed and confused; none of his Dommes have ever dressed him up like this before. But he still did it for me, like a good bitch, and the thought makes me smile.

"You look like a slut," I say, putting a razor edge on my smile. The words make him shiver. "And you like it. Don't you? Answer."

His hands clench and release, clench and release. "Yes. Yes, I like it." His hair, an unremarkable shade of red-brown, has been combed back from his face, but a single lock has escaped, draping across his forehead. He still won't meet my eyes, still keeps that face with those sharp cheekbones turned down and to the side, like a terrified child. I know the truth, though. I can see the way his cock is slowly unfurling in the panties, undoing all of his hard work just from that one word. *Slut.*

Oh, bitch, we're going to have so much fun together.

"Do you know what I do with sluts?" I don't tell him to answer, so he can't say anything. He hesitates and then shakes his head. His chest and neck are starting to flush, and he's leaning toward me, like a compass needle—making me a magnet. The black leather hilt of my crop is stark against the pale, freckled flesh of his neck, and I run it over his collarbone, along his sternum—between the lacy cups of the negligee—and flick at the loose folds of fabric around his waist. "I knock some sense into them. Would you like that?"

"Yes. Please."

I let the violation go, because he's finally looking at me now and we've got real progress. I crook my finger and walk away. He follows, still watching me like a good bitch, and I point to the prayer bench with my crop.

"There."

He's so good. So pretty as he kneels on the leather cushion, arms hanging loose at his sides. Since this is the first time I'll touch him, I take my time, sliding my hands down the long, slender length of each leg before I cuff his ankles and hook the cuffs to the rings recessed in the floor. I'd only guessed at some kind of exercise before, but I'd be willing to bet now it's yoga; you don't get this kind of trim muscle tone from jogging, and there's not a single quiver of instability as he keeps kneeling there, waiting for me to close the cuffs around his wrists.

Once I've pulled him forward, splayed across the bench like an offering, I stand behind him and admire the view for a few seconds. His panties are riding up, exposing more of his toned ass beneath the negligee, a teasing peek at what I'm going to have completely bare in just a few minutes.

I pick up the paper bag and pull out the baggie. He can only hear the rustling, and with the plastic still sealed, he has no idea what's about to happen.

"In Victorian times," I say, putting one foot in the middle of his back as I break the seal and dump ginger root and paring knife into my hand, "rumor has it that when a wife was especially misbehaved, her husband would put a peeled finger of ginger up her backside before spanking her, to prevent her from clenching against the pain. They say it has quite a strong sensation."

He whimpers. I dig my heel into his back, just a little, and start peeling. "Of course, it's been found that some people can actually enjoy the burn. In fact, clenching around the root releases more of the juices, increasing the experience. I wonder which you'll choose, the spanking or the burn."

And then I fall silent, concentrating on peeling the finger thoroughly. I have to rinse it a few times, do a little shaping, but this isn't my first rodeo, and it doesn't take all that long. Not that you could tell from the way bitch is squirming already; his hands are balled into fists, white knuckled and fierce, but his back is still relaxed, his breathing still even, so I know it's just eagerness. For a second, I almost break scene and laugh, tell him I hadn't been kidding when I said I was good at this.

But the urge passes, and I'm kneeling behind him and untying the bows to release his panties. He gasps, breath jumping, and I rub his ass with my free hand. Just me. Just me. Relax. He can't be tense for this part, not if he was telling the truth when he told me how long it's been since something's been up his ass.

Finally, I ease the plug between his cheeks. It's wet and the combination of water and juice from the ginger does the work of the missing lube. It takes care and patience, but I know it'll be worth it. It always is.

While I wait for him to adjust, and for the juice to take effect, I wash my hands. I haven't spoken a word to bitch in more than ten minutes, haven't let him speak in even longer. But he's been so good, and I know this next part is going to be hard enough on him. We can work on advanced stuff some other time.

Right when he starts squirming, head thrown back and lower lip caught between those perfectly straight teeth, I flip his negligee over his head. "Make as much noise as you want, slut." I tell him. "You're still getting this."

"Oh, god, *thank you*," he whispers, just as my hand comes down on his ass with a loud *crack*. I don't make the mistake of thinking he means to thank me for the permission to make noise.

I hit him again, leaving a pair of livid handprints on him, bright red blasphemy punctuated by the curl of ginger root between his cheeks. He's beautiful, unmarked by anyone else, and I feel a possessive surge within me—my bitch, my artwork, no one else's. A fresh and untouched canvas all my own, and the notion settles into my veins as I spank him again and again, raining down blows at odd angles, painting that beautiful, freckled skin with pain.

I'd wanted to use my paddle, especially considering how his ass is so toned it's like smacking into iron if I hit it just so, but he's moving too much. His legs and arms are so long, he's got more freedom than I'd like, and I'm worried I might hit the plug by accident. He's moving and clenching around the plug in between my strikes, letting loose these long and beautiful cries that make me think of orgasms and tears at the same time. And underneath it all, he keeps begging me for another, another, more, please. He keeps promising me that he deserves it, that he'll be good if I just keep punishing him.

By the time I stop, I've had to switch off hands twice, both of them aching from the effort of however long we've been at this. There are marks, various shades of angry red, as small as my fingers and as wide as my palm, from the tops of his thighs all the way up to the two unbelievably perfect dimples at the base of his spine. And he's sobbing, still begging me for more even though I know neither one of us can take it.

I grab the plug and pull on it slowly, twisting it inside of him to push a few more buttons that he needs played with. The root is kinked and curled, almost like a gnarled finger, and I use that to my advantage now. My bitch shouts, back bowing, and manages a single, garbled, "Please!" before he comes, the room abruptly smelling of sweat, spunk and spice.

The sound of him crying, soft and full of all the surrender I could have asked for, follows me as I throw the used plug out and wash my hands one more time. By the time I come back to him, he's pulled himself together enough to stop the tears. I undo his bonds, feet first, then hands, and ease him up onto his knees. I lift the negligee off his head, revealing a wet and blotchy face, his green eyes bloodshot and that perfect hair now utterly mussed.

"So pretty." I wipe his face and coo gently. He tries to sit, forgetting that his ass is a mess of welts, and bites off a pathetic noise. I shush him and run my fingers through his hair a few times until he's calm, until I see the man beneath the bitch creeping through.

And that's my cue.

I stand and offer him a hand up. He takes my hand, but stands on his own. With a laugh, I let him have that last, small rebellion; it's time to unlock the door, anyway.

"Clean yourself up," I say. "Keep the nightie if you want it, toss it if you don't. I won't need it."

"I—"

I stop with my hand on the knob, lock already undone, and turn back enough to look at him.

He straightens, and I see more of the successful businessman bleeding in. "Will I see you again?"

"If you want to." The answer is given lightly, but I can't help thinking *Yes, yes, yes. You're gorgeous and so good. I want to break you down so much more, see how much you can really take.*

"Good." It's the first time I've seen him smile.

"Good."

I leave the room and change my clothes, turning back into the other me, the boring me. There's still time for takeout and a movie at least, but I already feel like I've had an entire weekend's worth of down time. My hands are clumsy, the heels of my palms bruising already, but they're injuries I've earned. And every time I touch them over the next couple of days, I'll think about this. I'll think about him.

My beautiful bitch.

THE PRICE
OF EXPERIENCE

Kate Dominic

Although acquaintances rarely believe me, I was attracted to Adrian's wicked sense of humor rather than his money. Not that he isn't obscenely wealthy. He is. But I didn't need his millions. I'd known going into modeling that my career would, by definition, be short-lived. I'd found a good financial advisor and was at a point where I could live the rest of my life quite comfortably off the interest from my investments.

What I needed was Adrian the man. At fifty-five, he was a good thirty years older than I. His impeccably styled, thick, dark hair had gone mostly to silver and there were character lines at the corners of his eminently perceptive gray eyes. But beneath his designer suits was a firm, toned body he still worked to a hard sweat every morning before he left for his office. His razor-sharp mind had quickly seen beyond my shoulder-length blonde curls and 38D breasts to the brain that had always gotten me profitable contracts.

The night we met, he held me, and the rest of his dinner

guests, spellbound as he teased us to impeccably delivered punch
lines. Later on, when it was just the two of us watching stars
in his penthouse garden, I discovered what a truly marvelous
listener he is. As we sat on the brocade-covered swing, first next
to each other, then with me resting my head on his shoulder, he
pumped me for details on my life—everything from my child-
hood in the suburbs to my cover girl career to the out-of-the-
way castles I loved to visit on my frequent European getaways.

I was so smitten that I would gladly have stayed the night
with him. The kiss he gave me at my apartment door left my
knees weak. But he said he'd make reservations for dinner, then
got back in his cab and left. I stood at the window with my wrap
still on, touching my fingers to my swollen lips and smiling until
the sun came up.

Adrian told me later he'd been concerned about the obvious
difference in our ages. Given the unprecedented intensity of
his attraction, he'd been afraid he might be attracted too much
to the contrast between his maturity and my youth. He said it
was only when he realized the memories that most made him
smile were all related to our conversations rather than to my
looks that he'd made dinner reservations a second time. And
every night after that. The chemistry between us was explosive.
Our whirlwind courtship was so passionate that by the time we
married, two months later, my panties got wet just seeing him
taking off his jacket after work.

Two years later, our love had grown to the point where I was
no longer interested in the upheavals of international modeling.
I retired at the top of my career and started my own lucrative
consulting business. Adrian was not surprised at my business
acumen, though he reveled in teasing me, in private, of course,
about how delectable he found my designer suits to be. He was
fond of sucking damp spots on the front of my silk blouses or

sliding his fingers beneath my formfitting skirts to finger my pussy while we discussed the day's financial dealings.

I knew what he was thinking when his eyes once again turned molten as I paced the floor of our penthouse suite. We were enjoying a drink at home before we left to join friends for a late dinner. Adrian's look immediately made my panties damp, but I was too annoyed to let myself respond the way I wanted to—the way I knew he wanted me to as well. When I reached the end of the sofa, I deliberately turned toward the window rather than walking over to him. I glanced back over my shoulder.

"It's my own damn fault," I groused, taking a sip of my wine. "I was an asshole to Jonathan, all in a power struggle over an artistic difference I don't particularly give a shit about." I took another good-sized swallow of my wine and sighed heavily. "Now I've lost the services of the best graphics designer in town. I don't know how the hell I'm going to meet schedule."

Adrian was quiet for a long while, studying the swirl of the fine liquor in his crystal brandy snifter. I rarely swore. Adrian disliked vulgar language. But I was pissed enough, at myself and the world in general, that at that moment I didn't particularly care. The fingers tapping the edge of his glass let me know that now I wasn't the only one annoyed.

"I'm certain you'll do what you think is best." He took a slow, thoughtful drink. "Though personally, I think you need your panties taken down for a good, sound spanking."

I almost choked on my wine. At the same time, I was surprised at the unexpected surge of warmth between my legs.

"If I thought it would work, I'd try it." I laughed, pointing my wineglass at him. "Hell, at this point, I'd try it if *you* thought it would improve the situation!"

He raised his eyebrows at me. Then he set down his glass.

"Come here," he said quietly.

I gave him my best sultry smile. I was still irritated, but the heat between my legs was pronounced enough to distract me. I set my glass on the polished end table and moved next to him. His fingers trailed lightly over my hip.

"Lift your skirt."

I laughed and rolled my eyes. Adrian's expression was unreadable. His caress moved on to my bottom. With a sardonic smile, I worked the hem of my skintight skirt slowly up. I'd eschewed a garter belt that day in favor of thigh-high black stay-up hose with a delicate butterfly pattern at the ankle. Adrian nodded appreciatively as my stocking tops appeared. His breath caught momentarily as I pulled the skirt over my panties. I was wearing a tiny midnight-blue satin and lace thong that barely covered the neatly trimmed thatch between my legs. His eyes sparkled when I wiggled my bottom at him, though I was surprised at the hint of steel still lingering in his gaze. He sat on the couch. With no warning, he hooked his fingers in the waistband of my panties and slowly pulled them down.

"What are you doing?" I laughed, bracing my hands on his head as he deliberately drew my panties over my knees. "I'm wearing a thong. If you really think you're going to spank me, my bottom's already bare."

"Oh, I'm going to spank you." Adrian smiled tightly and lifted a foot. "However, regardless of her attire, a young lady who's going to get her bottom warmed should not be denied the anticipation of feeling her panties being taken down for the occasion." He lifted my other foot, setting my obviously damp panties next to him on the couch. Then he patted his thigh. "Over my lap, love."

I was amazed at the intensity of heat rushing up my face. I'd never been spanked before. The thought aroused me. At the same time, I felt guilty enough that a stinging bottom seemed like a decadent sort of well-deserved justice.

It was hard to maneuver in my heels, though. With my skirt scrunched up at my waist, no matter how I tipped, I couldn't bend without falling. I looked helplessly at Adrian.

"I'm stuck."

Wordlessly, he took my hand. I was again reminded of the muscles I'd been so surprised to see under his suit jacket and hand-tailored silk shirt the first time I slid his clothes from him. He drew me carefully over his lap, guiding me forward until my elbows were resting on the couch and my bottom was firmly ensconced over his thighs. His palm caressed my lower cheeks in warm, firm circles.

"I'm going to take your shoes and stockings off, in case you start kicking."

"Oh, indeed!" I laughed. That seemed silly, but I had to admit, what he was doing was turning me on something fierce. Adrian slipped off my right shoe and stocking, massaging deeply into my instep. I laid my head on my hands, moaning into the couch as he rubbed.

"That feels nice."

"Sensitized skin responds better to a spanking." The other spiked heel hit the floor, followed by my second stocking. I was relaxed bonelessly into the couch when he finally stopped rubbing. Through the soft wool of his pants, the damp heat of his erection pressed against my skin. I wiggled contentedly against him.

"What next?"

"I spank you," he said calmly. His watch jingled as he shook his arm. A moment later, the heavy gold timepiece rested next to my panties on the couch. His arm tightened around my waist. "I'll stop anytime you ask me to," he said quietly. I shivered as his fingers caressed my bottom cheeks. "But unless you ask me to stop, love, I'm going to give you the thorough bottom warming you so richly deserve."

I giggled and nodded. His hand lifted. The shock of a hard, sharp spank jolted into me.

"Ow!" I twisted around, looking back over my shoulder in total amazement. "That hurt!"

"A spanking is supposed to hurt." He ignored my shiver and stroked my tingling bottom. "Unless you're asking me to stop, lay your head back down. Lift your bottom when you're ready for the next stroke."

I eyed him dubiously. That swat had carried a definite sting. But my pussy was so turned on it was vibrating. And I was curious as to what a spanking would feel like—especially when I had so clearly earned one. I put my head down and tentatively lifted my bottom.

"Good girl," he said, his grip again tightening around my waist. "Wiggle and cry as much as you need to, but don't try to get away or cover your bottom." I gasped as a swat stung over my other cheek. This time, Adrian didn't stop. He spanked me again, and again, and again. I wiggled and squirmed. After the first half-dozen strokes, I started to yelp. I threw my hand back over my bottom.

"It hurts, Adrian!"

I was surprised when his hand simply caught my wrist and pinned it to my waist. "It's going to hurt a good deal more before we're done." I yipped as he swatted me again. The one after that was even harder. "Stay in place, young lady!"

Then the smacks rained over my bottom. Adrian swatted me a good three-dozen times, sharp hard spanks that quickly brought tears to my eyes. As much as the pain, what stunned me was that Adrian was really *spanking* me!

And he wasn't stopping. The louder I yelled, the harder he

smacked. The more I tried to twist away, the tighter he held me. My bottom hurt! I bucked up, howling at a stinging flurry on the tender spot where my bottom met the tops of my thighs. Adrian spanked me until I collapsed over his lap, sobbing my heart out as a river of tears washed away a tightness in my chest I hadn't even known was there.

"I dislike vulgarity, love. But you know that."

It took me a moment to realize Adrian had stopped. His touch was now a gentle caress. My bottom was so sore, even that light stroking made me shudder. Fresh hot tears leaked from my eyes.

"I'm s-sorry, Adrian." It was hard to catch my breath, but I struggled to choke out the words. I truly regretted taking my annoyance out on him.

"I forgive you," he said quietly. "Now I believe it's time for you to forgive yourself, as well."

I gasped as his hand slid between my legs. My pussy was so hot and slippery, I almost came when his fingers slid into me. Then his thumb was on my clit. I wailed as he teased me to the edge of orgasm—and held me there. My juices were running over his hand, down onto his thigh. He slid his index finger free. As his other hand held my excruciatingly tender bottom cheeks apart, his fingertip pressed against my anus. His erection poked up into my belly. I sobbed out his name, then screamed it as his fingers all moved at once, his thumb circling my clit as the fingers in my pussy pressed into my G-spot and the slippery finger on my anus slid deep.

The pain in my bottom segued into sensation so strong the orgasm exploded through me. I shrieked and bucked, clamping around his torturous fingers, my pussy spurting until even the lightest touch on my oversensitized clit was too much for me to bear. Adrian stilled the fingers resting in me, his other hand stroking my once more noticeably sore bottom. Beneath my belly, a large damp spot covered his softening shaft.

"It appears your husband enjoys spanking you almost as much as he enjoys making you come."

The disapproval was gone from his voice, replaced by self-deprecating amusement. I groaned as his fingers slid free, then I smiled and settled my face comfortably against the couch. I had no doubt I was going to find myself in the same position many more times in the future. But tonight, I was content to rest in Adrian's lap and savor the moment.

THE SPANKING SALON

Elizabeth Coldwell

Everyone on campus knew about the Salon. It was a story that did the rounds in freshers' week, like the one about the history student who had some kind of breakdown during his final exams, and turned in a paper consisting of the word *Aardvark,* repeated over and over on twelve sides of foolscap. But the Salon wasn't an urban legend, it was real—a secret, men-only club where you could watch and participate in the punishment of willing young women. Hence its more commonly used name, the Spanking Salon.

Becoming a member appealed to me on a level I couldn't explain. The thought of a woman having her bottom bared for an intense hand warming, or an extended paddling, turned me on like nothing else. But my chances of stepping through the Salon's door—hell, of even being told the location of those doors—were zero. No one knew quite how the club recruited its prospective members. Some said you had to be spotted browsing the collection of Victorian erotica buried deep in the library stacks. Others that it was a matter of family connections: only if your father had been a member of the Salon would you be admitted. Whatever the criteria for selection were, I knew I'd fail to meet them. That was confirmed the morning invitations to their initiation ceremony were stuffed into the pigeonholes of the lucky few.

Freddie Burleigh, who had the room next to mine and was the closest friend I'd made in my first few weeks at university, was checking his post at the same time as me. The bundle he pulled out included a thick, cream-covered envelope bearing nothing more than his name in neat copperplate handwriting.

"What've you got there?" I asked, watching him browse its contents with growing comprehension.

"You're not going to believe it, Ash. I've been invited to join the Spanking Salon." He thrust his invitation under my nose. Quickly, I scanned the handwritten note, envy gnawing at my gut. The pleasure of his attendance was requested on Friday night, at an address in town I didn't recognize.

"Well done, mate." I fought to keep the jealousy I felt out of my voice. It was no surprise Freddie had been recruited. He was prime Salon material: public school educated; father something in the diplomatic service; handsome in a sturdy, well-bred kind of way. More importantly, I'd seen the paperbacks he kept hidden behind his History of Art course books: lurid pulp novels with pictures of naked, blushing asscheeks on their covers, penned by authors with names like Ophelia Birch and Rosie Bottoms.

Glancing at the mail rack, I saw only one other similar envelope waiting to be collected. Hardly any of the pigeonholes had been emptied, it being Saturday and the lure of a lie-in after last night's excesses appealing more than the indifferent breakfast served up in the refectory. If the number of invitations issued was similar across the university's other five halls of residence, only a dozen or so initiates would be attending the Salon's next meeting. I longed to know who they were, what made them special. And what perverse delights awaited them on Friday night.

Of course, I had no expectation of ever finding out. Freddie might regale me with a watered-down version of events if I pressed him, but I was sure he'd be sworn to keep the real meat a secret. I'd simply have to stew in my frustration, lying on my bed, wanking and thinking of what I was missing.

Until a flu bug swept the hall. Half the people on our floor succumbed, including big, healthy Freddie. When he didn't make it down to breakfast on Friday morning, I popped my head round his door to find him pale-faced and shivering, too weak to make it any farther than the bathroom at the end of the corridor. One look at him and I knew he wouldn't be keeping his appointment at the Salon tonight.

"Anything I can get you on the way back from lectures?" I asked him, my concern genuine. We might have been chalk and cheese, but I really liked the guy.

"Paracetamol and orange juice should do the trick," he croaked in reply. "Thanks, Ashley, you're a true pal."

Instead of the paracetamol, I bought him an over-the-counter flu remedy, designed to soothe his aches, lower his fever and help him sleep. When I checked in on him again at seven, he was dosed up and dead to the world.

I know I shouldn't have taken advantage of him, but I simply couldn't help myself. That morning, I'd seen the tuxedo hanging on his wardrobe door, the outfit he'd planned to wear to the Salon. Along with it was a black domino mask. That gave me the idea. Freddie and I were roughly the same height, even if he was broader in build than me, and we both had short, fair hair. With the mask, in a darkened room, alongside a group of people who didn't know Freddie too well—and, in any case, would be more concerned about their own satisfaction—I reckoned I just might be able to pass for him.

Even so, my hand was shaking as I handed over the invitation, sure my deception would be picked up. The address on the card led me to a building just off one of the town's main shopping streets, with the kind of plain, black-painted door you could walk past a hundred times without ever noticing. I slipped my mask into position, knocked and waited.

The door was opened moments later by a tall, dark-haired man in evening dress, who looked me up and down.

"Yes?" he asked.

"The meeting tonight." I did my best approximation of Freddie's Sloaney drawl. "I have an invitation."

He studied it, then looked back to me. Could he tell I'd altered the fit of Freddie's jacket with strategically placed safety pins, worn an extra pair of socks so his shiny black shoes weren't too big for me and gelled my hair so it fell over as much of my face as possible in an attempt to conceal my real identity?

"Please come in."

Almost punching the air with delight, I followed him inside, through to a room with black walls and bare wooden floorboards, lit only by the light of flickering candles in wrought-iron holders. Masked men in formal wear stood round in twos and threes, chatting and sipping champagne. It struck me this place resembled nothing so much as a miniature version of the gentleman's clubs where discreet networking took place and business deals were struck. A haven where no women intruded and who you knew was more important than what you knew.

Looking at my fellow initiates, I realized any one of them could be someone I saw every day: a student on my course; someone who worked out in the union gym alongside me; one of the volunteers who served behind the Junior Common Room bar. Disguised as they were, I had no way of knowing. But, I reasoned, if I couldn't recognize them, by the same token they couldn't recognize me.

The man who'd let me inside took me over to what I assumed must be the president of this society, judging by the ornate gold mask he wore.

"Freddie Burleigh, Sir."

My hand was grasped in a bone-crushing shake. Slate-gray eyes regarded me from behind the mask. "Freddie, welcome to the Salon. I'm Martyn Salisbury."

The name didn't mean anything to me. I wondered whether Freddie knew him, and settled for a neutral, "It's good to be here," by way of reply.

"You're the last to arrive," he told me. "We were beginning to give up on you, to tell you the truth. You wouldn't have been the first potential initiate to get cold feet at the last minute. But now that you're here the real fun of the evening can begin." Martyn tapped his glass, attracting everyone's attention. Heads swiveled to look at him. "Gentlemen, tonight is a very special night for all of us. Every year, we select the cream of the new university intake to join the ranks of our little society. Tonight, those of you who have only ever dreamed of witnessing a bare-bottomed spanking in the flesh will discover what it really feels like to watch as a girl's ass turns crimson under the loving attentions of a firm hand—and experience the thrill of punishing her yourself."

An excited murmur ran round the room. Everything we'd heard about the Salon was true. This was a haven for spankos, carrying on its business under the noses of our lecturers and professors. Unless, of course, some of them were here tonight, hidden behind masks...

"Would the novitiates step forward to join me, please?"

Already at Martyn's side, I waited as another eight men made themselves known, almost ashamed of their eagerness in stepping forward. Fewer in number even than I'd expected, we didn't dare to make eye contact for fear of revealing just how stricken with nervous anticipation we were.

"Gentlemen, let me explain the rules for tonight. Allow me to introduce you to the lovely Scarlett."

At his words, a girl of around twenty was led into the room, dressed in a short, flirty white dress decorated with a cute cherry pattern. Her nut-brown hair was fastened in two pigtails at the nape of her neck, and she wore bright red T-bar shoes and white ankle socks. She looked the very picture of innocence, but a glint in her eye told me a saucy little pain slut lurked beneath the carefully constructed façade. Was she a student, taking part in tonight's ceremony for the love of it, or a working girl with a taste for submission? It didn't really matter. She clearly wanted to be spanked every bit as much as Martyn Salisbury and his cronies wanted to spank her.

A high-backed chair was set down in the center of the room, the other members of the Salon forming a partial circle around it. At Martyn's command, we took our places, completing the circle.

"First, you will watch as Scarlett is treated to a thorough bottom warming. Then each of you will have the opportunity to give her six of the best. Think of it, gentlemen, six hard spanks on her peachy, perfect cheeks..."

Glancing at the guys on either side of me as Martyn talked us through the pleasures to come, I couldn't help noticing they both already had distinct swellings in their evening trousers. I couldn't blame them; who could fail to be aroused in such surroundings, with the prospect of dishing out their first-ever spanking growing closer?

His speech at an end, Martyn sat on the chair, ordering Scarlett to drape herself over his knee. She made a halfhearted attempt to resist him, but it was all part of the game. Martyn simply grasped her wrist and hauled her into place. He'd made sure to position himself so the initiates had the perfect view of her round, plump ass, the dress straining across its curves. Edging up the hem, ignoring her protests that he simply couldn't do such a thing to her, he revealed Scarlett's white cotton panties, the spanking fetishist's undergarment of choice. Their crotch looked damp; proof, if any more was really needed, that she was enjoying this ritual every bit as much as we were.

"So, do you have anything to say for yourself before your spanking begins?" Martyn asked.

Scarlett's reply was simple and heartfelt. "Please, Sir, I need to be punished."

"Then punished you shall be. By me and my nine associates. I hope you're ready for that." Everyone in the room seemed to hold his breath as Martyn drew back his arm. A moment's tense silence, then his hand landed with an audible crack on Scarlett's panty-clad ass.

She gave a little "Ow," even though the blow didn't seem that hard. Still, it was what we expected. What we wanted.

Martyn repeated the action on Scarlett's other cheek, bringing another little mew of pain from her. Somewhere to my left, I heard a groan—part desire, part disappointment—and wondered whether the excitement had caused one of my fellow first-timers to come before the real fun started.

Ignoring the noise, Martyn concentrated on giving Scarlett's ass what my mother would have called a good skelping, slapping her cheeks hard through the thin underwear, over and over again. We didn't need to be told we were watching a maestro in action. His spanking motion was smooth, the strokes unhurried, giving the anticipation just enough time to build before the next one fell. For Scarlett's part, she wriggled prettily on his knee in reaction to her punishment, the crotch of her panties, aided by Martyn's thick fingers, slipping into the groove between her pussy lips to give us a glimpse of the delights to come once he pulled them down fully.

I heard the rasp of a zipper coming down, and glanced over to see the guy to my right extracting his cock from his fly. My companion to my left already had his dick out—as, it appeared, did everyone watching except me.

Martyn had noticed it, too. All the time, I thought he'd been concentrating on Scarlett and her reactions to the spanking, but it appeared he'd had an eye on his audience, too.

"A little slow in joining us there, Freddie." His tone made it obvious he expected me to be wanking publicly by now. "Don't tell me you're shy? And you a good Cavendish School boy, too. They're usually the first to start the circle jerks."

He was waiting, as was everyone in the room, but I couldn't bring myself to unzip my trousers. Not here, not in front of all these people I didn't know.

When my hand didn't move in the direction of my fly, Martyn decided matters should be taken into someone else's hands. He spoke to the initiate on my right. "Why don't you help Freddie out, Smith? He's obviously having first night nerves. Though I don't know why. After all, it's not as though he's going to have anything we haven't all seen before…"

This was the last thing I'd expected to happen, to have fingers other than my own undressing me. I tried to stop Smith grabbing for my zipper, but I was too slow. He pushed a hand inside my borrowed evening trousers, seeking for a hard, aching cock—and finding only wet, puffy pussy-flesh.

His baffled surprise lasted only a moment. "Fuck me!" he

bellowed, alerting everyone else to his discovery. "Freddie's a girl!"

Trying to back out of the circle, I was grabbed by Smith, who looked like he played rugby and had the brute strength to prove it. Without ceremony, Martyn dumped Scarlett off his lap and strode over to me.

"What's going on here?" He tugged the domino mask from my face, staring into my wide, panicked eyes. "Who are you, and where's Freddie?"

"I...my name's Ashley Powell," I admitted. "I'm a friend of Freddie's. He's ill, so I borrowed his invitation. I'm sorry I deceived you, but there was no other way I was going to be allowed into the Salon, and I wanted to come here so badly. I know I shouldn't have."

"Damn right you shouldn't. This place has secrets, secrets generations of Salon members have worked very hard to keep hidden over the years, and in you barge in your stolen clothes, spying on things that were never meant for the eyes of someone like you." For the first time, I became aware of Martyn's height, at six foot four a good six inches taller than me, and the way his muscular body bulked out his tuxedo. So strong, so dominant. His dark eyes stared into mine, and in that moment he knew me. "Of course, you know there's only one thing to do with someone who lies and cheats her way in here, don't you?"

I dropped my gaze, aware of a mounting excitement in the room. "Y-yes, Sir."

Martyn turned to Scarlett, who'd almost been forgotten about in all the ruckus following the revelation of my real identity. "I'm afraid we won't be needing you any longer, sweetheart. Someone will call you a taxi. Don't worry, there'll be a little something extra in your tribute by way of compensation."

So she was a tart—and a very disappointed one, from her

petulant pout as she was escorted from the room. Still, it left the way clear for Martyn to focus on dealing with me. I shifted from foot to foot, nervously awaiting his next instructions. They weren't long in coming, but to my surprise, they weren't directed at me.

"Gentlemen, as you all now know, we have an intruder. A very cunning one, but one who needs to be punished for this show of audacity. And the first thing we have to show her is that taking someone's clothes without permission is wrong. Smith, Berry, remove that stolen outfit from her, would you?"

"But I didn't steal it, I just—" I tried to protest, as Smith and the ginger-haired lad who'd been standing to my left began to unbutton my jacket. Just like Scarlett's, my protests were part of the game. Try as I might to deny it, my pussy was pulsing, fluid with desire as the two initiates stripped me of Freddie's clothing.

Shoes, socks, jacket, trousers, bow tie, shirt—all were removed from me in a matter of moments. I'd used bandages to flatten my breasts and aid in the illusion I was male, though in truth there wasn't too much to conceal. With a contemptuous flick of his wrist, Smith disposed of the fastenings keeping them in place. They slithered to the floor, baring my tits to the assembled guests. It was the most humiliating moment of my life, yet I'd never been so turned on. Martyn couldn't have known my most potent fantasies involved being stripped before a punishment while an audience looked on, though I'd never dreamed I'd ever find myself in this position.

Berry caught hold of my panties, preparing to lower them.

"Hey!" I objected. "Those are mine, not Freddie's."

Martin chuckled. "That may be so, but naughty girls who lie and steal shouldn't be allowed to keep them on. Otherwise they'll never learn their lesson, will they?"

With that, he told Berry to pull my underwear down. I stood

meekly as the shamefully damp garment was passed from man to man, eager noses sniffing at the cotton.

I attempted to cover my bare crotch with my hands, but Martyn ordered me to link my fingers behind my head so everyone in the room could take a good look at my naked state. "You're enjoying this entirely too much," he said, even though my cheeks burned with shame. "Maybe that will change once you're over my knee."

Taking me by the hand, he led me over to the chair. Sitting down, he guided me efficiently into position, rump upraised. Unlike Scarlett, I didn't try to resist. What was the point in pretending I didn't want this, that all the time I'd been preparing to watch another woman being punished, I'd been thinking how it would feel if I was the one whose ass was on the receiving end? I differed from everyone else who'd stepped through the door of the Salon for the first time tonight not just because I was female and they were male. They'd always wanted to give a spanking, but I'd always wanted to take one.

"Before we go any further, Ashley, do you have anything to say for yourself?"

"Only that I'm sorry, Sir."

"Believe me, you're not sorry yet, but you will be when this is over. As the stand-in for Scarlett, you'll be expected to take the same punishment she would. I shall be warming you up, then six spanks from each of the initiates."

It was a lot to expect a novice like me to take, but as Martyn's hand caressed the curves of my ass, acquainting itself with the texture and weight of my flesh, I willed him not to push me past my limits.

The circle of masked men had reconvened around us, clutching their cocks as they waited for my punishment to begin. For a moment, I gazed at them, proud and defiant. I'd infiltrated their all-male environment, breaking their rules, and I was unrepentant about that fact. Indeed, I'd have no qualms about doing it again.

My defiance lasted as long as it took Martyn to land the first smack. His open palm made contact with my bare ass, stinging more than I'd believed possible. When I yelled, it wasn't a cursory acknowledgment of the slap, like Scarlett's had been. It had bloody hurt, and I wanted everyone to know it.

Martyn's tone held a certain smug satisfaction. "Wasn't what you thought it would be, was it? Are you starting to regret this now?" His words were punctuated with smacks, each equally hard as the first. Falling in the same spot every time, they burned, making me writhe against the harsh twill of his trousers—and the substantial bulge lurking at his crotch. With every blow, the fists of our audience moved faster on their cocks, the sights and sounds of my punishment spurring them on to make themselves come.

But even though my spanking was so much more painful than I'd ever dreamed, already the endorphins were doing their best to soothe the hurt, and I was riding a wave of sweet, dark bliss. "No, Sir, I don't regret it," I told him.

"Well, I've done my best," he replied, even though I was sure the spanking he'd given me was only a fraction of what he could dish out, should he choose. "Let's see what someone else can do. Smith, would you like to take your turn?"

And so began my long, drawn-out punishment at the hands of the initiates. One by one, they stepped up to take Martyn Salisbury's place. A couple approached me with a measure of assurance, even if they didn't really feel it, while the others were endearingly clumsy in their eagerness to spank me. Each ordered me onto his lap, searching for the same authoritative tone Martyn had used. They stroked my ass, feeling the heat radiating from it. Some went further, letting a finger slip between my pussy lips to find the wetness there, rubbing my clit or exploring my juicy hole. One of them even slicked his thumb with my cream, before pushing it up my asshole. At least one of the wanking onlookers shot his spunk at the moment I cried out at the shamefully delicious feeling of being penetrated there.

Whatever else they did to me, they all made sure to treat me to six spanks. Most were tentative at first, but by the sixth, they were swinging their arms with confidence, palms falling with unerring accuracy on my sore, blotchy cheeks.

By the end, tears were rolling down my face, and my ass felt so hot and swollen I knew I'd have to sleep on my front that night. Between them, these men had broken me down, but in their appreciation of my submission, the resilience with which I'd taken all they had to give me, they'd put me back together stronger and more alive than before.

What happened now? I wondered, as the last of the initiates helped me off his lap. Did I get down on my knees and suck every single one of them until they came, by way of thanks?

It seemed not. "Thank you, gentlemen," Martyn said, applauding their work. The other members of the Salon joined in, welcoming their new brothers in spanking. "And that concludes the evening's proceedings. I look forward to seeing you again in a month's time." As they began to zip themselves up and prepare to leave, presumably to spend the rest of the night reliving what they'd just witnessed, he turned to me. "As for you, Miss Powell, we still have unfinished business..."

He waited until everyone else had left, letting me wonder what else he had in mind for me. Unzipping his fly, he brought out the only cock I hadn't yet seen. His self-restraint was amazing, not to have touched himself at any point, despite the punishment scene he'd orchestrated so spectacularly. I'd gained some idea of his dimensions as I squirmed on his lap, but still I smiled at my first sight of that long, unyielding column of flesh.

"Suck it," he ordered.

Without a murmur, I sank down, taking him deep in my mouth. All my gratitude at having been chastised so thoroughly and so publicly was expressed by my lips and tongue, sucking and slurping from root to tip. He tasted of spice and brine, and when I gazed up I saw his eyes half closed, his expression one of wonder. Grazing my teeth along his length, I gave him a teasing hint of how it felt to have your pleasure mingled with sweet pain.

Unable to deny myself what I'd been craving since Martyn's hand first caressed my bare ass, I dabbed at my clit. He realized what I was doing and laughed.

"Greedy girl, aren't you?" Those were the last coherent words he managed before his orgasm overtook him. Fingers curled in my hair, he held my head steady as his load jetted down my throat, his willpower no match for my oral skills. The taste, the feel of him climaxing in my mouth was all it took to have me coming, too, the perfect end to this most extraordinary evening.

As I was dressing to leave, Martyn surprised me with his next words. "So we'll see you in a month, Ashley."

"I'm sorry?" The last thing I'd expected was to be allowed anywhere near the Salon's premises again.

"It's always nice to find a girl who loves to be spanked as much as you do, and who doesn't expect to be paid for the privilege. And after tonight's performance, I think a few of our older members are going to want the opportunity to warm that gorgeous ass of yours. Oh, and bring Freddie with you. He's still got to pass the initiation, after all."

Poor Freddie. I had some explaining to do, when he was well enough to hear it. He'd be annoyed when he realized how I'd used him to get what I wanted. Annoyed enough to punish me? Despite the dull throb of my recently punished ass, I couldn't help hoping so. And with any luck, I wouldn't have to wait 'til the next Salon gathering rolled 'round to learn how that felt.

THE IMPACT OF CHANGE

Maggie Morton

I found, one late, midsummer afternoon, that I was sick of Ryan spanking me, which came as a huge surprise. I'd always loved it, always gotten so hot, so wet, so, so, so turned on by each mouthwatering, cunt-wetting *smack* of his hand. Or our paddle; or our strap; or a spatula, once; or a dildo, which happened more than a few times, each with him taking turns sliding it in and out of my pussy, then hitting each cheek with a walloping thump. But this afternoon, bent over his knee, one whole year into our relationship, it just wasn't doing it for me. Well, fuck. I knew it was his favorite act, knew his last girlfriend had hated it—that had been one part of why they'd broken up. So I took each spank like I always did, pretending that I was having a hell of a lot of fun even though no, I really wasn't.

Once he was done, Ryan put on a condom, and I found I certainly still enjoyed this sex act, still enjoyed having his lovely cock fuck my pussy. I came, quick and intense, with only a few rubs of Ryan's skilled middle finger. He came only moments later, growling and bucking against me.

We cleaned up and went out to dinner. But what to do about this problem? Did this mean more trouble down the line?

During dinner, Ryan noticed I wasn't my usual talkative self, and he tried to pry the reason out of me, but I refused to reveal what was causing my lips to mostly stay shut. After all, how could I tell him? Especially in a fancy restaurant like this.

"Maybe this will cheer you up, Toni," Ryan said, one corner of his mouth turning up in what I'd always thought of as his "sexy-time grin."

"Oh?" I asked. I swallowed the last of my chardonnay. I was more interested in what kinds of desserts the restaurant was serving than anything sexual at this point in time, but it certainly wasn't *dessert* that always came along with said "sexy-time smile."

"Yeah, it's something waiting for us at home. In our bedroom. Consider it an anniversary present. Which, well, is kind of what it is."

Now, a gift—that I could get behind. He'd always had exquisite taste in whatever he picked out for me, and while we'd agreed not to get each other anything for our anniversary (we were both a little light in our wallets at the moment), I had already thought once or twice that he might go ahead and get me something anyway. That was just what Ryan was like, always wanting to show me how much he loved me, even though all I needed to be reassured of his love were his words and his affection, something he still hadn't realized, obviously, or he wouldn't have gotten me something.

"Then I suppose I'll skip dessert." I took Ryan's hand and kissed it. "I already know I'll love it, whatever it is. But you know you didn't have to get me anything."

"Yes, I knew that, but I worked out a deal with someone, so you don't have to worry about it costing us this month's rent. It may not have been very pricey, but I have a feeling you'll just love it," Ryan said, and then he winked at me.

"Good. Well, let's pay the check and head home, sweetie. I'm dying to find out what it is!"

We had walked there; the restaurant was only about three blocks from our building, and luckily, the night was pleasant, with a slight, warm breeze carrying along the scents of summer. Admittedly, I felt a little giddy at the thought that some kind of delightful (and probably sexual) surprise was waiting for me at our place. Whatever it was, I was sure it would align with Ryan's always perfect taste. And it did, in a way, although it was nothing like what I'd expected.

When we got home, Ryan told me to wait about five minutes and then join him in the bedroom. I did as he said, and then, not knowing what to expect, I turned the doorknob and went inside. Ryan stood near the bed, completely naked, and sitting on the bed, wearing just as much as Ryan was—in other words, nothing at all—was one of the most gorgeous men I'd seen in all my days. Instead of being delighted, or overjoyed, maybe, that such a lovely specimen sat on our bed, I gasped, suddenly feeling a little light-headed. Ryan's gift to me was a *man*? What on... what on earth had gotten into my boyfriend?

Yes, we'd talked, while fucking, about a third—always a man, because while Ryan was bi, I mostly wasn't—but talking was quite different than doing. Obviously. Why didn't Ryan realize that?

But when Ryan approached this fine, fine man, when the man stood, and reached up to Ryan's head, trailing his fingers through Ryan's thick hair, when he grabbed my boyfriend's ponytail and yanked, hard, and when Ryan's back bowed back from the pull of this man's hand, I practically soaked through my panties. "Oh, my god..." I said, my voice quiet—reverent, almost. This was, quite possibly, the hottest thing I'd seen. Ever. In my entire life.

"Am I..." I slowly took a few steps forward. The man watched me, his beautiful, full lips slightly parted, and then his tongue darted out and he licked them, turning what was already perfection into something close to a religious experience. "Am I allowed to make requests?" I continued. And then I surprised myself by reaching out my arms. One of my hands came to rest on the man's side, slightly above his subtle curve of hip. I used the other one to trail my nails down Ryan's side, and I didn't choose to do it very gently. I watched my boyfriend swallow, his Adam's apple bobbing as he did, and it was then that I noticed how hard he was—no, how hard they *both* were. Well, this was obvious proof that Ryan hadn't been lying when he said men turned him on. And my arousal when I'd thought of him with another man, well, it was about doubled at actually seeing my man with another cock so close to his own. I mean, god, they were almost touching.

"Requests are more than allowed," the man said, finally answering my query. "After all, as Ryan has told me, this is a gift. For you." He slowly loosened his grip on Ryan's hair, causing Ryan to stumble a little, causing their cocks to brush against each other.

Now I was the one swallowing, my entire mouth wet and hungry for more. "I want...I want to watch Ryan suck your cock. And then..." I knew what I wanted to happen next. But I wasn't all that sure that Ryan would agree. I had always been on the bottom up until now. I'd thought of asking Ryan, asking him to present his ass to me, to let me attack it with my hands, or the implement of my choice. I'd thought of it, but when I'd pictured asking him, his answer always, always was "no." Would he turn down my request now, though? It was a gift, this experience, and gifts are all about giving, not taking away. So, here went nothing. "And then, I want to watch you spank him, while I touch myself. Is that...Ryan? Is that...?"

"Of course," Ryan said. "I was guessing you'd ask for that. I've...I've been hoping you would ask for that, actually. I want to know what it feels like, to be the one getting spanked. I want to know how it feels to you."

"It feels..." and I looked down for a moment, trying to figure out what to say. Then, still unable to find the words, I just nodded at them and stripped off my dress and underwear, sitting down on the bed. "You'll see soon enough."

"Are you ready to suck my cock?" the man asked him.

Ryan nodded, then said, "Wait, let me get out a condom." He went over to our "sex drawer" and removed one, then handed it to me. "I want to watch you put it on him," Ryan said, and I didn't pause for a second, taking the condom from him and freeing it from its wrapper. Then the man turned toward me and grinned, placing his hands on his hips, framing his perfect, hard cock. I placed the condom around its tip, then gently rolled it down, making sure to squeeze his dick a little as I did, enjoying the sounds he made as I squeezed—a grunt, then a gasp—and I looked up then, watching as his grin widened. Then he turned away from me, just a little, and I watched as, for the very first time, I got to see Ryan get down on his knees for someone other than me. He wasn't getting ready to eat me out this time, no, he was getting ready to suck cock, and I couldn't possibly have been more excited, waiting almost breathlessly for that first moment where his lips would meet the tip of the other man's dick.

Ryan wrapped a few fingers and his thumb around the base of the man's cock, slowly tightening his grip. Then he took his lips and opened them, just enough for the head of the man's cock to be able to slip inside. Inch by inch it went in, until I learned that, just like me, my boyfriend was a cocksucking queen, and like me, he was quite capable of deep-throating. I looked up as the last of the cock disappeared in between Ryan's lips, watched as the man tilted back his head, his thick black hair sliding even farther down his muscled back. I couldn't wait any longer; I spread my legs and began to touch myself, my clit already well past engorged. It was just as hard as the two men in front of me were, and I proved, yet again, that women were visual creatures, too. Fuck, yeah, we were, judging from the fact that no one had even touched me, and yet, here I was, soaking wet, with a clit that was threatening to send me screaming over the edge any moment now.

But I didn't want that moment to come yet. And I was the one calling the shots, after all. So I did something that may have surprised Ryan, but which certainly surprised me—in my first move of real topishness, I reached out and grabbed Ryan's pony-tail myself, yanking back his head. I did it just as he had come up for air, his lips not around the man's dick anymore, but just touching the tip of it. "Spanking time," I told him.

"Yes, Ma'am," Ryan said with a grin. The little imp. Well, I'd show him what happened to little imps. I walked over to the open drawer and removed what was my very least favorite item from its contents. It was just a paddle, after all, but it was full of holes. This was the spanking tool that made me squeal and shriek. This was the one that made me stand instead of sit the next day. This was the one I hated, but put up with, out of the goodness of my heart. Out of the wetness of my cunt, too, because it may have hurt like a motherfucking bitch, but god, did it ever turn me on. But how would Ryan like it?

It was *my* game right now, though, and so I enjoyed the look on Ryan's face, a look of fear, as I turned around and revealed my implement of choice.

"That's the one?" Ryan gulped. I didn't know if he did it as a joke, or if he was really that worried.

"Yes, this is it. You probably have a good idea how much it hurts when you smack my ass with it. You probably remember how I always prefer to stand instead of sit the next day, don't you, sweetie?"

"Y-yeah. Are you...are you sure you don't just want to use the strap? Or the paddle? Or just Lorian's hand?"

Lorian? So, I finally knew the man's name. Interesting, to have gotten this far into things and not have known it, although I quickly realized that knowing his name wasn't really all that important—as long as Lorian did what I asked, his name didn't matter in the least. Not the usual way I thought, no, but nothing about this situation was "usual" for me. Or for us.

"Yes, I'm quite sure. Lorian, is it? Here." I handed over the paddle, touching Lorian for the third time this night, and I found I hoped there would be more touching following the spanking, if it was okay with my guy. I guessed it would be, but after all, sexual boundaries are important in a relationship, so I would make sure to ask this time, instead of order. Because would Ryan be comfortable with another man burying his dick deep inside me? I hoped so, but this whole situation was so surprising, I didn't really know what to think at this point.

And then thinking ceased to be all that important and watching took its place, as Lorian sat down on the right side of the bed and slammed my boyfriend down across his knees. I got ready, positioning myself close to where Ryan's head was, reclining against the pillows, and then lovely, lovely Ryan surprised me by inching forward a little and beginning to eat me out. My whole body shuddered at the first touch of his tongue, and then it shuddered along with his, as I watched Lorian stroke the paddle back and forth across Ryan's ass, going gently from cheek to cheek. I knew this move, knew about the tease that came before the first smack of whatever the current implement was, and so I knew that in mere moments, it would come down with a loud, lovely noise, and Ryan's head would shove itself against my cunt.

And there it came; there it was. The first impact of the paddle against my boy's ass, the shove of his head against my wetness. But lucky me—through an amazing show of skill, or perhaps willpower, he continued to eat me out, to lap at my clit, and as the paddle came down again, I felt his tongue skip a beat, felt it thrust, hard, against me, and I knew that it wasn't intentional, this added pressure of his tongue, which made me love the feeling all the more.

I placed my hand on Ryan's neck then, my fingers making delicate circles against his skin, and the shudder it caused brought me immense arousal. Oh, I was close, and then Lorian made eye contact with me, his eyes seeming to tell me that he knew— he knew how close I was. And then the paddle came down, again, again, *again*, in a quick, cruel, volley of smacks. They were loud, hard, and mean, and I barely needed any help from Ryan at all, as the orgasm came pouring out of me, so strong it seemed as if it was going to flood the room. I lost control in that moment, grabbing the only thing I could—Ryan's head— and I pulled his face against me, his eager tongue somehow still managing to help me ride out the orgasm for as long as possible, even as Lorian dropped the paddle and took over with one of his hands. Or at least, that seemed to be the case, because as the orgasm faded into nothing, leaving behind just a very wet cunt, his hand was spanking Ryan, and now Ryan raised up his head, yelling out "Red!"

"Had all you could take, then?" I asked him, my voice sounding thick and dreamy.

"Yes! Yes...oh, wow. You're tougher than I give you credit for," Ryan sighed, his voice weak, as he lay his head down on my thigh. Then I was gentle with him, slowly stroking his head, his hair soft and lovely to touch, like always.

"Do you have any more requests, my sweet?" Ryan asked. "You haven't had either of us inside you yet, after all. Do you want to get fucked?"

I paused for a second, just a second, then smiled down at Ryan. "I do, yes, I do."

"Well, just give me about ten minutes and then your wish, which I suppose I kind of planted in your head, and which I guess is kind of my wish, too—"

"And mine," Lorian said with a chuckle. He began to massage Ryan's ass, something that Ryan always did after using that paddle. It always felt good, although it always felt a little bad, too, as that fucking evil paddle made your ass nice and tender. And I had to admit, it would be nice to have Ryan be the one hesitating for a moment before he decided he had no choice but to sit down, to put pressure on his poor, aching butt. *Tit for tat, motherfucker*, I thought with a smile.

"What're you smiling about?" Ryan asked me, as he inched his way upright.

"I'm smiling about...lots of things, I guess. Thank you, Ryan, this has been a wonderful gift."

"'Has been,' she says?" Ryan glanced at Lorian, then back at me.

"Yeah, 'has been'? Did you change your mind about getting fucked, Toni?"

"No, no, not at all."

"Good. Because I would have been incredibly disappointed."

Lorian rose up off the bed and walked toward me, then lay down, easing me toward the bed's center. Then Ryan got on my other side, and I was surrounded by two gorgeous men. One of them loved me, and for this I was grateful. This was a wonderful entry to the next year of our relationship.

And as Ryan slid his dick into my ass, and Lorian slid his dick into my pussy, thoughts began to enter my head, thoughts about how maybe I wanted to give Ryan an anniversary gift, too. Maybe one with tits? And then I stopped thinking and just got lost in the feeling of being fucked, got lost in pleasure, and we didn't come up for air for many, many hours.

WRITER'S BLOCK

Evan Mora

Parker is my patron, my lover and my muse. I live with Parker in her beautiful three-story century home downtown. I sit at her antique desk, with the laptop she bought me, and I write her stories. Dirty stories. Because that's what Parker likes. Sometimes I write about Daddies and their little girls, dirty little girls who like to be fucked. Sometimes I write about rock-hard butches in low-slung jeans and pouty femmes with short skirts and bright red lipstick. Sometimes, there's even romance. I write about dominance and submission and bondage and pain. Because Parker is a sadistic fuck, and because you have to write what you know.

I want them to be perfect, these stories I'm weaving, these pictures I'm painting with my words. I want every word to bind seamlessly together and be precisely the right one. I want sentences and paragraphs to create images so vivid that Parker's eyes go from smoky gray to nearly black with desire. But sometimes the words don't do what I want them to do. In fact, sometimes the words don't come at all. Anger and frustration quietly amass somewhere deep in my belly, roiling and churning and slowly rising until their taste is like bitter acid at the back of my throat. And when I erupt, when I snap—because it happens, how can it not?—I snap at Parker. And I shouldn't. It's never anything she's done.

She catches my chin between thumb and forefinger, studying my face with those all-seeing eyes. I bristle, I chafe; I want to tell her to get her damn hands off me. I open my mouth to do precisely that, knowing—still knowing—that it's not her I'm angry at, but she beats me to speech with a cold clipped: "Get your things. We're leaving in ten—" and my mouth snaps shut with enough force to make my jaw ache.

We're off to a place far from big-city lights. Our cabin in the woods. Our lake house. Does it matter that it's the middle of the week? It might, if Parker wasn't so very, very good at what she does, or if she or I had anyone to answer to other than her. But she is, and we don't, so we get in the car, her sleek black machine, and head north, where the sounds of the city can't find us.

I hate the drive. I hate everything right now. The waiting, the silence, my own stupidity, the anger that beats at me so fiercely that I want to cry. I know what's coming, and I hate it, too. Even knowing that at some distant point on the other side of this I'll be grateful, transformed, weeping with joy—even knowing that, I'm angry. I hate that she's right, that she's *always* right, at least about this. About what I need.

And she's so damn calm that I want to scream. A primal, animal, ripped-from-my-bowels kind of scream. Anything to shake her up. To make her fight. Perversely, as much as I hate what I'm feeling, this out-of-control, directionless rage, right now I don't want to give it up. I want to sink deeper into it. Let it consume me. It's a powerful force surging through my veins, and if I give it up...

If I let it go...

What if all I'm left with is despair? What if that's all that remains?

It's dark when we get here, and dark here means dark, not the ever-present twilight that permeates back home. It suits my mood.

"Get inside," Parker says.

"Fine," I snap, too far gone to care that I'm compounding my mistakes by even opening my mouth.

This place is like Parker, all clean lines and rugged beauty, glass walls and stone fireplaces and massive timber beams. But underneath there's a foundation built on solid granite, and it's strong and unyielding to its very core.

"Wait here," she says, and I want to turn around and leave, let the night swallow me whole and vanish without a trace. But I wait, like I'm told, because that's what I do. Then Parker's back, dressed in leathers and harnessed already, judging by the sizable bulge in her pants. My cunt comes to life, like some Pavlovian dog; that's how well trained I am, how Parker's made me. I wish we could just bite and tear and fuck each other senseless, but I know her too well to think I'll get off that easily.

She drops a leather duffel bag beside me and plants herself squarely in front of me. Steely gray eyes assess me shrewdly, and I tip my chin up defiantly, refusing to look away, even when better judgment tells me I should.

"You have no words," she says to me, and hers are sharp like razors and cut me to the quick. That's the problem, isn't it? I can't *find* the words, I don't *have* the words, not the ones I need. It's what's brought us here, to this point, and my silence says what I can't.

Parker undresses me, removing each article of clothing with slow deliberation, stripping me of more than simply dress and stockings and underthings.

"Your name is not Callie tonight," she says. "You have no name. Callie means beauty, and right now you have no beauty. No grace. You are anger and self-pity and petulance." She leans in close, looking into the portal of my eyes at the swirling mess of emotions clawing and tearing through my insides. "And I will drive you out," she says.

I hear myself snort derisively and somewhere in some tiny hidden corner inside I start to cry. Parker's hand is up lightning fast, twisting into a fist in my hair and dragging me down to my knees.

"You just can't help yourself, can you?" she asks, striding toward the sofa and pulling me behind her so that I have no choice but to crawl awkwardly on hands and knees after her.

"I was going to work you over with the things in my bag, but now I think you just need to be turned over my knee," she says, planting herself on the center cushion and hoisting me bodily over her lap.

I fight for all I'm worth, thrashing and kicking—there's nothing I hate more than being spanked like that, it's humiliating—but it does no good. Parker's got several inches and about thirty pounds on me and she subdues me quickly, trapping my legs between hers and throwing a strong arm over my back.

I switch tactics, becoming absolutely still. Parker's hand falls on my ass with a resounding crack, but I don't so much as flinch. I won't give her the satisfaction. I may as well be carved from ice. Again and again her hand falls with precision, covering every inch of my ass, lighting my skin on fire, testing my resilience. But I won't give in. I *can't*. I'm not even sure it's something I have control over anymore.

"You don't like this, do you?" Parker says, running her hand over the hot, pulsing landscape of my ass. "You'd rather be strung up and whipped, because you know how pretty you look all stretched out and striped. You like to show me how sweetly you suffer, don't you?" I say nothing, and Parker reaches between my legs and pinches my labia between her fingers. I cry out, caught off guard, but then stubbornly resume my silence.

"Still no words, hmm?" Her fingers probe deeper, tunneling between my slicked folds and into the hot wetness that's accumulated there. It's practically running down my thighs, I'm so well conditioned to Parker's particular brand of sex and violence, but I wish I could turn it off right now. Heat floods my cheeks and I'm glad Parker can't see my face.

"Or maybe I'm wrong. Maybe you like to be humiliated? Turned over my knee like some bratty novice sub and taught a lesson?"

All the things I can't say are lodged in my throat, stuck like something half chewed that I'm choking on. Tears prick at the corners of my eyes, and I squeeze them shut, willing them away, willing my anger to hold.

Parker delivers another barrage of smacks to each cheek and then trails a finger down the crack of my ass, swirling it around my asshole and lower, sinking it deep in my cunt. She adds a second, then a third finger, pumping my slit, holding me down when I would have bucked my hips and tried to dislodge her.

Everything's getting so jumbled up in my head, too many feelings, too many emotions, and they're all getting lost every time Parker pushes into me. A tiny sound escapes me, but doesn't escape Parker.

"You *do* like it, don't you?" She pulls her fingers from inside my body, smearing the wetness across my cheeks and then my lips.

"Do you smell how turned on you are?" My lower lip starts to quiver; I will *not* cry. "Do you taste it?" As she pushes her fingers into my mouth, the salty sweet tang of my arousal is ripe on my tongue.

I know she wants me to let go. I know everything she's doing right now is meant to strip me down, to force me to get rid of all the anger and ugliness I'm carrying. And at this point? Honestly, I wish I could. But I'm stuck. And I can't even find the words to tell her that. She knows, though. Like I said, she *always* knows what I'm feeling, what I need.

Parker pushes me off her lap and onto the floor.

"Bring me my bag." I retrieve it on hands and knees, red ass in the air, wet pussy exposed. "With your teeth." My heart sinks a little, even as I lower my head and gather the leather handles delicately in my mouth. It's light, as I suspected, and light is never a good thing.

I deposit the bag at her feet and sit back on my heels, waiting. If I'd been good, Parker's bag would be too heavy to carry with my teeth. It would be filled with the heavy silver-handled flogger that I love and maybe a wooden paddle. It would contain wrist and ankle restraints, yards and yards of rope, and if I was really good, a pretty body harnesses or corset for me to wear. Instead it contains all the things I hate, things that pinch and sting and burn.

"Sit up," Parker says, clover clamps in hand, and I sit taller and thrust my chest forward, even though I hate them with a passion. Parker pinches my nipples until they are tight little nubs, then affixes a clamp to each one. It hurts like a sonofabitch, but I give nothing away, holding everything deep, deep inside.

She's watching me, holding the chain that connects the two clamps loosely in her hand. My mouth flattens into a thin line and I raise my chin up a little.

"Don't," Parker says, yanking on the chain with enough force to make my breath whoosh out and fresh tears gather in the corners of my eyes. She lets the chain fall then places her hand on the cushion beside her.

"I want you on your knees here." I take my place, facing the back of the sofa, and for a moment our eyes connect and I think I see compassion in hers, but then she stands up and I'm only left with a fleeting impression and my own misery.

Parker lays two items next to me: a vicious neoprene cane, by far the worst tool in her collection, and a short leather whip that looks like barbed wire, with five twisted, barbed and seriously mean tails.

"Choose," she says, and I think about refusing, but there are limits even to my self-destructiveness, and I incline my head mutely toward the whip.

"Lean forward," she says, and I lay my torso over the back of the couch, gritting my teeth against the pain as my breasts, still clamped, mash against the firm surface.

"Tell me you're sorry," Parker says.

I can't.

The whip whistles through the air and lands on my ass with a crack, every single barbed knot digging into my skin like a rifle full of buckshot. I bite down on my lip to keep from crying out, and the whip falls two, three, four more times.

"Tell me you're sorry," Parker says again, and I feel them fall then, the tears that I can't control anymore. She's massaging my clit with the tip of her whip, and I want so much to tell her I'm sorry, to feel her inside me, pushing out this ache. But I don't know how, and Parker lets the lash fall again, and again and again, punctuating each blow with the same four words and a maddening caress of my clit.

Everything inside me and everything Parker's making me

feel—all the frustration and anger and sadness and arousal—
they're all swirling together in my gut, gathering force, climbing
higher. And Parker doesn't relent, she keeps saying those words
and slipping her hand between my legs and then letting the whip
crash down again and again. It's too much—it's all too much.
My body's not big enough to contain it any more. It's at the back
of my throat, and the lash falls again and I scream the words
Parker's been waiting to hear.

"I'M SORRY!"

I'm sobbing, gut-wrenching cries ripped from my very core.
Parker's hands are gentle, and she guides me down, laying me
on the sofa.

"Ssshhhh..." she soothes, stroking my body, whispering
tender words of comfort. "It's all right, Callie. It's all right
now." She's tasting my tears, kissing my lips, absorbing my cries
into her.

Parker shifts position and I hear her zipper open, and then
the silky smooth head of her cock is pressed up against my cunt.
She enters me slowly, fully, deeply, until she's buried to the hilt
and her body blankets mine.

Her weight pushes my poor tortured backside deep into the
sofa, and the crush of her chest against my clamped nipples is
an agony that pulses directly into my clit. The walls of my cunt
contract against her cock, and Parker begins to move inside me
with deep, powerful thrusts that I feel in every lost, forgotten
corner of my body. She's driving it out, all the chaos, all the
rage. She's cracking me open, pouring herself into me, and it's
blinding and brilliant and cathartic and I'm crying and coming
and shattering into a million points of light in the darkness.

It's a long time before I come back down, and when I do, I'm
tucked snugly in Parker's embrace, surrounded by the smell of
sex and leather and her.

"Hi," she says, brushing the hair back off my forehead, kissing me tenderly. "Feeling better?"

"Mm-hmm, much."

I feel better than better. I feel relaxed. Grounded. And wonderfully sore. I run soft fingertips along Parker's jaw, thinking I must be the luckiest girl in the world to have someone who knows me so well; who can take care of me the way I need to be taken care of.

"Parker, I'm so sorry—" I begin.

"Sshhh…" she says, placing a finger over my lips.

"Write it down," she says. "All of it. What you were feeling. What you were thinking." She smiles, a deliciously dirty smile that tells me we are far from finished.

"It'll make a hell of a story."

LESSONS
LEARNED

Jade Melisande

He says he wants you to teach him how to tie a girl up and spank her," Sabine told Julian. Julian was in the middle of a complicated tie, holding her arms firmly behind her back as he secured them in place. He gave the rope a firm tug and spun her around to face him.

"Down on the floor," he said. With his hand on her arms to steady her, she sank to her knees obediently, and then, at his direction, farther down, so that she was lying flat on her belly with her chest on the floor. For a moment he held her head down, preventing her from looking up; all she could see was the front of his booted feet and the floor beyond. She loved the sensation of being bound, of the strict rope biting into her flesh, of his hands on her, holding her in place. He moved behind her and bent her legs at the knees to bring them over her back. With a few deft movements, he wrapped her ankles tightly and secured them, heels against her ass, to her wrists. Next he pulled her hair back into the tie, arching her neck and back into a bow and exposing the long line of her throat.

He stepped back and admired his handiwork for a moment, then moved out of her line of sight. A second later she heard the click of his camera as he immortalized his vision in film. She could just see him out of the corner of her eye, stepping in closer and then moving farther back, the camera clicking away the whole time. He finally came back into her field of vision to stand in front of her. She strained to look up at him where he loomed over her, but the ropes restricted her movement and finally she just closed her eyes, forcing herself to relax into the tie, and felt herself begin to drift.

"You'd like that, wouldn't you?" she heard him say.

"Hmm?" she murmured, eyes still closed, still in that half-dreaming state that rope so often put her. It'd been so long since either of them had spoken that she'd lost the thread of their earlier conversation.

"This," he said, and delivered two stinging slaps to her backside. She yelped, her eyes popped open and she jerked against the ropes in surprise. Her lover did not favor a subtle approach. "You'd—like—me—to—teach—Rick—how—to—do—this." Each word was punctuated by another *smack!* of his hand against her backside. As his hands, small for a man's but meaty and dense, connected with her bare skin, Sabine felt a familiar warmth spreading through her. As her ass warmed to his touch, so did the rest of her.

Julian paused and ran his hand over the curve of her ass, soothing, or perhaps only admiring, the heat in her tender skin. The hog-tie did not allow for much movement, but what she could do, she did, wriggling her butt at him in what she hoped was a suggestive manner. The suggestion being: *Spank me! Spank me more!*

He seemed to understand her body's unspoken language

perfectly. First, though, he reached down and loosened her hair from the tie, allowing her to drop her head to the floor so that she could catch her breath. Then he crouched next to her and started in again.

This time he did start slow, patting her round, full ass from the curve where it met her thighs to the dip in her lower back and down again, striking every inch of flesh that the hog-tie left exposed. He slapped the skin on her thighs and hips and what he could reach of her calves, warming every bit of her. She sighed in pleasure, giving herself over to the feel of his hands on her flesh, to the rhythmic *rat-a-tat-tat* and the heat it was generating. Without changing the tempo, he began to ratchet up the intensity, smacking her harder, the pats becoming slaps and then deep, steady blows that threatened to take her breath away. She grunted as each strike connected, her body jerking involuntarily, and felt her cunt begin to throb in time to his slaps. Soon she was panting and moaning beneath his hands, writhing helplessly in the ropes on the floor, alternately trying to wriggle away and to expose more of herself to him, to open herself up from within the ropes even as her body flinched, even as she felt the blows reverberating throughout her entire body. She was no longer sure if she wanted him to continue or to stop.

He stopped and without a word slid a hand between her legs. She gasped as he pushed two fingers against the opening he found there. The folds of her cunt opened easily for him and she felt her wetness drenching his fingers as her body spread wide, like a greedy mouth, to accommodate him. She pushed back against his hand, moaning softly, fighting the ropes that kept her immobilized, wanting so much more.

He laughed and pulled away. Standing abruptly, he looked down at her. She struggled to steady her breathing. He leaned down and put his fingers into her mouth, letting her taste her own excitement.

"Oh, yeah," he said, "I think you'd like that a lot." And then: "Set it up."

A week later Sabine perched on a bar stool at her favorite wine bar, tapping her foot nervously as she waited for Rick to arrive. She checked her cell phone for what seemed like the tenth time. He was only five minutes late. She sipped her wine and told herself to be still.

A moment later Rick walked in. She waved at him as he came in the door and he hurried over. "Sorry I'm late," he said, giving her a somewhat awkward hug. She hadn't seen him in a month or more, and she looked at him curiously, trying to figure out what was different about him.

He saw her looking at him curiously. "Contacts," he said, pointing to his face.

"Aha!" she said. They both laughed, their initial awkwardness broken.

While he ordered a beer, she discreetly gave him the once-over. A handsome man with blond hair and startlingly green eyes (she wondered how she could have missed their color before, even behind glasses), he towered over her own five two by at least a foot. She had never felt intimidated by his size before, however, and wasn't now. She felt comfortable with him, even knowing that within the hour she would most likely be naked and bound before him. Her gaze dropped to his hands, which were large and long-fingered; thinking about what those hands would surely be doing to her soon, Sabine shuddered delicately.

They'd met several months before at, of all things, a book discussion group. The book they'd been discussing had had some oblique references to a D/s relationship, and Sabine had felt compelled to correct some of the group's misconceptions about the lifestyle of which she was a part. She had noticed Rick's rapt attention as she had been speaking (as well as several others' obvious disapproval) but she had only exchanged pleasantries with him in the months since.

That is, until he had emailed her and asked her to tell him more about what she and Julian did. She had known instinctively that his inquiry wasn't for wank material, but that there was a genuine interest there, and they had exchanged several long emails before he had finally asked her if she and Julian would be willing to meet him in person to give him a "lesson."

BDSM 101, as Julian had called it.

"When did you get interested in spanking?" she asked, when his beer arrived.

He took a sip and looked thoughtful. "To be honest, it was your description of your relationship with Julian that intrigued me," he said. "What he does to you, what you share, is so unique. So powerful. I haven't stopped thinking about it since. And now...well, I've met someone. A woman who says she wants me to tie her up and spank her. It's like a dream come true! Except..." He spread his hands wide and shrugged helplessly. "I don't know how to do any of the things she wants." He actually blushed as he said it, and Sabine felt her stomach do a little flip-flop. She remembered now, how quiet and reserved he had always been in their book group and she found it both amazing and endearing that he had worked up the nerve to do this.

She placed a hand on his arm. "We all had to start someplace," she said.

That someplace was Julian's house a little less than an hour later. Sabine stood in the center of the room in only panties and a chemise, while Julian demonstrated different rope techniques on her. First he would tie a limb or other body part, then he would have Rick do the same to her. Rick was a fast learner, and although the setting was not in and of itself erotic, Sabine couldn't help reacting to the feel of his and Julian's hands on her, to the feeling of being a life-size doll, put there only to be moved around like an inanimate object, turned this way and that and maneuvered between them by their hands and the rope. She felt a slickness between her thighs, her pussy ached to be touched and the room was redolent with the scent of her arousal.

If either man noticed, he wasn't letting on.

Occasionally though, as she was spun around or moved from one position to another, her arm or hip, or even, once, her cheek, brushed against a groin, and she felt an erection there, both Julian's and Rick's.

You're not as unaffected as you seem, she thought with a gleeful inner smirk.

Finally Rick asked Julian about the "correct" way to give a good spanking. Sabine listened quietly as Julian went over the basic techniques for a "safe but effective" spanking. As he talked he re-coiled the rope and tossed it aside. Standing off to the side a little, Sabine stifled a yawn. She was much more of a hands-on kind of girl. She sighed, shifted from one foot to the other and wondered if he was ever going to actually *show* Rick how to spank her.

Suddenly, and with no warning, Julian grabbed her by a handful of hair. Sabine let out a startled yip as he dragged her unceremoniously over to the spanking bench that he had set up in the middle of the room. Ignoring her protests, he pushed her roughly down across the bench and pinned her there with one hand.

Sabine gasped as he landed the first blow across her ass, but when she jerked instinctively away he held her down more firmly and said, his voice cracking as sharply as his hand had across her ass, "Don't move, slut!" as he continued slapping her ass with his other hand, striking heavy blows on first one cheek and then the other with a ferocity that made her flinch and struggle futilely against his hold on her.

"Julian!" she finally managed between gasps and grunts. "Please!"

He stopped. "What?" he asked. "You want more?"

She swallowed, still panting. Her backside was on fire, and her mind reeled, but the truth of the matter was that yes, she did want more. Yes, she liked a good, long, warming-up-to-full-on spanking, but she loved this, too, this balls-out aggression that Julian exhibited at times. But the thing was, she knew that Rick was looking for something else. He'd told her about the talks he'd had with his new love interest, and it didn't sound to her like this was exactly the sort of spanking she was looking for. Something more...civilized...was in order.

She looked back over her shoulder at Julian, with Rick standing right next to him, his mouth hanging open. She knew that with her legs spread like this over the spanking bench, both men could see very well how wet she was, how much the spanking had excited her.

"Yes," she said, because there was no sense in lying, "I do want more. But..."

She had a sudden inspiration. An inspiration and a conviction that had been growing in her since she had sat next to Rick at the bar and watched him blush when he talked about what it was that he wanted.

Straightening up from the bench, she turned around to face the two men and cocked her head. "I have an idea," she said, rubbing her tender ass. "May I show him something, Julian?"

Julian looked from her over to Rick and back again. "Sure," he said.

Sabine took Rick by the hand. "I like what Julian was doing, don't get me wrong," she said. "But...there's another way I like it, too. Can I show you?" She tugged on his hand to lead him toward a chair that stood in the corner. He hesitated a moment, then followed her. Eagerly, she thought.

There was a mixture of anticipation and trepidation on his face that she recognized—she knew she'd worn just that expression, had had just that wonderful mix of conflicting feelings herself. And she felt something unfurling inside her chest, something waking up in answer to the hesitant, excited look in his eyes.

She stepped close to him and slipped her hands inside the waistband of his shorts, caught the bottom of his shirt and tugged it gently out. "I want to feel you," she said, her voice a husky murmur. She stood on tiptoe, allowing her breasts to brush against the springy blond curls on his chest, sliding her hands from his belly to his shoulders as she pulled his shirt up and over his head. Out of the corner of her eye she caught Julian watching them closely.

"This will work so much better if you can feel it against your skin," she said. *And*, she thought, *if I can feel it against your skin*. She was shocked at how much the idea of spanking him was turning her on. She reached for the waistband of his shorts again, noting how his breath caught as her fingernails grazed his belly. She looked up at him as she unbuttoned his fly and felt a tug low in her own belly as she saw the beginnings of a smile cross his lips. Delighting in his reaction, she pulled his shorts and underwear down. His cock sprang out from the confines of his shorts as though seeking her mouth, but she only chuckled and shook her head. She saw a slight flush creeping over his chest and up his neck, and looked into his beautiful, green, inquisitive eyes, seeking an answer there.

And found it. Never taking her eyes off his, she stepped forward again, drawn toward him as though pulled by a wire thrumming taut between them.

A breath away from him she stopped and placed a hand against his chest, lightly, so lightly. Her face tilted up to his, they stood that way for a moment and simply breathed together. Then, putting a hand on his shoulder, she turned him around. Taking his wrists, she guided them to the arms of the wooden chair so that he was bent slightly at the waist. She trailed a hand down his back and over his haunches.

God, his skin felt so good. Warm and surprisingly silky, with soft, downy hairs that tickled the palms of her hands. A sigh bubbled through her. She heard him take a tremulous breath as though in answer. She stroked a hand across his ass, cupping the roundness of it, admiring its firmness beneath her fingers, before lightly patting first one cheek and then the other. She lay against his bent back, stroked the skin of his ass and the backs of his thighs and just breathed in the strong, male scent of him.

When she felt him relax beneath her, she straightened and began to spank him.

She started with pats, just testing the water, and loved the way her hand sprang back with each blow, the way he sighed and submitted to her, all the tension seeming to drain away from him. His ass was firm and round, but not too hard. Just the way an ass should feel, she thought. She spanked him harder, slow and steady, and harder still, deeper, until she was delivering sharp stinging blows, over and over across both cheeks. His ass began to glow, warm and pink. His breathing quickened, became a panting that matched the timing of her hand. She relished the sting in her palm, the crack of sound that her hand made each time it connected with his backside. She wanted to go deeper yet, but wasn't sure if either of them was ready for that.

She paused, taking a breath, then slapped him sharply, once more, and felt him flinch. She liked the way his muscles tensed as she drew her hand back again, liked the way he seemed to be holding his breath, liked the way she could see his testicles between his legs, swinging back and forth as he moaned and swayed slightly.

Instead of the smack he was expecting, that she wanted to deliver, she brought her hand down softly and stroked his heated flesh, then, simply held her hands against his hot, red, tender skin.

She stood that way for a time while their breathing slowed. After a moment she felt Julian's hand on the back of her neck, his lips on the top of her head. She leaned into Rick, slipping her arms around his waist, feeling the heat from his skin against her belly, and Julian leaned against her, wrapping his arms around her just as hers were wrapped around Rick. The three of them stood that way for a long time, while Sabine's and Rick's breathing slowed. Finally, she pulled away and turned Rick around to face her.

The wonder she felt was reflected in his face.

"I think," she said, touching a hand to his cheek and then to his lips, touching the smile that hovered there, "that that concludes Lesson One. For both of us."

INVITATION TO A SPANKING

Andrea Dale

Jill bent over the bed, palms flat by her face, her right cheek resting on the purple-and-gold brocade spread. Her eyes were closed, but already she had a beatific smile on her pretty face.

It was her ass I was more interested in, though. Mildly obsessed with, you could say.

High, heart shaped and firm, slendering down to thighs toned by bike riding. A hint of dark, trimmed pubic hair peeking out. Best of all, a constellation of freckles dusted her smooth flesh. I don't know why that aroused me so much, just that it did. Mm, yes, it did.

Oh, how my hand tingled, anticipating the first smack just as much as she did. The feel of that skin against mine, the resultant jiggle, the way the imprint would bloom.

I tortured us both by delaying. I glanced at her husband, but his gaze was also riveted on her inviting cheeks.

I raised my hand...

It started with a personal ad.

Happily married couple seeking female spanking aficionado to warm wife's bottom. No sex involved.

That made me sit up straighter in the hard wooden coffee shop seat—and squirm a little, too. I love giving a firm, hard spanking. I can't say I dislike getting my own ass blistered from time to time, but doing the spanking myself? I imagine it's like how an opera singer feels performing a perfect aria: soaring.

My heart beating just a little harder, I took a sip of my steaming cappuccino and scanned the ad again. It could be a crock—personals in the city weekly paper often are—but something about it spoke to me. Sent me tingling all over, including the good places.

It felt right in my gut...and below.

So I made contact, they responded and we arranged a meeting the next day.

My pussy hummed as I waited in the park, admiring the pretty red and white flowers spilling from the baskets that hung from the faux-antique light posts.

An attractive couple pedaled up on bicycles and dismounted a few feet away. The woman approached me.

"Shar?" she asked with a hint of hesitance.

"Sharon, actually," I said, rising and shaking her hand. I hadn't used my full name, either, in case this was some sort of scam.

To my growing delight, it didn't look like a scam at all. They introduced themselves as Jill Tomita and Christopher Carlisle. They were, like me, in their early forties. While they didn't seem to be gym rats, they were clearly active and fit. She was Asian American, with straight black hair and a smattering of freckles on her nose and high cheekbones. He had dirty blond hair cropped close and warm brown eyes.

Time to get down to business. I asked, and they answered.

Jill wanted to be spanked. Christopher was hesitant. He'd read about it but still felt unsure. He'd been ingrained with the concept that you didn't strike a woman—not a bad tenet overall, really, just not one that meshed when the woman in question craved having her bottom blistered.

So they'd come up with the idea that if he saw Jill enjoying a proper spanking, it would help break down his barriers. They'd both agreed that they'd be more comfortable with a woman doing the deed. Jill was nominally bi: she'd had the obligatory college experiences, but was monogamous in her marriage.

Of course, sex itself wasn't in the agreement—at least, not between them and me. What they did after I left was up to them.

So then I asked to speak to each of them individually, to be extra sure they were both doing this for the right reasons, that neither had talked the other into it.

Christopher went first. I ogled Jill as she walked away. Her ass really was perfect. She wasn't so skinny that her thighs didn't touch. I mean, where's the fun in that? For a spanking, you've got to have some juicy flesh.

I noticed Christopher watching, too. A good sign.

"Fess up," I said. "What's the real reason you don't want to spank her?"

He looked down at his hands. They were broad, capable, solid. Perfect for caressing, holding...and spanking, absolutely. I sometimes get crushes on men just from their hands. Jill was going to be a lucky woman, provided this little plan worked.

He reiterated what he'd said before, about not wanting to hit a woman. I waited. I knew there was more.

Finally, he said, "I know it's what she wants, and I'd give her the world if I could. I just...I don't want to do it wrong, you know?"

Aw. That was just adorable. I patted his arm.

"Don't worry. I'll give you pointers…and afterward, I'm sure Jill will let you know what she likes."

Jill was even more forthcoming. There was no question that this was absolutely what she wanted—craved, even.

It was clear they loved each other, that they both wanted this to happen, but they didn't know how to do that. They needed a fulcrum, a catalyst, an instigator.

They needed me.

That's how it started, and now I was here—we were here— and the world narrowed to my raised hand and Jill's waiting ass. Christopher was silent; I think he was holding his breath. I think we all were.

As if apart from myself, I saw my hand flash through the air, nails painted OPI Diva of Geneva hot pink. Felt the sting against my palm as I connected with her ass. Saw the judder of flesh, the rise of rosy blush.

My own cheeks clenched, savoring the memory of what that sensuous blow felt like.

I caressed the pert globes of her ass, petting away the sting. Preparing her for the next flash of delicate pain.

The scent of her arousal—hot musk and spices—tickled my nose. My own panties—I'd worn lavender lace with a bouquet of tiny flowers in the front, even though nobody but me would see them—were damp with desire.

I struck her again, glorying in the sensation and in the sound of her tiny gasp.

This wasn't about hard-core BDSM. This wasn't about whips and chains and dungeons. It wasn't, really, about bondage at all: Jill's hands were flat on the bed, although her fingers twitched, and I guessed she wanted to reach down and explore the wetness created by nothing more than the throbbing of her spanked, hot flesh. If she caressed her swollen clit, she'd probably come in no time.

But she didn't. This was about pain and pleasure and arousal and need and...not quite denial, no. Anticipation. A hint of submission.

Mostly, though, it was about the smarting ache of her flesh and the feel of my hand connecting with it again and again.

Throughout the scenario, I'd been explaining to Christopher what I was doing and why. How the flesh of the upper thigh, just beneath the curve of the ass, is especially tender. How each strike has to be controlled but confident. Trust yourself. Trust your partner.

A whimper escaped her, and my clit twitched. I liked it when pretty women reacted to what I did to them.

She was almost ready. She rolled her hips, and I rolled mine, as slick and wet and needy as if I'd been the one receiving the spanking.

We'd set out a paddle and a soft, red suede flogger. Nothing too hard-core; if they decided to try a cane or a whip, that would come later. But honestly, right now, the paddle and flogger were superfluous. My desire was hand on flesh, and clearly Jill's was the same.

I spanked her again, delighting in the feel, the sound, the scent. And as I did, I tipped my head at Christopher.

In a flash, he was on his feet. I stepped aside to let him take my place. Jill's eyes were closed, a faint glisten of tears on her cheek and a faint smile on her lips. She didn't know what would come next, but I suspect she knew it would be better than what came before, if only because that's the way the evening had gone so far.

Christopher raised his hand then looked at me. Beneath his

hesitation, he was as ready as Jill. He just needed to believe. I nodded.

His hand, his perfect broad hand, connected smartly with Jill's ass, exactly right.

There was a brief moment when she froze, and then I saw her body shudder and crack beneath the force of an orgasm she didn't expect. Her eyes flew open, but appeared unseeing; her mouth formed an O as she keened, high and stunned and overwhelmed by the force of it.

It was all I could do to stumble out of their bedroom, pulling the door shut behind me before I half collapsed against the wall, the shimmerfall of something akin to an orgasm turning my thighs to delicious mush.

As I staggered my way out their front door, fumbling for my keys, I realized how my reading that personal ad had changed their lives.

Now I was off to find a sweet young thing who craved a spanking—or maybe a sweet young thing to focus on my tender bottom.

Female spanking aficionado looking to warm your wife's or girlfriend's bottom. No sex involved...

A TIMELY CORRECTION

Dorothy Freed

Vincent, my husband and Master, is a punctual man. To him a seven-thirty dinner date means exactly that. The same goes for movies, the theater or other social events. He considers lateness to be not only rude, but a passive form of control.

As for me, I'm prone to lateness. Try as I might, time gets away from me—I tend to think I have plenty of it, even when I don't. So, with minutes to spare before keeping an appointment, I'll decide there's time for a phone call, an email check, or restyling my long red hair. And surprise! Wherever I go I end up rushing—particularly if Vincent's involved.

He doesn't take kindly to lateness.

"That'll be ten, hard, with the paddle, when we get home," he'd say, his dark eyes cool and distant, his bearded, high-cheek-boned face stern, hustling me out the door to the car—knowing the specter of impending discipline would keep me aroused all evening.

Later, at home in our playroom, bare-assed and repentant,

I'd yelp and squeal my way through ten hard—which hurt like mad while it was happening—that left me dripping, every time, rubbing my stinging, reddened ass tenderly; pussy tingling, panting to come.

But the penalty for misbehavior would be no orgasm for me that night—although I was permitted to suck Vincent off.

Each time I was disciplined for it, I'd swear off lateness for life, but before long, I'd be late again—or worse, make *us* late— and the cycle repeated itself. Punctuality was an ongoing issue in the early years of our BDSM relationship.

That is, until the final evening of our visit to Switzerland a few years ago. With our return flight to San Francisco confirmed for the next morning, Vincent, who knew me well, emphasized the need to be at Zurich International Airport two hours before our ten a.m. flight.

"Do your packing tonight, Lucy. The travel alarm's set for six a.m. We'll dress, have breakfast and be on the airport bus by seven fifteen at the latest, arriving at the airport by eight. Security lines are long and slow these days. We *don't* want to have to rush," he said, giving me a look.

"Of course not, Sir," I agreed. "I understand."

But I found it hard to wake up the next morning and stood in the shower until my eyes finally opened. Then I dressed, applied makeup and packed a few things I'd forgotten the night before. In spite of my best efforts, everything took a little longer than I thought it would. Vincent was tapping his foot by the time we sat down to breakfast. That's when I remembered that the book I'd planned to read on the plane was still in our room.

"It will only take a minute," I said, rushing back for it. "We're early; we have plenty of time."

Well, we had less time than I thought. We missed the hotel bus to the airport by one minute and had to wait for the next one. Even with the delay, we might have had sufficient time, but for the bumper-to-bumper traffic we encountered along the way.

I smiled ingratiatingly at Vincent through my lashes, but he wasn't having any of it.

By the time we reached the airport and made our way through security, we were so late we would have missed our flight, but for the kindness of a flight agent, who held the plane for us.

"Hurry, they won't wait long," she said, waving us on. And we were off and sprinting, hair flying, shoes clattering, luggage rolling crazily behind—through the entire, enormous terminal, to our departure gate—*at the opposite end of the building.*

We rushed onto the plane, disheveled and undignified, seconds before the doors were locked.

Once we were seated I looked up at Vincent with a little grin, willing to laugh about it if he was. He wasn't. His eyes were narrowed, his full lips drawn tight. Steam came from his ears.

He barely said a word to me during the long flight that followed. I sat beside him, sipping wine, watching the movie, leafing through magazines—and thinking about the ten hard I expected to get when we got home.

If I'd known what Vincent had planned for me, I might have stayed on the plane. But he said nothing until we were settled in at home. Then, before kissing me good night, he gazed into my eyes and said in that low, *Godfather* tone he uses when he's really pissed, "Tomorrow afternoon at four, *sharp,* I want you stripped and kneeling facedown, ass up, at the entrance to the playroom—waiting to be invited in. And this time, sweetheart, expect more than ten."

I woke the next morning to immediate anticipation of what was coming, moving through my day in alternating states of arousal and apprehension. Little electric currents of excitement crawled over my skin and between my legs. I knew I wouldn't trade the strange delight I shared with Vincent for anything— but still, pain was pain, and I was worried.

Will you really submit to this? I asked myself. *Well yes, we have our rules.*

At four sharp, I knelt at Vincent's feet as directed, repentant and trembling. "I'm *so* sorry, Sir," I whispered, not daring to look up.

"I know you are, Lucy," he said softly, "but I want you sorrier." I looked up, and he extended his hand to me. "Get up. Come this way."

Heart thumping, eyes down, I rose, took his hand, and followed him. Minutes later I was collared, cuffed and bound in the black leather sling that hung from our playroom ceiling. My arms and legs were spread high and wide and secured to the chains supporting the sling. Vincent carefully positioned me so my pussy and asscheeks hung slightly over the front edge of the sling, leaving me, in his words, "completely accessible."

The wooden blinds were drawn, the lights low. Vincent, shirt open to his waist, stood looking down at me, feasting his eyes. I could hardly breathe with all the excitement and he knew it. Half grinning, he reached between my legs, slipping two fingers inside me, making me moan, and brought his fingers, slick with my juices, to my lips. I licked them clean, and he bent, kissed me lightly, and left the room—leaving me to reflect on my transgressions.

Time slowed down for me. The warm air in the room felt cool against my naked skin. The sling swung a little as I shifted my weight. I stole a look in the full-length mirror on the closet door and flushed at the sight of myself—long red curls tumbling over my shoulders, my shaved pussy swollen and exposed, sapphire-blue eyes wide—like something from the *Beauty* books. A drop of sweat broke out behind my neck and trickled slowly down my back. My limbs were taut but nothing hurt yet. I don't know how long I waited there, dreading and craving Vincent's return, but it felt like a long time.

I trembled, and my breathing quickened when I heard his footsteps coming down the hall and into the room. He stared at me without speaking, before opening the red chest of drawers we called "the toy chest." He selected a flat wooden paddle I loathe, and the hard-core nipple clamps he uses when he means business. I tried being brave when they crashed down on my hardened nipples, but whimpered in spite of myself, and looked up at Vincent beseechingly.

His heavy eyebrows arched up. He circled the sling silently, like a one-man wolf pack, inspecting me from all angles while slapping the paddle lightly against his palm.

"Because of you," he said from behind me, whispering in my ear, "your forty-nine-year-old top was forced to race, like a teenager, through an *entire airport terminal*—not to mention being chewed out by an airline hostess for lateness. I think, Lucy," he said, standing before me again, looking me in the eye, "we'll be pushing some limits this time."

"Yes, Sir," I whispered.

Vincent nodded. "Good," he said. "We agree."

I was gazing up at him when the paddle came down on my firm round asscheeks—striking first one, then the other, then the first one again. Not hard—not yet—but landing with a sharp slapping sound, and making me gasp for breath.

The next several swats were more widely spaced and landed directly on my crack. I yelped, arms and legs stiffening, causing the terrible nipple clamps to sway as the sling swung to and fro, chains rattling.

"Oh, please, Sir," I squealed. "Please not so hard."

Ignoring me, Vincent brought the paddle down again and again, harder now, moving with carefully controlled force from my flaming asscheeks to my tender inner thighs. It hurt so much when it splatted against my pussy, I screamed. "Keep it down. You have this coming," he said.

The spanking continued. My wrists and ankles strained at the leather cuffs. My nipples burned. I'd quieted down, as ordered, but the tears in my eyes spilled over and streamed down my face.

I can't, it's too much, I thought, as my pain level escalated, pushing at my limits. My safewords presented themselves in my mind. *Red! Say it and he'll stop. Yellow! Say it and he'll slow it down!* But I stayed stubbornly silent, riding that pain like a giant wave, aware of nothing in the world but me and Vincent and the spanking of my life.

When it was over, he brought me down slowly, soothing me with his lips and hands. He removed the nipple clamps carefully, sucking at my nipples to ease the pain as the blood rushed back into them. Uncuffing my wrists and ankles, he stroked my quivering arms and legs, then bent and held me, kissing my mouth, my eyes; stroking my hair; telling me I was his good, good girl.

I can't say I was never late again after that. But I will say Vincent got my attention that night—and for the entire week that followed, when I was allowed to service him, but not to come. I was half crazed with desire by the time he hung my ass off the edge of the sling again and swung me back and forth onto his cock. I came so hard I almost passed out.

From then on I treated time, and my top, with new respect, and began being on time more often than I was late.

SPANKING
THE MONKEY

Cynthia Rayne

I want Lynn. Desperately.

Watching her surreptitiously through the kitchen doorway as she sips coffee with my wife, Jane, is a temptation in itself. Their heads are bowed and they speak in low tones that I can't discern over the roar of the college football crowd on ESPN. I press the button and lower the volume a bit. I bet they are talking about Lynn's latest conquest. Overhearing a detail always gives me a painful sort of pleasure. Both jealousy and a bit of a thrill. Yes, I ache for her in ways I would be ashamed to admit—especially to my wife, Jane.

Lynn is my wife's best friend and her antithesis. Jane is short, barely over five feet, with curly dark brown hair and warm olive skin. She is feisty and charming. I love her laugh and the way she smiles when she sees me. She is everything I wanted in a wife. Except for one thing...one fairly large and unspeakable thing.

But Lynn? Lynn is tall, nearly six feet, with long blonde hair and a cool presence. She is always so measured and controlled. It makes you wonder what she'd be like if she ever let go. Let herself feel. What would she look like when she came? Would her face be fierce? Full of lust and abandon? Dreamy with orgasm and at peace?

I met Jane long before I came clean with myself about my sexual desires. Before I realized I was submissive. Sure, I'd had the odd thought about being tied up and ridden by some Amazon of a woman, but I thought it was just a passing masturbation fantasy. A whim. I'd had a very normal sex life until I came across a website that changed everything. A man was on all fours at a woman's feet. She held a wicked-looking leather flogger and rained blows down on his ass.

I'd gotten hard. Hard as fucking granite. From then on out, I've been unable to help myself. I crave discipline.

I brought it up to Jane once, just once, after a bottle of wine, a shared joint, and delicious lovemaking. Our sex life was good but strictly vanilla. We were cuddled up in our bed. I had whispered my request in her ear. She laughed off the suggestion that we tie each other up. In actuality, I had wanted her to tie me up, but I thought taking turns would be less threatening. I never had the nerve to bring it up again.

Instead, I fantasized. No harm in a forbidden, five-fingered release, right? I'd get up late at night, leaving her sleeping in our bed. In the anemic glow of the computer screen, I'd beat off to images of women bending men over tables and couches and paddling their asses red and raw. I was obsessed with the thought.

But Lynn was better than any cyber fantasy. The way she dressed: on more than one occasion I had seen her dressed in leather pants as she picked up or dropped off my wife on the way to a girls' night out. I pictured myself perched over her lap as she slapped my ass while wearing those. One time, I'd overheard her talking to her flavor of the week on her red Black-Berry and she had murmured something in a low decadent tone about what happened to "bad boys."

That had set my imagination afire.

I started wondering what other naughty secrets she possessed. She had to be dominant. Had to be. The way she walked, the cool way she looked through men. She had a full-throated, head-back laugh, along with a powerful career as a lawyer and a take-no-prisoners way of dating. In short, she was a challenge.

I was taken with her and wondered what she'd be like in bed. Most of all, I wanted her to discipline me. Every time I think about it, I get hard. Hard as a fucking piece of stone. And achy. I picture myself bent over the cold stone of her granite coun-tertop. I picture her artfully tying my wrists together, maybe with something she's taken off like that pink and black scarf I'd seen her wear once. I bet it would hold her scent, tickle my nose, as she exploited my body for her own pleasure. The scarf would be enough to hold me. It wouldn't dig into my wrists, but it would leave me helpless. I picture her squeezing my asscheeks. Teasing me. I picture her slapping me with her palm. I want her to grease my asshole and fuck it raw for good measure. With her fingers. With a dildo. Jesus. Or a strap-on.

I was getting hard in my chair. I looked at them again and noted they were oblivious. Thank god. I adjusted myself, but it didn't really help. My cock strained against the fabric of my jeans. I pictured her grabbing that cheese board she had hanging from the rack over her kitchen island. The one she brought over laden with brie and Camembert for parties, along with the dark red wine she favored.

It would be perfect for spanking.

Just wide enough to cover both my asscheeks in one blow.

The small handle would snugly fill her palm, giving her ultimate control. I imagined her, fully clothed, maybe in a business
suit. I liked that. Liked feeling vulnerable while I was naked
and exposed. Pictured her dragging the smooth wood over my
vulnerable ass. Imagined her giving one cheek a little tap to
warm me up before she let me have it. No mercy. She'd rain
blows on my vulnerable butt while I writhed against the cold
stone. My cock trapped, unable to get away.

My cock was straining. I grabbed a throw pillow from the
chair next to me and covered my lap. I watched Lynn smile
slyly and my dick twitched in response. I wondered if she'd do
it bare-handed. Would she lay me across her lap? Would she
bare my ass and stroke it first? Run her hand over the vulnerable mounds? Give me teasing little slaps that would make me
groan and push my cock farther against her thigh? Would she
manipulate my asshole with her clever fingers, maybe slide in
a plug? Yes, a thick plug that stretched me. Made me feel full.
Then she'd lay into me, slap my ass into submission, again and
again. My tortured cock would be engorged, pressed against her
thigh and aching to be inside her.

Lynn stood up from the chair in the kitchen and kissed my
wife on the cheek. They exchanged pleasantries, then she stalked
toward me and my breath caught. Her breasts bounced as she
moved and I briefly wondered what color her nipples were.
Pink? Beige? She stopped by my chair and then leaned down.
My cock twitched again, so deliciously painful against my fly.

She pressed a kiss to my cheek. I inhaled her scent and closed
my eyes. Jasmine. "Goodnight, Kevin." She walked to the door
and I breathed out slowly and deliberately, trying to make my
body calm down.

It wouldn't.

While my wife loaded the dishwasher, I snuck to our

bedroom and lay down. With a groan, I unzipped my jeans and shimmied them down my hips. I jammed my hand in the night-stand drawer and withdrew a small bottle of lube. I squeezed a couple drops on my dickhead and began to stroke. I like the cold contrast of gel against my heated skin.

Once more, I was on Lynn's granite countertop and she was letting my ass have it. She told me I was a naughty boy and I deserved my punishment. God, I loved it. Yes, I needed her paddle on my vulnerable skin. Craved her discipline. I worked my hand up and down the shaft. Faster and faster, my breath bellowing out in harsh gasps. I groaned as the come poured out in hot, wet fits. I pumped my shaft empty and lay there, hot semen on my stomach.

And a sinking feeling.

I always felt guilty afterward. Masturbating to images of my wife's friend spanking me? How low could you get? I can only imagine what Jane would say.

I heard my wife's footsteps outside the door and quickly shucked off my pants and wiped up the mess. I tossed the jeans on the floor and the lube in the drawer. She walked in and sat down beside me. Her fingertips traced my lips. "You tired, honey?"

"Yeah, a bit." I grabbed her hand and pulled her down and onto my body. I love my wife and I would never, ever cheat on her. I consoled myself with that thought. And fantasizing isn't a crime, is it? But occasionally, just occasionally I need to be spanked.

Even if it's only in my own mind.

SHINE

Shanna Germain

Inventory:

One round leather paddle. Check.

One rawhide flogger. Check.

One metal zester, curved in the shape of my ass. Check.

Each piece is laid out before me on a thick towel. This isn't our entire spanking kit, but it is the collection of toys that Rob uses most often, and I want to make sure they're perfect. Like wiping the china and shining the best silver one extra time before company arrives.

It is my job to keep our toys clean and organized, to make sure they are ready for Rob at a moment's notice. It might seem silly for a woman who spends her days heading a big company to spend her nights naked on her knees rubbing saddle soap into leather, but I take this job just as seriously as my day job, even on the days that aren't as special as this one. Tonight we're celebrating our one-year anniversary, and I want to do my best to make sure it's perfect.

Rob is the best master I've ever had, maybe the only real one. Before him, I went through a lot of guys who just wanted to break me or fuck me or beat me, pseudo Doms with power issues. They never lasted, of course, and I started to think that what I wanted was impossible. That I'd never find someone who could fuck me and spank me *and* respect me and love me. That all those people talking about soul mates with a sadistic streak were just making it up.

And then I met Rob.

I was at a play party, the kind of event where I stayed in the corners, watching. I'd broken up with my last Dom, a jerk with more women issues than I could count on both hands, and I wasn't really interested in finding a new one. I felt broken, in all the wrong ways. But I hadn't wanted to sit at home by myself. And so I spent the evening staring at the erotic black-and-whites on the walls, watching seemingly happy couples out of the corner of my gaze. I was standing in front of a retouched black-and-white photo of a woman bent over a man's lap, her skirt raised, his hand caught in the action of going down or coming up. The only spot of color in the photo was her ass, with bright red spots on both cheeks. It made me ache for something I didn't have, and it almost made me angry because I thought it was all a farce.

And then this man came and stood beside me. Taller than me, short blond hair that looked like butter curls. Dressed in dark jeans, and a button-up shirt that fit his shoulders perfectly, that showed off the curve of his back. A thick silver ring glinted on his middle finger.

He didn't say a word. Not a cheesy pickup line, not a mention of the photo or the spanking or the couples getting off all around us. He didn't seem to take his gaze off the photograph or even notice me at all. But his presence, his…I didn't even know what to call it…charisma sounds cheesy, essence sounds odd…but whatever it was, it was as though it spoke right to me. Power and pleasure, a quiet strength that instantly made the back of my knees sweat. I could actually feel myself breathing, not just in and out, but deep in my chest, an odd experience, one that heightened every time I tried to quell it, until it seemed like all I could feel was this man radiating next to me, and my own breath entering and leaving my chest.

I don't know how long we stood there, silent. It was fast as my heartbeat and slow as the dew that was gathering between my legs. It was as though he was already wrapping me up in his binds, invisible ones that tugged at every wet and aching part of me.

At the end of it, he turned and caught my gaze. It felt like he was asking for permission, and I nodded. A tiny gesture. He cupped his hand softly around the curve of my ass; I could feel the heat of his palm through my skirt, the cool of his metal ring, and instantly wanted more. Harder. Stronger. Hotter. I was only a little ashamed to realize I was sticking my ass out, pressing it into the curve of his hand, asking for all of those things.

He took his hand away, but not his gaze. "When you're ready," he said.

And then he left me there, in the club. Just walked away.

Still kneeling, I pick up the big, round leather paddle and begin to slowly spread saddle soap over its wide surface. I know what each of these toys does to me, what they do to Rob, how they make my body—and his—respond.

When Rob has had a long day or I've had a long day, he usually chooses this paddle. It's larger than a Ping-Pong paddle, but the same shape, and made of leather so smooth it feels like velvet. Rob says it's just big enough to cover one of my asscheeks perfectly. It certainly feels that way when he lays me down on the bed, two pillows under my hips to push my butt and hips into the air, and begins to use it on me. Slow, long swats at first, the kind I can barely feel, one side and then the other. Soon, he's hitting with the kind of speed and arc that makes my ass ring with every slap. The heat spreads through my skin fast, and I know I'm growing first pink and then deep red and then a nearly bruised purple. He likes to watch my skin change colors, likes to make me squeal and squirm.

When I get like that, I start begging him to fuck me. I can't help it. I want him inside me so badly, to feel his strength counteract the open, slippery thing that I'm becoming. Sometimes he obliges me, flipping me over with a sudden quick movement, driving himself into me so hard and fast that I'm left momentarily breathless with the way he fills me.

But most of the time, he just laughs, that evil wicked laugh that I only hear when we're playing, and he rubs the tip of his cock against me, crooning at how wet I am. Then he pulls away and goes back to the paddle, leaving me whining like a dog.

He's a dick, Rob is. He's been a dick since the day I met him. But there's a difference between being a dick and being a *dick*. Rob is the good kind.

After he left me at the club that night, I went home by myself. Feeling lost and slightly dazed, the inside of me a wet hollow, a vibrating hum of hope and desire. I came almost as soon as I touched myself, a quick hard orgasm that brought a growl from my throat, but it was still missing something. That hand. That ring.

I didn't know if I'd find him again, but I thought he'd given me something just as important: hope that there was someone out there who could want what I wanted, who could give me what I craved, without being a total asshole.

It took me a month to get up my courage to go back to the club. A month before I felt ready to open myself up to what might come my way. I almost didn't go—work was kicking my ass, and I was tired—but something in me made me shower, brush my dark hair back off my face, slip into a low-backed dress that swung around my thighs as I walked.

The artwork this time was pinup girls, new and old. I found myself drawn to a picture of a Rubenesque woman bent over a chair while a man spanked her with a hairbrush. The expression was what caught me, more than anything: two faces filled with pure bliss. As I was standing there, a few men came up and tried to talk to me, but it felt dull and flat, nothing like the power I'd felt the last time.

As soon as I felt a certain presence beside me, I knew it was him. And I knew that was what I'd been hoping for, waiting for, even if I hadn't been willing to admit it to myself. It wasn't like true love or happily-ever-after or meant-for-each-other. None of that. It was a magnetic field between us that made it hard for me to stand upright. I wanted to lean into him, to press myself against him to relieve the pressure. The power poured over me, infiltrated me until I was all breath and pulse and the wet place between my thighs.

We stood, as before, a long time. Quiet. Still. The world moved around us, and all I could focus on were the small things. The glint of his ring. The way his sky-blue shirt set off his blond curls. The tiny lines at the corner of his mouth.

Eventually, my breath turned into something else and I said, "I'm ready."

And just as though he'd expected me to say that, he smiled at me, sweet, dreamy and just a little wicked. He put his hand,

that hard and wonderfully purposeful hand, on my ass again.
And just like that, he led me from the club.

I finish the paddle and move on to the flogger: a thick leather
handle with suede tails. It's not very big, but it's a mean little
toy, with a sting that makes me do this high-pitched squeal like
nothing else. I use a leather cleaner on its long strips, taking
each one in turn.

Rob is the most anal man I've ever had a relationship with.
And I don't just mean that he's an ass man. I mean that he's *anal*.
As in obsessive-compulsive anal. As in, even with a flogger, he
can hit the same exact spot over and over and over again, until
I don't think I can stand it anymore, until I'm begging him to
just move his aim a centimeter to the left, until I'm crying and
blubbering into the comforter because it hurts so bad. I swear
he's going to break me, to split me apart so completely that I'll
never be able to go back together.

But he knows. He knows just what I can handle, how many
times he can hit me in the exact same curve of my ass, before
I'm at the edge of saying, yelling, screaming my safeword. Only
then does he say, "Breathe, baby." And he flogs my ass just. One.
More. Time. And I take it, sweating and squirming, because
I can trust him all the way, even when my ass is searing and
my mascara's smearing the sheets, even when I think he's never
going to stop. And then he stops and he leans down and kisses
the tender skin, so soft I'm not sure I can even feel him, he kisses
and kisses the hurt away until I'm all blossoms and desire and
the squirm I'm doing is a different kind of movement entirely.

We left the club that night, but he didn't take me home. Not
right away. We walked instead, saying nothing, his hand on my
ass like it had always belonged there, moving with me every time

I stepped. It had rained while we'd been inside and the night was awash in damp city lights, cars that trailed white streaks through the streets and people, laughing, smoking, moving.

Everything became hyper-real, surreal. I saw it all, as if for the first time, guided by his hand, and yet I could only focus on my own breath, my blood, the heat and wet of my body. I felt as though I was drunk, stumbling and wide-eyed. Awake to the possibilities. And yet I'd had nothing more than a glass of wine at the club.

Beside me, he walked. Power. Presence.

I was afraid to look down, sure if I did my desire would be rivering down the insides of my thighs. We walked for what must have been hours, until I was unsteady on my feet, until desire was fighting with exhaustion, until I could no longer resist the magnet between us and I leaned into him, his heat, his strength.

Then he took me home. He put me into his big bed, like something out of a fairy tale, and I slept. Naked and dreaming and safe.

I didn't even know his name.

The last toy is a zester. Less than five bucks at the local kitchen store. A long tool full of little metal points. Curved in the shape of my ass. That's how many times he's hit me with it, how hard. I open the rubbing alcohol and clean its metal surface, each groove and nick.

This is the toy I like least at the beginning of a session and the best by the end. It is both sting and smack, the way it lands. It scores my ass with a million little wasp bites. I beg him to stop almost as soon as he begins, writhing in his lap as he holds me by the hair. I want to put distance between my skin and the toy, but I know that would only make it worse, and so I writhe and breathe between the swats.

"Almost there, baby," he says to me, his free hand sliding between my legs to finger my clit. Sometimes I don't even know how wet I am until he touches me, until I feel the slip of his skin against mine. "Almost there."

I believe him, every time, because he's never lied to me, because I know I can take it, because in his eyes, I become my whole and true self, my best self.

Somewhere, the pinpricks of pain become a flush, a burn, a test that I have endured and won. My ass radiates heat as though I have a fever. And the rest of me moves into a space that is beyond anything else, beyond pain, beyond the soft brush of Rob's fingers along my clit, beyond the soft mews that come from my mouth.

It's hard for me to come from spanking alone—I like a hand on my clit, too, a pair of fingers on my nipples—but this space, this space is like living on the verge of an orgasm. I ride the precipice; stay crested at the very point. Rob keeps me there, keeps me there, keeps me *there*.

And then, when he finally slides himself into me, the zester laid aside, both hands clutching my aching, burning ass to pull me back onto his cock, it is like being reborn. No, like dying and then gasping for breath again. I have lived through a thing meant to break me, and now I am being rolled over by the man I love, kissed by the mouth that belongs to me, held in arms that know exactly how to hold me down while still letting me rise.

Inventory:

Three toys, cleaned and ready. Check.

Me, in my favorite dress and nothing else. Check.

The man I love, who I've loved for a year, since he first brought me here to sleep in his big bed, that man coming through the door at any moment to bend me over his lap, to choose a toy that pleases him and to bring me to the one place that I truly want to go? Check.

When Rob opens the door, I feel the pull of his power, our power, from across the room. It never fades; it never wavers. And neither do we.

PAPERS
TO GRADE

Thomas S. Roche

Kelsi had papers to grade. We'd planned to celebrate the end of the term, but my little schoolgirl had procrastinated 'til the very last minute. The grades for Japanese Postwar Cinema were due at the University at 8:00 a.m. Thirty very unhappy undergrads awaiting their grades would be looking for her with pitchforks and torches if they didn't get there in time.

I was beat after a long day at work. I was also horny as hell and had promised her, earlier that day, a long night of sin if she got the grades in on time. She promised she would, and I'd spent the day with a bona fide throbber packed into my chinos, anticipating the curve of that perfect little ass getting nice and warm under my hand, and her snug lips—two different snug, also moist and delectable, sets of them, actually—wrapped around my cock.

Instead, she'd spent the afternoon and early evening playing Diner Dash, and alphabetizing her porn.

I wasn't having it. Undergrads with pitchforks are famously

hard to fight off when you live in a crappy new-build complex three blocks from campus. So I told her, "Sayonara, sucker!" and went to bed, boner throbbing.

I lay there thinking about Kelsi, wondering *Jerk off? Don't jerk off. Jerk off? Don't jerk off. Jerk off?*

I feel asleep.

She woke me up about three in the morning, squirming under the covers with me. Something was wrong.

She purred in my ear and woke me up. She said, "Tell me a story?"

I came out of sleep without much trouble, but I was still groggy. I tend to get boners while I sleep, and I had one in spades. I reached out for her and grabbed her and pulled her slim tight body onto me, and...something was wrong.

"What the hell are you wearing?" I asked.

She straddled me and kissed my neck and purred, and mewled, and whimpered.

"Tell me a story?

"What are you wearing?"

My eyes started focusing; they adjusted to the bedside light that Kelsi had turned on...and I saw what she was wearing. Oh, I *saw*, all right. I saw, and y'know that hard-on I mentioned? It didn't go away.

"What the *hell* are you wearing?" I repeated.

"Please, Daddy, tell me a story?"

I frowned. I sneered. I scowled.

I asked, "What kind of a story?"

Kelsi laughed, a soft whimpery musical sound that wasn't quite a giggle—far too girly for a tomboy like her. I say "tomboy," but she's always been a bit of a hesher—when she started teaching college she bought a set of schoolmarm blouses only after I convinced her that Judas Priest T-shirts were not what you wear to teach film at a major university. So what I'm saying is, my juicy little slut-cum-professor—future professor— Kelsi Greene can give you a lube job, belch the alphabet and put a .22 LR slug in a tin can at roughly fifty meters...but she's got some girly-ass hair.

And it was in pigtails.

Cute, blonde pigtails, tight and perfect.

I guess she did the pigtails to match her face. She'd done it up like a barely legal slut, the kind of schoolgirl who goes to Catholic school for one reason and one reason only: to get practice for the day she gets hired at the strip club. Kelsi had put on layers of heavy, horny eye makeup—liner, shadow, mascara— and plenty of blush. And in case whoever got to see her missed the *message of the medium*, as they say in film studies...my little college professor schoolgirl whore-stripper girlfriend had planted a slash of slutty sex across her face that didn't rightly belong there. It wasn't what I was quite sure I'd left there just a few hours ago when I'd gone to bed. It's not that it wasn't a mouth, it's that it wasn't the mouth of a college professor—or at least it wasn't *just* the mouth of a college professor. This was a mouth that said to anyone out there who would listen: *I'm a mouth. Fuck me.*

A similar thing was said by her very short, tight and mildly pleated plaid skirt. It came maybe one inch lower than her white lace-top stay-ups, and as to whether she was wearing panties underneath...well, I'd found that out. As she'd slid her thigh over me, slid her body onto me, gotten in my lap and wriggled atop me, my hard cock got a wet, smooth slick little brush from her puss that said *No, Daddy, I'm not wearing panties. Wanna fuck?*

She was freshly shaved.

Like...*freshly* shaved.

As in, she must have *just* finished shaving, and putting on slutwear and skanky perfume—slutty musk and horny flowers, like you'd expect to huff if you visited a brothel—and putting her long blonde hair in pigtails. Who the hell *does* that at three in the morning?

I'd felt Kelsi up about eleven o'clock, in an attempt to inspire my procrastinating girlfriend to get a fucking move on. I'd just kinda snuck up behind her, caught her looking at porn instead of reading papers, and leaned over her, grabbing her hair, pulling her jeans open, shoving my hand in her cotton thong.

She'd had a full tuft of snatch hair then, curly-wet and blonde, the way I loved it. I'd felt her up and fingered her a little, felt her getting wetter, felt her squirming on my finger and trying to hump her clit onto my hand. She tipped her face back and purred at my neck, and lapped and licked and kissed and bit and whimpered, "Fuck me, Daddy?"

"Are you done grading papers?"

She pouted. "No," she said miserably.

"Then not a chance," I told her. "Not until you're done."

"It'd help me focus," she whispered naughtily.

"When you're done," I told her. "I'm going to bed. Sayonara, sucker."

That was eleven o'clock, like I said, and she was *curly*. Now she was *shaved*. Nice and smooth, legs and pussy both, straddling my cock and saying, "Tell me a story."

"A story?" I said. "What kind of a story?"

She glanced down at her outfit and smiled at me, her deep red lips saying *Fuck me* some more.

"What kind do you think, Daddy? Schoolgirl's been *bad*."

She gave a giggle, then—not the almost-giggle she'd given before, not a chuckle, but a *giggle*, girly and innocent.

Kelsi did a shimmy and rubbed her sex against my cock.

She didn't let me *in* her, though it wouldn't have taken much for me to grab her and pull her and position her and shove her and jostle her into exactly the right position. But she was just *teasing* for now…in the absence of *grabbing*, we were still in the foreplay phase. And the foreplay phase, with Kelsi, can last for *hours*—quite a few of them—if not *days*. She, my hesher professor, is a procrastinator in all things.

She sat up, knees at my hips and puss at my balls, tits hanging out of her plain white blouse with the bottom tied up right under those scrawny rocker-chick teacups in their girly white lace prisons. It was a push-up number, with pink little bows, and the blouse was so thin they showed right through it even in the obscure light from the bedside lamp. When I say *push-up*, I don't mean *push-up*, I mean *motherfucking push-up*. Her steamy little teacups, short and stout, overflowed the world's sluttiest pair of tea cozies.

She bounced a little, rocking her hips, sliding her smooth-shaved pussy over the length of my cock. She moaned and looked down at me.

"Do you like my shaved puss, Daddy?" Kelsi asked eagerly.

She saw me staring back at her, not the nice Daddy but the mean Daddy. What the hell was she expecting?

I growled viciously, "Schoolgirl better define the term 'bad' for Daddy."

Kelsi looked blushy and squirmy. She decided right about then was a good time to ease her tits out of her bra and start playing with them "Don't you like your naughty girl's puss, Daddy? Don't you like your dirty girl's tits? I shaved my pussy just for you, Daddy, and I bought this bra—"

I moved on her then, faster than she could see or react to with anything more than a squeal. I moved like a boyfriend kind of lightning, like a guy who had either an undistinguished semester on the junior varsity wrestling team, or a hundred pounds on his opponent. Or possibly both. It wasn't really much of a struggle.

In no time at all, I got her pinned to the bed, faceup. Her thighs came together as she fell, and apart as the cheap bed frame protested our struggle with a tortured metallic whine and a dull thump against the wall.

She only struggled a little as I pinned her, my hands on her wrists. She stopped fighting, arched her back and spread her legs.

"Fuck me, Daddy."

"Maybe," I said. "Depending on how bad you've been. Define bad, schoolgirl. Just how bad a girl has little Kelsi been?"

I saw the real Kelsi in her face for an instant...understanding that I really was going to be mad, or at least disappointed. Mad was easier than disappointed. Hence the total blowing off of her appointed tasks to do something frivolous and stupid like shave her pussy and dress up like a schoolgirl for me. My own personal procrastinatrix follows a very strange bliss, sometimes.

She said, "I'm sorry, Daddy. I was trying to grade papers, but—"

"Stop right there," I said. "How many did you do?"

"Well," she said. "I've got thirty. I did some."

"How many?"

"Some," she said defensively.

I shook my head, knowing full well that "some" couldn't be "one," so it probably meant "two."

"Turn over," I told her.

Kelsi got a thrill in her voice. She positively whimpered as she obeyed.

"Yes, Daddy. What are you going to do to me?"

"Ass in the air."

She looked back over her shoulder at me, coquettish, looking genuinely scared.

"Eyes front!" I said. "I said ass in the air!"

"Yes, Daddy!" She hurried to comply, getting up on her hands and knees. She put her ass in the air and knelt there doggy-style, staring at the headboard.

I reached out and tried to grab her pigtails—have you ever tried to grab pigtails? It's hard to do, at least with one hand. And I needed my other hand for a task far more important.

So I grabbed the neckline of her blouse. The buttons were half undone already so there wasn't much to hold...but that didn't matter. Kelsi wasn't going anywhere.

I growled: "How many papers did you do, *Professor*?"

"Two," she said. "Well...one. I finished one."

I hit her *hard*. I cupped my hand just so to make the maximum possible noise—which I knew would shock her. She yelped. I hit her again, then again—this time flattening my hand and smacking her right on the stinging part of her ass, maybe an inch above her sweet spot. She squirmed.

I said, "Those three are for lying. Now you get twenty-nine. If you lose count—"

"I said I did two!" she squealed.

"You said you finished one!" I said.

"I *almost* finished another!"

"Fine!" I snarled. "You get an extra for pussing out early when you were almost done! Count them, Kelsi, and don't you lose count or—"

She started whining, shaking her ass back and forth. She said, "Daddy, please, Daddy, don't, Daddy, I'll be a good girl, I'll go do them right now, I'll do my papers, Daddy—"

I interrupted her with a thundering blast of rage.

"Slut!" I yelled. "If you were wearing panties I'd take them

off you and shove them in your mouth! The only thing I want to
hear from you are numbers, and—"

"Thank you, Daddy," she whined, glancing back at me, her
hips rocking in building arousal.

I said, "Precisely." Then, more loudly, I snapped, "Eyes front!
Front, damn you!"

She turned her face to the headboard and started saying,
"Yes, Daddy," but she stopped with a squeal when I spanked
her again. I spanked her hard this time, no longer interested
in making a big noise. I wanted my hesher professor to feel it,
feel how bad she'd been, how profoundly she'd disappointed her
Daddy.

"Ow! Ow! One," she whined. "Thank you, Daddy."

"Did I tell you to say 'Ow,' slut?"

"No, Daddy."

"Every time you say 'Ow,' you lose a piece of clothing. And
I'll be *very* disappointed if you finish this spanking without all
your clothes on."

"But Daddy—" she tried to whine, but I silenced her with
the first blow—or fifth, depending on how you were counting.
I swatted her *hard*.

She had to fight not to *Ow*...but she did it.

She just counted and said, "Thank you, Daddy," whimpering.

In fact, she did pretty well. I spanked her harder each time—
there was no warm-up intended, but the first round, for lying,
had served as way more warm-up than my dirty schoolgirl
deserved. I hit her hard enough to make her shudder, and whine,
and spread her legs quick when I told her to open them farther.

She made it to five before she lost it.

"Ow! Ow! Ow! Fuck, Daddy, Daddy, ow, Daddy, thank
you, Daddy...ow, ow, ow, ow, ow."

"Take down your hair," I told her. "Undo your pigtails."

She whined: "But it took me an hour to—"

Smack!

"Sorry, Daddy...ow. Ow, ow, ow, ow, fucking ow..." she clawed at the bands that held her pigtails, pulling them off and fluffing her hair. I gave her only seconds, then I started spanking her again.

"Ow! Six, six, six, Daddy, ow, ow, ow—"

"That sounds like four or five *Ow* sounds to me," I said. "But then you'd be naked. Undo your blouse."

She did, as I spanked her again. Whining, "Ow, Daddy, seven," she opened her blouse.

I told her, "You said *Ow* again, slut. Take your blouse off."

She tried to wriggle out of it, but couldn't. I spanked her hard and then helped her. She looked good in that white and pink push-up bra with her tits spilling out. She resumed the position.

I spanked her again. She whined, "Eight, thank you, Daddy," no *Ow* this time. So I hit her harder, and she gave me what I wanted.

"Ow! Ow! Ow!"

"Bra," I snarled. "Off. And one more for not counting!" I gave her two in rapid succession as she undid her bra and let it fall forward onto the pillow. Her little tits hung free, the nipples erect, as she whimpered, "Nine, Daddy," keeping her *Ow*'s to herself through ten, eleven, twelve and thirteen.

I fingered her perfect buns and watched them turning red. I touched her cunt—smooth, fresh shaved, dripping. Slit all slick with her juices, lips swollen with desire. I circled her clit with my finger.

She moaned, distracted. Then, *Wham!*, and Professor Kelsi Greene—*future* professor Kelsi Greene—whooped out a storm of *Ow*'s that shook the windows.

I reached down and pulled off one shoe.

"Fourteen, Daddy...thank—Ow! Ow! Ow! Thank—ow! Thank you, Daddy, fifteen, Daddy, thank you." I had hit her with the shoe, and now I tossed that shoe on the ground and took off the other and spanked her with it—harder, much harder.

She squealed, "Eeek! Fuck fuck fuck, ow, fuck fuck, ow, ow ow ow ow, Daddy, ow, um, sixteen, ow, ow, Daddy—ow!"

Her toes curled up in the sheer white stockings with the faint little white-on-white heart pattern. I hadn't even noticed it before. It looked so sweet as she curled her toes in pain like that...

I spanked her. Harder than ever, right on the sweet spot where her red buns could take it. She counted like a good girl, and struggled successfully not to complain or say *Ow* for quite an impressive number of very hard smacks.

At twenty-six, she broke again. My cock surged as I heard her whimpering her way through the pain...and thanking me for it.

"Time to lose your stockings, baby. Isn't this easy?"

"Yes, Daddy, thank you, Daddy." Kelsi sounded out of her mind, horny and desperate and wanting to be fucked. I knew that sound in her voice. She wanted cock...anywhere would do, but she wanted it hard and rough and fast. And when she got it I knew she'd come.

I wanted her naked first. Plus...she'd said *Ow*, like the bad girl she was.

So I eased the lacy band of one pink-bowed white stay-up down her thigh, caressing her sex as I did. She was fucking *dripping*. She was *throbbing*. I touched her clit and Kelsi nearly popped off, pushing her ass back to rub against my hand as I drew the stocking slowly down her thigh, then over her knee, which she lifted obediently. I brought the ephemeral white stocking over her calf and over her ankle and down her perfect feet and caressed her toes so she shivered all over right before I spanked the fuck out of her.

To be fair, this time she had not a chance. I spanked her so hard she couldn't have helped but yell *Ow*—I'm surprised she even managed to count. But she did; she even said, "Suh-suh-seven, twuh-twuh-twenty-suh-seven, D-Daddy, thank you, Daddy," before she started the cascade of yowls and *Ow*'s and grunts.

So then I took off her other stocking. She was naked except for the skirt.

"Just two more, girl. Can you do it? Can you?"

I caressed her butt slightly more gently, giving her several very gentle false starts, just to give her a sense of accomplishment, like she was closing in on twenty-nine, and she'd be able to handle it without breaking again.

None of those false starts connected. I was just playing with her. At times, I'm a very bad Daddy.

When I finally hit her, she screamed, "Ow!" at the top of her lungs, so loud I thought I'd hurt her for real. But while she was shivering and shuddering and moaning her way through the pain, she said, "Thank you, Daddy, thank you thank you, Daddy, thank you thank you—"

"Skirt off," I snarled. "And then get your ass up high and keep your legs spread."

She unzipped her skirt and wriggled out of it. Then she reassumed the position...spreading her legs and lifting her ass and resting on her elbows and staring right at the headboard, obediently waiting for her final blow.

What she got was my cock. I gave it to her fast, so she wouldn't have time to adjust her expectations. It's such a satisfying feeling when a naughty schoolgirl squeals as you insert your cock in a very naughty cunt. And this cunt was naughty, maybe the naughtiest part of a very naughty schoolgirl—naughty for being shaved, naughty for being wet, naughty for having distracted its owner from a more important task. Or... more immediate, at least.

Except at that moment, with Kelsi's very tight cunt, smooth and snug and dripping wet, around my cock, there was nothing more urgent than this. I fucked her deep and hard, making sure she didn't have time to get mellow and romantic about being a stripped-naked schoolgirl taking it from behind from Daddy, right after he'd spanked the living hell out of her. Romantic was not what I had in mind... if Kelsi wanted oxytocin, she'd have to look for it once I'd finished with her...and so had the university.

So I gave it to her fast, never thinking that Kelsi is as much a tomboy as I am a girlyman. I love teasing and taunting and cuddling and talking about my feelings and all that girlie shit... and Kelsi likes being banged hard and deep and humiliating with her asscheeks lovely and red against my body as I pound cruelly into her.

She came just before I did.

She howled as she came, moaning, "Please, Daddy, thank you, Daddy, I'm bad, Daddy, your schoolgirl is bad, Daddy, spank your schoolgirl, Daddy, spank me, Daddy, please spank me, Daddy—"

So I did, whacking her hard on her ass as I pumped my cock into her. I felt her pussy clenching, arrhythmically, randomly, muscles going crazy as I fucked her fast and let out a squeal of my own.

I came in her, wet and full, a load that said *We were supposed to fuck at eight o'clock*. It felt like a white-hot blast of pleasure shooting up through my body from that perfect cunt that

Professor—future professor—Kelsi Greene had shaved instead
of grading papers.

I stretched myself out on the bed, reaching out to squeeze
Kelsi's very red butt. She gasped and sighed and smiled at me,
working her hips softly and rhythmically, as if she still sort of
had a cock in there or something.

She smiled at me beatifically and said, "Thank you, Daddy."

I looked at the clock—four-thirty.

Naked, bun-warmed Kelsi cuddled up on top of me and
yawned and shut her eyes.

I said, "Don't you need to file your grades?"

Kelsi sat up and smiled at me, put her head back down.

"Nah," she said. "I turned everything in about one."

I looked at the top of her head, her blonde hair scattered
everywhere.

I said, "Huh? But you told me—"

She said, "Hmm?"

I said, "You told me you'd only finished one."

She planted her face against my chest, kissed me, yawned
and said, "Did I?"

We went to sleep.

LEAN ON ME

Adele Haze

L it only by the screen of Sam's netbook, our room seems vast, a cavern of promised wonder. I stand in the doorway, a dripping umbrella in hand, and watch my lover sleep, curled around his laptop on a too-short sofa.

"Hey," I say gently. Then, a bit louder: "Hey. Sam."

He stirs and sighs, waking, and murmurs back a sleepy greeting. As he stretches, he shuts the lid of the laptop, flooding the room with darkness.

"Mind your eyes," I say, and flick the light switch.

Not a cave of wonder, but a cramped studio apartment with mold on the walls, coffee ring stains on the coffee-colored carpeting. A sliver of London too small for two, too expensive for one. I lean the umbrella against the door, step out of my wet interview heels.

Sam unfolds from the sofa—six feet of skinny, pale boy—and comes to give me a hug. He's wearing his brother's old army jacket, an incongruous uniformed hippie. "How'd it go?" he asks, as he wraps his arms around me.

"It was fine. They're seeing more people. They'll call me. You know how it goes."

He knows how it goes. 'Round and 'round, email after email. *Dear Sir or Madam. I would be grateful if you considered me. It would be an honor to be allowed to wear a suit in your illustrious presence.* We have both been at it for weeks.

"How about you?" I ask, unzipping my smart skirt.

"Same," he shrugs. "Shall we eat? I've made a tagine."

I open my mouth to ask for details—How many new listings had he found? Had he called back that guy from the temp agency?—but instead I just nod. "Food sounds great."

He doesn't want to talk about it, and no wonder: rejection is hanging about the apartment like a roommate with bad personal hygiene, unbearable yet unavoidable. At university, we had believed the talk of our brilliance, but it's getting hard to clutch to any shred of self-esteem while choosing whether to spend the unemployment check on lunch or the Internet bill.

Chicken is cheap, and so is couscous, but spices make the meal into a treat. When I cook, I stick to bland recipes, as though punishing us for being poor. Sam may spend his days in black despondence in front of his netbook, but when he cooks, he lives, and that's how I know we are not yet lost.

Our place is too small for a table; we eat on the couch in affectionate silence, knees touching. Hungry after having faced London, I clear my plate in minutes; Sam is playing with his heap of couscous, picking out apricots.

"Eat your food properly, young man," I chide.

"Meh. I cooked it, do I have to eat it, too?" He sounds petulant.

I guess it's my turn to be in charge tonight.

"Sam, darling. You've got to finish it."

"Meh." He puts the bowl on the floor by his feet.

I know what he needs: to be made to eat, made to feel like his life is worth sustaining.

"Do you need to feel the back of my hairbrush, Samuel?"

Furrowed eyebrows, a pout to make a toddler proud. The request couldn't be clearer.

"Very well. Go and get the brush, then."

"Don't wanna."

"Sam. You know better than that."

"Fine!" He stomps to the bedside table—three paces, no more, but he makes them count—and stomps back holding my antique oak brush, the one that's kept in the drawer, and never, ever used for the brushing of hair. We both know the burn of its wood all too well.

I make him stand in front of me and reach to pull down his jeans. They've become loose enough to slide over his hips without undoing, belt and all, but I unhook every fastening, peel them down to his knees with ceremonial deliberation. He's wearing thick, warm boxers, but I leave these up for the time being, just for the pleasure of taking them down later.

"Over my knee, boy."

"All right, I'll eat," he says quickly.

"Too late. Over you go." I give his thigh a sharp swat with the brush.

He stretches over my lap, upper body resting on the sofa, boxer-clad backside elevated by my slightly raised knee. I stroke it in a smooth circle. He gives a small whimper of anticipation.

"Do you know why you're here, in this position?" I ask. My voice is quiet, in contrast with the loud crack the brush makes when it lands on his upturned behind.

"Because you're mean?" he says sulkily.

"No. Wrong." I land a few sharp swats in a row, making

him suck in air through his clenched teeth. My heart swells with tenderness. "Try again, boy."

He is silent, and I take it as a sign to step up the spanking, to make every smack count. I know what it's like to need pain, to crave the fire that washes away the day's disappointments. I grip him around the waist and apply the brush with vigor, peppering the seat of his boxers with crisp blows. He tenses and hisses, but doesn't cry out, and I take that as my cue to put some weight behind the smacks.

It doesn't take long. Whatever silent battle had been waging inside Sam's head, it seems reason has won. "All right, all right! I'm here because I wasn't eating my dinner!"

"That's right." I pause the spanking to give his behind a good squeeze. "And why is that bad?"

"Because it's not healthy!"

"There you are. You know all the right answers. Good lad."

"Can I get up now?"

"Nice try. Boys who refuse to eat their food have to finish their dinner standing up."

I grasp his boxers by the waist and work them down to just beneath the swell of his cheeks. The newly exposed skin is already pink and blotched, but I'm not quite ready to stop. I run my fingernails over the sore skin; Sam grinds his hips into my lap, hard against the soft flesh of my thigh. I tighten my hold against his waist and slap the brush down onto his exposed skin. With the protection of the boxers gone, he will be starting to feel the burn of the wood so much more keenly now. It takes three swats to make him yelp, and once he has given in, he can't stop.

"Ow! Ouch! I'm sorry, okay?"

"You will be," I say calmly, steeling my heart against his protests. "Ask me nicely to be allowed to finish your food."

"Please! Can I finish my food?"

"'May I,'" I correct him impassively, aiming my swats on the underside of his cheeks. "Try again."

"May I finish my food? Please? Please?"

"In a minute." He is playing along, but he hasn't yet surrendered, and he needs to, if he is to sleep tonight. I hold him tight and crack down the brush hard, fast and merciless against his bucking. It takes time, and it takes a certain amount of willpower on my part, but eventually his cries start to sound genuinely pained rather than merely indignant. I can hear tears in his voice. He welcomes the tears, I know, and so I spank him until he dissolves into sobs, until he lies limply over my lap, letting the pain wash away the ache in his heart.

Only then do I stop and let him cry, stroking his back in soothing circles. "Shh, Sam. Shh. There's my good boy. Hush now." His sobbing calms, and as I stroke him, I become aware again of his growing hardness against my thigh. My own sex responds with a tingle, but to drag him off to bed would be counterproductive at this stage. Instead, I stroke his flaming-hot ass and give it a fond final pinch.

"Now then, boy. On your knees, and hand me that bowl. You clearly can't be trusted to feed yourself properly, so I'm going to feed you myself."

He kneels by my feet, naked from the waist down; his face is flushed with tears, and his cock is jutting forward like an obscene figurehead. I feed him forkfuls of barely warm couscous.

He chews and swallows, and smiles up at me, his eyes still wet. "We'll be okay, love," he says quietly. "I'll take care of you. You'll take care of me."

I lean in to kiss his brow. "I know." And I guess I really do know. It will take time. We'll have good days and bad. Some days, he will lean on me; some days, I will be the one to ask for pain, and pay it back with trust and tears. And then, somehow, we will be okay.

I look at the chastened young man at my feet, and in his eyes I can see hunger of a different kind, the kind I will be only too happy to satisfy as soon as the last of his dinner is gone.

PROXY

Lucy Hughes

Zach wandered around the house with his morning cup of coffee, too restless to sit still. The place felt huge and empty without Ryan. He hadn't noticed how joined-at-the-hip they'd become until Ryan left to attend his family reunion alone. Zach had no right to be mad about it, since he'd gone home for Christmas without Ryan the year before, but he was starting to feel like a dog who'd been left at home alone too long. Pretty soon, he was going to be tempted to chew on the furniture.

The phone rang. Zach scampered into the kitchen and checked to see who was calling. Ryan. He scooped up the handset and said, "Hello, dearest."

"Hey, cutie. How's it going?" Ryan asked with a smile in his voice.

"Quiet. I think I'm going to finish painting the kitchen this afternoon." He flicked on all the lights and examined the uneven layer of sage green. "How's the family treating you?"

"It's official. Every one of my relatives, without exception, is mentally ill." Ryan sighed theatrically.

"Cool! You could start a reality show and make millions." Zach touched the wall to make sure the coat of paint he'd rolled on yesterday had dried completely.

"Hmm. Maybe I should get you to write something snappy and pitch the idea to the networks for me." It sounded like Ryan had more to say, but he paused for a couple of seconds, then changed the subject. "Did you notice it's the first Saturday of the month?"

Zach's buttcheeks clenched reflexively. The first Saturday of the month was when Ryan spanked him so hard that it hurt to sit down for the rest of the weekend. There wasn't a reason, beyond the fact that Ryan enjoyed it, and Zach liked to be reminded, on a regular basis, who his ass belonged to. Still, the break that he was getting because Ryan was out of town came as a welcome relief. "I guess I get off easy today."

"Nope."

"You're coming home early?" Zach perked up.

"No. Somebody else is going to spank you."

"What?" Zach was too flabbergasted to string a sentence together.

"Her name is Kelly. You don't know her. She'll be there in a few minutes. Short black hair. Tribal arm tattoos. Twentysomething. Super cute." His voice had a leer in it.

Zach felt something warm on his foot, and realized he was spilling his coffee. He set the cup on the counter. "You can't be serious. You can't just invite a stranger over without even consulting me and expect me to automatically drop my pants for her."

"I'm completely serious."

"I won't let someone I don't even know spank me, Ryan. That's ridiculous. Why would you even think such a thing?"

Even as he argued, though, he started to get hard thinking about it.

Ryan persisted, undaunted. "You'll do it because you do what I tell you to. I got the video chat working on my tablet thingy before I left, so I can watch."

"Um..." Ryan's total confidence that Zach would obey this unreasonable order was a huge turn-on, but the order was still unreasonable. "We both know I'll do just about anything for *you*, but this is different."

"Go downstairs and turn the computer on."

Zach headed for the basement stairs, realizing as he moved that Ryan was right about him. Again. He was a total pushover for this man. "What am I supposed to say to this Kelly person when she shows up? I can't think of a single thing that doesn't sound ridiculous."

"You don't need to say anything. You're going to answer the door with your mouth taped shut. To her, you're just a piece of meat to play with, and meat doesn't talk."

"You're mean." Zach ducked to avoid bumping his head on the low door frame at the bottom of the stairs.

"And you love it," Ryan cooed.

Zach didn't argue with that, because it was true. He turned the computer on and paced around the basement study, straightening things up while it booted. Ryan insisted that he start the video chat ahead of time. After a few minutes of Zach poking at the computer, his lover appeared on the screen, bathed in sunshine and surrounded by trees. It was a good picture. Zach could even see Ryan's freckles, and the colors of his mismatched eyes—blue and green. His light brown hair took on a golden hue in the sun.

Ryan waved. "Great! I see you now."

"I see you, too. How's the sound?"

"Good." Ryan broke into an impish grin. "Go get the tape. While you're at it, grab the paddles, the cane and the strap and bring them all downstairs. I don't know what she'll want."

"Yes, dear. You realize Hell would freeze over before I'd do this for anyone else, right?"

"I know how lucky I am. Now go."

Zach went. He found the things Ryan asked for in the trunk at the foot of the bed. For a moment he considered leaving the nastier of the two paddles in the trunk, or even hiding it so that Ryan couldn't tell Kelly where to find it. Then the moment passed, and he brought both paddles to the basement, along with the other toys. He loved feeling like Ryan's bitch too much to disobey.

According to Ryan's instructions, he laid the spanking implements out on the basement couch where Kelly would see them, then cut a strip of duct tape and gagged himself with it. *Should I change into something besides my jeans and T-shirt?* he typed in the chat window.

"Nobody cares what you're wearing," Ryan answered aloud.

The doorbell rang. There was actually a stranger at the door, ready to spank Zach without ever hearing him speak a word. He found it a little too surreal and froze in place on the computer chair. Ryan raised his eyebrows and looked at him expectantly until he got up to let the stranger in.

Before he opened the door, Zach checked through the peephole to make sure it was actually Kelly on the doorstep, not a Girl Scout selling cookies or something. Indeed, the woman was exactly the way Ryan had described her, except that "short" was an understatement. She was barely five feet tall, if that, with a delicate build. Her dyed black hair, heavy eyeliner, and black jeans gave her a bit of a goth vibe.

Ryan knew that Zach was attracted to that kind of woman.

He must be feeling awfully secure if he was comfortable sending
her over while he was gone. Where did he find her, anyway, and
how did he rope her into this? Was this her occupation, or was
she just odd? He'd have to ask Ryan later. For the moment, he
opened the door and stepped aside silently to let her in.

The woman slipped past Zach and leaned on the wall to
unlace her boots and toss them in front of the coat closet. Her
perfume reminded him of cathedral incense. "Hi. I'm Kelly.
You must be Zach," she said, with her back to him. Thin silver
bangles on her arms jangled as she worked on the laces.

"Mm-hmm." He nodded even though she wasn't looking and
studied her back, looking for clues as to what kind of person
she was. Her multipierced ears suggested that she didn't have
a conservative corporate job, but that was as much as he could
guess.

Kelly turned around and surveyed the house, peering through
the French doors to the living room, and down the hall toward
the bedrooms. "Where are we going?"

Zach beckoned for her to follow and headed through the
living room and kitchen to the basement stairs.

She trailed after him, looking around as she went, and
moving more slowly than he'd like. "You guys have a really nice
place. Kinda supports the stereotype that gay guys know how
to decorate."

Since his mouth was taped shut, he had to just take the
compliment instead of pointing out that technically, they were
bisexual guys, and the half-finished paint job in the kitchen was
the only decorating either of them had done since they'd bought
the house six months ago. "Mm," he said, and continued on
down to the basement.

Kelly bounced down the stairs after Zach and gave Ryan a
wave when she spotted him on the computer screen. "Hey, Ryan.

You really do have a cute boyfriend. Oh, and a nice collection of toys!" She skipped over to the couch to take a look.

Ryan grinned. "Tip of the iceberg. We've got a whole trunk full of trouble upstairs."

The duct tape got in the way of Zach pointing out that the trunk was actually only half full of trouble, and half full of blankets and a stuffed walrus named Ian.

"Cool. I plan to have one of those someday. I guess it'll have to wait until after I finish college and move out of my mom's attic, though." Kelly grabbed Zach by the wrist, and asked Ryan, "So how do you want him arranged so you can see?" If she found the situation at all strange, she hid it well.

"Don't worry about it too much. I know what he looks like up close, so just do whatever works for you."

Zach bounced on the balls of his feet and hummed a few quiet notes. *Perfectly normal Saturday, here.*

"Hmm. Okay." Kelly towed Zach over to the couch and shoved all the toys to one end so she could sit in the middle. "Do you have a safeword or..." She turned around and her eyes focused on Zach's taped mouth. "...Something?"

Zach shook his head no.

Kelly's forehead furrowed with concern and she looked past Zach toward the computer.

"He's free to decide not to cooperate, isn't he? But don't worry. I'm sure he'll be good for you," Ryan said.

Zach nodded. He would be good. It wouldn't be easy, but he would rather be totally humiliated than embarrass Ryan slightly by not doing what he was supposed to.

"Yeah, I guess you have a point there." She plopped down in the middle of the couch and patted her thigh. "Okay, Zach, pull your pants down and lie across my lap."

He looked down to avoid their eyes while he unbuttoned and

unzipped his jeans. Zach was finally used to Ryan knowing all his perversions, but with Kelly in the room, it was like the first time all over again. He felt them watching him in expectant silence. The blood that hadn't already rushed to his groin rushed in his ears, and his heart thudded. He gathered up his courage, and pushed his pants down to his knees.

"I think he likes me," Kelly remarked.

Ryan said something that sounded like agreement, but his quiet voice was slightly distorted by static, and Zach couldn't hear it over the rushing of blood.

Zach put his knees on the couch and started to lower himself onto Kelly's lap, but she put a hand on his shoulder to stop him. "Other way. I'm a lefty."

He stood back up, shuffled to the other end of the couch and draped himself over her lap. Something about having his pants pulled down made him feel more naked than if he'd been wearing nothing at all, and it was impossible to forget even for a moment that he didn't know this person. Kelly was half the size of Zach's stocky, powerfully built boyfriend, she smelled different and she made him lie down a different way. She slipped the bangles off her arms and handed them to Zach. "Hang on to these for me."

Zach tried to put the bangles on his own arm, but they didn't fit over his hand. He clutched them with three fingers instead—one more thing to remind him that he wasn't with Ryan.

She laid a slender arm across Zach's back and gave him a gentle pat with her other hand. Ryan made a casual remark that Zach couldn't hear well enough to understand. Whatever he said seemed to be what prompted Kelly to start spanking Zach.

At first, her tentative slaps just warmed his ass up, without really hurting him, and he wondered if he was going to get off easy after all. The spanking was only getting him more worked up. Zach squirmed and his toes curled. He tried not to be rude and hump her leg too much, even though he really wanted to. Ryan would have enjoyed humping, but he didn't know about Kelly.

Kelly's tentative slaps gradually transformed into confident smacks that hurt enough to make Zach jumpy and elicit an occasional involuntary squeak. She pressed down firmly on his back with her right arm to help keep him in place, and she started to smell like sex and breathe a little harder. Zach turned his head so that he could see Ryan on the computer screen. His lover watched them, apparently captivated, with his lips slightly parted. Zach loved the fact that both of them were enjoying themselves at his expense.

He imagined getting on his knees between Kelly's legs and licking her to orgasm afterward, tasting the excitement that she got from putting him in this embarrassing position and hurting him. Ryan could take him from behind at the same time, but for the slight problem of three hundred miles in between them.

Kelly stopped. "This is starting to hurt my hand too much. Let's see what else we've got here." Kelly pulled a toy out from under Zach's feet, but he couldn't tell which one until she tapped his ass with it. The cane. "Hmm, that's a bit of an awkward angle. Too bad. These always looked fun to me."

"Yeah, that and the strap will work better if you get him to stand and lean on something," Ryan told her, "but the paddles ought to work well on the couch."

Stuff moved under Zach's feet, and Kelly applied a paddle to his ass next, giving him a few tiny experimental taps. He couldn't tell which one it was. "You're right. This works," she said.

Curiosity got the better of Zach, so he looked over his shoulder to see what kind of trouble he was in for. Uh-oh. She'd picked up the evil one. He buried his face in the throw pillow and gripped the arm of the couch, bracing himself.

Kelly experimented with a couple of different angles.

"Go ahead. He can take it," Ryan said.

Zach pushed his feet against the arm of the couch and held his breath. The next time Kelly smacked him, it hurt more than her hand, and he flinched, but he knew that still wasn't half of what this toy could do. Eager anticipation and dread tied his insides in knots. He hated that paddle with a passion, but he also needed to feel it, and knew that he would submit to a beating he could barely tolerate, just because it entertained Kelly to dish it out, and Ryan wanted to watch. He lay there braced for it for what felt like several minutes, wondering what in the world Kelly was waiting for.

A swish in the air warned Zach that the next time she hit him was for real. It gave him a fraction of a second's warning before the spike of pain overwhelmed his senses. He squealed, because he needed some kind of outlet for the pain, and Kelly didn't seem strong enough to hold him if he struggled in earnest.

"That must've hurt a lot. It's really red." She didn't sound the least bit sorry.

Zach nodded rapidly and hyperventilated. It still did hurt, though it was tapering off toward a pleasant warm glow.

"This is a good experiment." Kelly brushed the tingly spot with her fingers. "I definitely get off on this. Even better than being on the receiving end, I think." She took her fingers away and paddled him three times in quick succession.

Each time she struck him, a fresh jolt of electric pain came with the sharp, high sound of the paddle hitting his skin. It was more than Zach could handle without trying instinctively to protect himself. He bucked and rolled halfway off her lap.

"Zach. Face down, ass up." Ryan reminded him.

Kelly helped to steady Zach as he composed himself and

resumed his original position. "Feels like he's going to go through the roof," she commented.

"Yeah. Try slowing down. You don't need to ease up. Just give him a couple seconds to get a grip before you smack him again. That will make him a lot easier to handle."

"I know that, Ryan. Been there, done that, remember?"

"Sorry."

Zach had a moment to wonder whether Kelly was one of Ryan's exes and try to decide how he felt about that before she took Ryan's suggestion and he couldn't think anymore. The new rhythm left Zach without an excuse to be uncooperative. With a couple of seconds of respite, he had enough willpower to stay with his face down and his ass up, subjecting himself to whatever she chose to inflict. That didn't mean he could hold still or refrain from yelling through the tape, of course.

After about the tenth stroke, he turned partway around to beg for mercy with his eyes, but she growled and grabbed him by the hair, shoved his head back down and kept paddling him until his skin burned continuously. He kept telling himself that he could stand to be hit once more, then once more after that, until he stopped thinking about resisting.

Zach got so lost in the task of processing the pain and allowing Kelly to keep hitting him that it confused him at first when she tried to get him to sit up. He rose, wobbling to his knees, using the back of the couch for support. Kelly hopped up and pulled his pants and T-shirt the rest of the way off, undressing him like a doll because he was too dazed to be a lot of help. "Okay, that's good. Stay there."

Zach half turned to look at the computer again. Ryan blew him a kiss. Then Zach felt the cool plastic of the cane against the backs of his legs. Kelly slid it up over his ass. Even that light touch made him gasp. He was definitely not going to be sitting

down anytime soon. Still, getting caned at the end of a session
like this, when his brain was swimming in endorphins, was one
of his very favorite things. If he could have made a request, he'd
have asked for this. He faced the back of the couch, still on his
knees, then spread his legs a little farther apart for balance and
put his head down.

Once again, Kelly gave him a couple of light practice swats
before she hit him for real. She was going for the backs of his
thighs this time. Zach willed her to hurry up and not hold back.

She laid the first stripe across his thighs and followed it with
a second before the wave of heat and pain had time to peak.
She worked her way down his legs at that rate, so it felt like the
fire was rolling over his skin. He moaned and arched his back,
trying to encourage her, but she stopped when she got close to
his knees.

Zach growled in frustration as the burn faded from his legs.

"More?" Kelly asked.

"Mm-hmm."

"One more, then, but it's going to be on your butt, okay?"
She touched him there with the cane to remind him how raw his
skin was.

He whimpered, but followed it with another "Mm-hmm." It
was insane to ask for this, but he couldn't help himself.

She gave him what he asked for: a taste of Heaven and Hell
blended together, and once it started, mercy was impossible. He
screamed and panted, helpless to do anything but ride it out. The
throbbing heat radiated through his body, and for a moment,
he got a tight feeling, almost as if it could push him over the
edge and make him come. He wanted to ask Ryan permission to
bring himself the rest of the way there, but since he was gagged,
he squeezed the back of the couch instead and let the moment
slip away. As he fell back to earth, he wanted to kiss Kelly all

over to thank her for spanking him, and Ryan for inviting her over to do it. He wanted to worship them as his sex goddess and god, and spend his life making love to both of them.

Kelly laid a hand on the back of Zach's thigh, and he shuddered with pleasure. She explored the texture of the raised welts with her fingers. "That was really intense. I bet you fuck him senseless afterward." Her voice slithered over the words.

"Always," Ryan answered.

"I hate to just walk away." Her touch wandered to Zach's inner thigh, and her fingers brushed against his balls. She withdrew her hand abruptly. "I guess I'd better get my own boyfriend, eh?"

Zach accidentally let out a disappointed whine. When he'd dropped his pants for Ryan and Kelly, he hadn't followed things to their logical conclusion, where, instead of spending the remainder of the morning in bed with Ryan, he'd be left alone, throbbing and wanting.

Kelly sighed. "Awww, sorry, Zach. I'm all worked up, too, but you're not mine." She stroked his hair.

Ryan made a soft, appreciative sound. "I'm tempted to let you fuck him senseless for me, but I might regret it later. Better not."

"Probably sensible. But if you change your mind..." She trailed off and left the carnal possibilities to Zach's capable imagination.

"I'll let you know," Ryan said.

Kelly grabbed a handful of Zach's hair and hauled him up until he was standing. "Thanks for being my guinea pig." The look in her eyes said she wanted to rip the tape off his mouth and swallow his tongue, but instead, she stood on her toes and kissed his cheek. "I'm going to burn through a lot of double-A batteries thinking about you."

"Mmmm," Zach said, for lack of other options. He felt dizzy.

She pried her bangles from his fingers and slid them back on her arms. "Maybe I'll see you again sometime." With that, she left, taking the stairs two at a time.

Zach steadied himself with a hand on the arm of the couch and listened to her let herself out the front door.

"You can take the tape off now," Ryan said.

Zach dropped to his knees on the floor in front of the couch and tore the strip of tape off. "Oh. My. God."

"Did you enjoy that?"

"Yes." Zach stared at the deep indentations that Kelly's bangles had left on his fingers.

"Me, too. Should I have let her fuck you?"

"Don't know." The question was much too complicated to think about.

"You look like you need it."

"God, yes."

"Me, too. I think actually I'm going to drive home right after dinner instead of waiting until tomorrow. I can probably make it back before midnight. Oh, and sweetie?"

"Hmm?"

"Leave these toys out on the dresser. I'll want to inspect her work when I get home and make sure you've been spanked thoroughly before we do anything else."

Zach's buttcheeks clenched reflexively. "Yes, dear." He knew without a doubt that Ryan was going to decide Kelly hadn't quite done a good enough job. No matter how many stripes and bruises she'd left on his backside, no matter how raw his skin already felt and no matter how hot that was, it wouldn't count until Ryan came home and marked his territory.

BAD BOY

Isabelle Gray

When we met, he told me he wasn't going to change. He told me he loved taking risks, loved living on the edge—the kind of nonsense women normally go for. I was at the salon where I work as the head stylist. He was dropping off his sister for a cut and color. I've gained something of a reputation as a colorist—I know what hues and tones look good on a woman's head. He tracked a slimy trail of mud and grass clippings into the salon with his big leather boots. I paused in the middle of applying a foil to a thin section of hair, grabbed a broom and made a beeline for where he stood next to the reception desk, leaning arrogantly, taking up too much space. He looked down at me with a smirk. I thrust the broom into his chest.

"What's this for?" he asked.

I snapped my fingers and pointed at the mess he'd made. "We expect adults to clean up after themselves around here."

He stepped in closer, smelling like motor oil and cigarettes and sandalwood. He was a very big man—a good foot and then some taller than me, broad in the chest, thick logs for thighs, long hair, a strong jaw, pale blue eyes, surprisingly full lips. His sister focused intently on the magazine she was reading, slowly flipping the pages.

"Is that so?" he asked.

I nodded and he laughed and that's when he explained he was a *bad boy*, the kind of man who could never change, and I told him I was not impressed. I grabbed his wrist, letting my fingernails dig into his skin, and forced his fingers around the broom handle. "I don't really care what you think you are so long as you clean your mess."

As I walked away, I gritted my teeth, willing myself not to look back. I wondered if I could smell him on my fingers. Before long, I heard the soft swish of the broom moving back and forth. At the end of my shift, he was standing in the parking lot, leaning against a motorcycle.

I held my purse tightly against my ribs as I made my way to my car.

"Hey, bossy."

I stopped and turned around, glaring. "Who the hell are you calling bossy?"

He closed the distance between us. The smell of sandalwood was stronger. His long hair was pulled into a ponytail, revealing an elaborate tattoo on the back of his neck. "I'm calling you bossy."

"What do you want, sloppy?"

He laughed. "Who the hell are you calling sloppy?"

My lips stretched into a wide smile before I could stop myself. "I'm calling you sloppy."

"I'm taking you out tomorrow night."

I looked up at him again, taking in his broad chest, admiring the way he towered over me. "I'll go out with you if you figure out where I live."

"Hey," he called out. "What's your last name?"

As I drove past where he stood, I rolled down my window. "Tick tock," I said. I reached out and pressed my hand against his breastbone, patting lightly, enjoying the warmth of his body seeping into the palm of my hand.

The next evening, I took a long shower and shaved my legs and otherwise behaved as if later, a man might be seeing me without my clothes on even though I had no intention of letting this particular man see me naked that evening or any other evening for that matter. I wore a pair of tight jeans and a silk camisole, lots of dark eyeliner, big hoop earrings, and ridiculously high heels. I enjoy being impractical. I enjoy being looked at when I know I look good. Then I waited, watching something ridiculous on television, staring at the clock every two or three minutes, pretending I did not care if the bad boy showed up. Finally, near seven, there was a knock at the door. A strange rush of energy filled my chest and spread down my arms to my fingertips. I waited until he knocked again, then stood slowly, snapping my fingers again. I snap my fingers whenever I'm angry or excited so I do it a lot.

When I opened the door, he said, "Goddamn," and let out a long, low whistle.

I smiled, raised my hand high in the air, snapped and said, "That's a good start."

His motorcycle was parked at the end of my driveway, a big old Harley, the kind that rumbled between my thighs and made me wrap my arms around him even tighter, the leather of his jacket soft against my cheek. We drove to the lakeshore as the sun was setting and sat on his bike, staring out at the shocking stretch of red and pink and orange as it slowly sank into that dark expanse of water. As the night stilled, he turned to face me and pressed his lips against mine as he wrapped his fist with my hair to hold my mouth against his. I slid my hand along his muscled thigh and it flexed in response. His tongue was warm and solid against mine. I nipped at it with my teeth and he laughed deep and low.

"I can see I'm going to have to tame you," he said.

I planted my hands against his chest and pushed him away, jumping off the bike. "Excuse me?"

"I'm a bad boy who likes to tame bad girls. I can tell you're a bad girl."

The spaghetti strap of my camisole fell down my shoulder as I blew my hair out of my face. "Who even talks like that?"

He beamed proudly and traced the line of my bare shoulder with just one finger. I resisted the urge to shiver or lean into his touch.

"What makes you think I am a bad girl?"

He grabbed the belt loops of my jeans, pulling me against him. "I can just tell."

I tapped his chin with one of my perfectly manicured fingernails. I enjoy painting myself pretty. "You have so much to learn. In fact, I don't believe you properly apologized for getting my salon floor dirty." I sank my fingernail into his skin harder and harder and held his gaze. I watched as his jaw tightened. I still held his gaze.

"Am I supposed to apologize now? Or are you trying to draw blood?"

I lightly rubbed my thumb over the dark red crescent I had made and stood on the tips of my toes, flicking my tongue against his chin. He slid his big hands beneath my camisole, brushing his lips against my neck as he murmured, "That's more like it. You like bad boys. Admit it, bad girl."

I arched my neck into his lips and then his teeth and sighed as he sucked hard, pulling at the skin. I hoped for an angry bruise in the morning. His hands slid higher until he cupped my breasts. As he was about to squeeze my nipples, I pulled away, grabbing his wrists and pushing his arms down. "You owe me a proper apology."

He offered a charming grin, one I'm certain had charmed many women before me. I noticed his dimples for the first time. The night grew darker and stiller around us. The air was cool but not uncomfortable.

"I'm sorry," he said, his voice lowering into a lazy drawl.

I looked him up and down, crossing my arms over my chest. "I'm not convinced."

He crossed his arms across his chest, too. "What would it take to convince you?"

I walked around his motorcycle, running my hand along the bike's solid curves. When I reached him again I turned him around and guided his hands to the bike seat. I pressed my chest against his back and slowly unbuckled his belt.

"That's more like it," he said.

I unbuttoned his pants and found his cock thick and hot, standing at attention. He hissed as I began stroking him slowly. I stroked harder, pressing my thumb gently against the tip, and he groaned, leaning his weight against his bike. With my other hand, I began squeezing his balls, warm and soft and heavy. He leaned into my hand.

He muttered something invoking a deity along with several curse words. Suddenly, I stopped. He tried to turn around.

"Don't move," I said.

I tugged his jeans down around his ankles and, crouching behind him, I kissed the muscled rise of his calves, the soft and sensitive spots behind his knees. His legs began to tremble. I drew my tongue against the backs of his knees in wide circles then drew a line up one inner thigh and down the other with the tip of my tongue. He breathed hard and fast. When he tried to reach for his cock, I smacked his thigh.

"Don't move," I repeated.

I dragged my tongue along the underside of his asscheeks and smiled as I felt him clench those muscles. Then I stood and began running my hand over his ass in a lazy circle.

"Are you really sorry?"

He nodded. "I'm really sorry."

"Are you a bad boy?"

"Hell, yes, I am," he said.

"I suppose I do like bad boys."

I raised my arm, and swiftly brought it down against his firm ass, rounder than I would have expected. My hand tingled pleasantly.

He tried to turn around, but I reached around and tugged on his cock once, hard.

"What part of 'do not move' are you having a hard time understanding?"

"You just smacked me."

"And I'm going to do it again. You said you're a bad boy, right?"

"Damn right," he said, his voice faltering slightly.

"Bad boys should be punished."

His shoulders slumped slightly and he chuckled. "I get your game."

I slapped his ass again, spreading my fingers a little wider. "I'm not playing a game and if I am, it would seem you like to play."

Slowly, I dragged my fingernails between his thighs and squeezed his balls from behind. He pressed back into me again.

I began to stroke his cock with one hand while I slapped his ass over and over, alternating from cheek to cheek until his ass was nice and warm. The moon had finally risen. In the dim light, I could see the pink spreading.

"You know you deserve to be punished, don't you?"

He was silent. I raised my arm high, and brought my hand down against his ass as hard as I could.

"Do you deserve to be punished?"

He nodded.

"I cannot hear you." I pressed my fingernails into his ass and dragged them roughly from one side to the other.

"Yes," he said, tightly. "Goddamnit, I do." I watched his grip tighten as he held on to the motorcycle.

"Do you deserve to be punished very badly?"

Again he was silent. I let go of his cock and squeezed both asscheeks in my hand, then scraped my nails back across the warmly worked-over flesh, leaving bright, angry streaks. I spanked him again and again and again.

"Why do you keep making me repeat myself? Do you deserve to be punished very badly?"

A strange sound caught in his throat. We were both silent and still for a moment. Finally, he said, "Yes."

"Do I hear a question in your voice?"

I slapped his ass again, then his thighs.

"No," he stuttered.

I reached down for his pants and slowly pulled his belt free from the belt loops. He groaned. I wrapped my arms around him from behind, my breasts to his back, and held him tight. He trembled against me but he did not try to move. Suddenly, he lowered his head and exhaled loudly. I kissed his shoulders and pulled away.

Carefully, I folded the belt in half, slapped it against my bare hand. The sharp sound filled the air around us, echoed lightly.

"I'm glad we understand each other," I said, slapping my hand again. "I would hate for there to be any misunderstandings between us."

"There is no misunderstanding. None at all."

I stepped a bit farther back, drew my arm back and lightly allowed the belt to fall against his ass. When the muscles flexed, I admired the deeply carved indentations on each side of his ass. I drew my arm back again, this time letting the belt fall harder. He jumped a little, but pushed his ass toward me.

"You like this, don't you, bad boy?"

He shook his head. I whipped his ass with the belt again, letting a good length of the leather sink into his skin. A white streak appeared then grew bright red. I aimed the belt for the same spot and smiled widely when a deep and guttural sound rose out of his chest and into the night.

"I think it's time for us to get serious, don't you?"

He coughed. "This feels pretty serious to me."

I slid my hand through his hair, tousling it gently.

"Baby, you haven't seen serious yet."

His head sank lower, his chin against his chest.

"Say thank you, bad boy."

Before he could answer, I brought the belt against his ass once and twice and a third time, hitting the same freshly bruising spot.

His breathing grew rapid and ragged. Each time I hit him, a new and stranger sound fell from his lips. My arm began to ache. A thin sheen of sweat spread across my forehead and between my breasts. There was so much heat between my thighs I thought I might burn. Finally, he said, "I can't. I can't take anymore."

I let the belt fall to the ground and dropped to my knees,

pressing my lips against the hottest bruises. His shoulders shook. Gently, I squeezed his thighs and whispered, "Turn around," and he quickly obeyed. His cock was as hard as it had been the entire time. Without ceremony, I opened my mouth wide and welcomed him inside me until my lips pressed against his body. He held my face softly with one hand and planted his other hand against his bike. As I began bobbing my head, wetly flicking my tongue against the swell of the head, he stuttered.

"Please," he said.

I paused, grazing the length of his thick shaft with my teeth as I pulled away.

"Please what?"

"Please let me fuck you."

"Bad boys don't deserve to fuck me, do they?"

He grabbed me by my shoulders, pulling me to my feet. He didn't answer. Instead he crushed his lips against mine, forcing his tongue between my lips as he held me so tightly against him I thought my bones would collapse in on themselves. I moaned softly as his rough, calloused hands slid beneath my camisole. He brushed the pads of his thumbs across my nipples. They instantly hardened. He rolled my nipples between his fingers, harder and harder. I leaned into his touch, offering my breasts to him. He lowered his mouth to my neck, grabbing at the sensitive skin between his teeth, tracing the small indentations with his tongue, sucking the skin so hard I thought he might tear the skin from the muscle beneath.

"I want you," he growled.

He slid one of his hands down my body, deftly unbuttoning my jeans.

"How badly do you want me?" I asked as his hand drifted over my neatly shaved mound and he spread me slickly open, teasing my clit with his fingertips.

He stopped teasing and roughly shoved his fingers into my mouth. I sucked them wetly, enjoying the taste of my desire, the taste of his.

"I want you about as badly as you want me."

I slid around him so I was standing next to the bike. After pulling my camisole off and tossing it over the handlebars, I draped myself over the seat, cool and firm against my chest. I spread my legs, arching my back so he could get a good look. I turned back to look at him, my hair falling into my face.

"You can fuck me so long as I get to punish you again. Bad boys aren't very good at learning their lessons."

He pressed his thumbs along the base of my spine and slowly pushed his hands along that curved line of bone like he was trying to push me out of my skin. His cock throbbed against the cleft of my ass and then he was inside me, stretching me, filling me. I gasped, reaching back to hold on to him, pull him deeper into me. He covered my body with his and nibbled my ear. He said, "Yes, please punish me again."

I reared back against him, rocking my hips in a lazy circle. He grabbed my hips, pressing his fingers into the skin just above the sharp edges of my hip bones. In the morning, there would be light purple bruises.

"Good boy," I said, biting my lower lip, inhaling the scent of motor oil and leather. "You are a very good boy."

MARKS

Rachel Kramer Bussel

S top it!" Emma squealed as Russell's blows with the belt went
from slaps with more noise than sting to ones that seared her
skin, ones that would surely leave marks all over her pale backside. Normally she loved knowing that he wasn't just spanking
her in the moment, but was giving her a parting gift as well,
something she tucked into her panties and skirts as she went
to work or was reminded of as she sat down at a restaurant for
lunch with a friend.

The tinge of afterglow combined with being able to admire
her ass were added bonuses to the thrill she got from being
spanked, the rush of delicious sensation that she could rarely get
enough of. Even on her most off days, when the world seemed
askew, a spanking from Russell could set her mind at ease,
could right her world. As wonderfully painful as they were, she
balked, sitting up and shifting so she was sitting on the hotel
bed. "They're all going to know." Yes, even at an alternative
venue, Emma wanted to be liked and not judged, to fit in. She

was all too used to feeling like the odd woman out for liking things like being spanked, slapped, tied up, choked and verbally degraded. She'd found a community of like-minded people who gave her the support she needed, who understood that after a long day she liked to come home and sometimes wear nothing but a collar. This was a new adventure for Emma and Russell, a welcome pleasure after eight years together.

"Know that you like to be spanked? Honey, I'm sure they can tell just by looking at you," Russell coaxed her. The idea of being "found out" in nonkinky company had always been something they'd talked about in bed, but now it wasn't having its usual arousing effect on her. "And besides, so what? We're adults and we're at an adult resort. The point is to do whatever we want. And I know you want a spanking." He was right; she did, very much so, and she knew he wasn't talking about a simple over-the-knee hand spanking, but the kind of blistering session that made them both breathless, the type of spanking that fueled their relationship and, Emma thought, kept it solid and secure.

Spanking was something they could always turn to—and did. But showing off her ass after a full round of Russell at his most vicious wasn't on her agenda. The bruises and welts he tended to leave on her pale ass were special to her, marks of her endurance she treasured with pride, but they were for her to see in the mirror or him to admire around the house. She'd wanted to come here, but she was still feeling out the crowd, and didn't want to jinx herself and be seen as separate because of her spanking predilection. Sure, most of these people maybe engaged in a few slaps before and during sex, but Emma liked it hard and rough.

"Well, it's fine for them to suspect, but I can't walk around in a nudist hotel the way I normally do, with marks and bruises all over me. It's one thing if I show off my tattoos or maybe bend too low and they see a bruise or a few lines so quickly they could almost think they imagined it, but what would these people think if they saw exactly how red you make my ass? They're exhibitionists, sure, but that doesn't mean they're kinky. I don't want to scare them." Still, even as she said the word, the idea of scaring them filled her with a sense of excitement, a sense of power. She was an exhibitionist, but she was also a perfectionist and competitive at everything she did, from her job as a party planner to finding the best-tasting coffee in town.

If she was going to do something, she wanted to be the best, and if you're at a nude resort, the goal is not so much to have the mythical "perfect" body as to score the most attention. If Emma hadn't known that when they walked in, she'd have figured it out from the parade of people, classically beautiful and not, strolling through the hotel in their altogether. The truth was, to really stand out in a place like this, you'd have to not just wear clothes but dress like Lady Gaga. Emma liked her size-ten body, liked the way it felt when she draped herself across Russell's lap, liked how her large breasts bobbed as she walked around topless, as she had last night, their first at the resort. She'd been too nervous to go bottomless, but eating dinner in public with her tits hanging out had been freeing, and exciting, and they'd both enjoyed seeing so much naked flesh, whether they were interested in touching it or not. Russell had moved his seat next to Emma's so they could whisper and discuss their fellow diners, and who they'd want to kiss or spank or fuck.

"Fine, for tonight. No marks. But I'm not letting you go to dinner until I've enjoyed your ass, one way or another. What'll it be, Em?" He was asking her if she wanted to get spanked or have him spread her cheeks and shove his cock deep into the hole he opened up there. She liked both of them, though spanking was her favorite. She'd never been spanked before meeting him save for a few light smacks, and those hadn't done what his smacks did for her. Russell's spankings were a work of art, from the way he teased her to the way he made her ass feel like it was coming alive under his hand.

When she didn't answer, he took her silence to mean she was letting him decide, and he bent her over the hotel bed, first stroking her pussy, then slapping her sweet spot, where her cheeks met. Emma used to make noise when he spanked her, thinking, based on previous experience, that that was what all men wanted, that that was what a true sub did. She'd thought that until Russell had ordered her to be quiet or he'd make her be quiet, and she'd realized that the act of suppressing her noises turned her on as much as holding off on coming when ordered to. She wasn't just a spanking slut, but a glutton for being ordered around, told what to do, made to obey automatically. Even thinking about having to ask a question, knowing Russell would get to decide the answer, made her pussy clench whether she was in line at the drugstore or just waking up.

So she stayed quiet as his hand swiftly beat her bottom, faster and faster, harder and harder. No matter how many times Russell did it, Emma found something new to enjoy about his smacks, and at that moment, if he'd dared to ask her, she'd have been so far gone in the pleasure of what he was doing she wouldn't have cared about the marks. But Russell was true to his word, and he merely left her ass burning with heat that made its way to her cunt. He ignored that, telling her she'd get fucked when he was allowed to mark her. She smiled, an ironic, secret kind of smile, the kind only a fellow submissive or intuitive dominant would understand. It was a smile of delighted denial, a smile that promised her pleasure for obeying, or the pleasure of pain for disobeying. She sucked his cock on her knees, her heels pressed against her warm buttocks, knowing they wouldn't last the whole vacation without her being marked.

And then they ventured out into their first morning at the resort. Many of the guests at this hour were wearing swimsuits or some light form of clothing, fluttering white dresses blowing in the breeze, thong bikinis nestled between tight bottoms. Emma gasped when she saw a stunningly gorgeous woman, statuesque and curvy, with a mane of glossy, beautiful honey-blonde curls tumbling over her breasts. But it was when the woman turned around that Emma's heart started to beat faster, because her ass looked like what Emma's looked like after a particularly rough spanking session. There were dark stripes of red set against an overall paler shade of pink, as if the woman had gotten sunburned and then spanked, but the otherwise pale skin surrounding the redness told Emma otherwise.

As they made their way to the buffet table, a tingle of excitement swept through Emma. There was something about being around so many naked people that made exhibitionism a whole different ball game. It was one thing to playfully flirt with having a wardrobe malfunction while on the subway, or to be the girl getting beaten the loudest and longest at a kinky play party, but when nudity was simply the norm, it made you notice all sorts of other things about people. Emma had trouble selecting from the sumptuous feast in front of them because she was so excited about having spied the woman. She didn't consider herself bisexual exactly, but there'd been a few times in her life when the sight of a stunningly gorgeous woman had made her reconsider the label, or at least made her want to drop everything and immerse herself in the woman in question.

Emma and Russell had agreed that, while they were mostly monogamous, and had only indulged with one other partner each in the time they'd been together, this vacation was their chance to be free, unfettered from their daily lives, including the constraint of monogamy. As long as they told each other what they were doing, they were free to indulge. So as Emma spooned some macaroni and cheese and salad onto her plate, she was already cooking up opening lines. She scanned the room for the woman, who was seated next to an older man with a bushy salt-and-pepper beard. "Let's sit over there," she said to Russell, who was a few steps behind her.

"Is this seat taken?" Emma asked, knowing it clearly wasn't. The couple introduced themselves as Janet and Paul, and they chatted easily, as if they weren't all sitting there topless. When Emma's hand reached for Russell's beneath the table, she also felt how hard he was, and that intimate knowledge made her squirm. She picked at her food and tried to sound intelligent as she patiently waited until there was an appropriate moment to ask Janet about the state of her ass. For all the flesh on display, it wasn't like they were at an orgy, and the chatter around her was on much more mundane topics than belts versus paddles.

Finally, they'd finished eating and Janet suggested she and Emma head over to the women's spa and soak in the hot tub for a while. "You'll be all right on your own, won't you, honey?" asked Emma. At Russell's nod, she went off with Janet, feeling her skin tingle before they'd even stripped down and planted themselves in the almost-scalding water. Emma couldn't help but ask, "This doesn't bother you? I mean, I noticed your marks..." She trailed off, hoping she hadn't said too much.

"Oh, those?" Janet said, laughing as her hair fell into the bubbling water. "Doesn't hurt any more than it did getting them."

Emma let that sink in before saying, "I like it, too. Spanking. Getting spanked, I mean." She laughed nervously. "I was actually worried about being too marked here. I didn't know how kinky a place this was. I've been to a few swingers events, and every time, kink was definitely frowned upon. I didn't want to be the odd girl out, and I actually stopped Russell from using anything too heavy this morning. And then I saw you..."

Janet stood and thrust her ass out toward Emma for her to admire. They were the only ones in the spa, and when Janet said, "Go ahead, you can touch it," Emma did, finding the woman's skin warm to the touch. She cupped her palm around Janet's perfectly, lush curve, smiling as she saw up close exactly what Janet's welts looked like.

"I can take a lot," she said. "I mean, I pay for it when I sit down, but it's worth it. What about you?" Janet was as casual as if they were talking about knitting.

"Me, too. We tend to only play to our limits on the weekends, when there's some downtime to recover."

"What about here?" Janet asked, floating across the water so she was right in front of Emma, her lower lip jutting out and her lips parting in a way that even not-so-bi Emma could read as desire. "Did you come prepared?"

"Yes," Emma said, the word catching in her throat. "We have some equipment." She swallowed, suddenly light-headed, her pussy throbbing.

"Do you only play together, or does he ever loan you out?" The way she asked made Emma's whole body tingle with the assumption that Russell owned her.

"We're allowed extracurricular activities, though mostly I'm just with him. It's so intense that...well, most other people don't tempt me. But that doesn't mean I wouldn't."

"Wouldn't what?" Janet asked as she leaned in and before Emma could even think of an answer she was kissing her, her tongue sliding easily between her lips, hot and seeking. Janet pressed herself right up against Emma, mashing her into the

edge of the hot tub. Emma gave herself over to the kiss, and to
Janet's knee pressing against her pussy.

"Wouldn't...I don't even know, actually."

"Wouldn't let me spank you?" Janet's words hung in the air.
"Just because I can take a lot doesn't mean I can't dish it out.
I don't top too often but this ass"—she reached down to grab
it—"would be an honor to spank."

Emma smiled at her, still stunned at how fast this was
moving. "I'd like that. A lot," she said, realizing that in all her
time with Russell, no one else had given her anything more than
a light slap on the ass. And she'd never played like that with
a woman. Emma was a good eight inches shorter than Janet,
petite to Janet's tall, commanding presence. From the way Janet
leaned down and sucked on her lower lip, then shifted to her
neck, sinking her teeth in, Emma had a feeling Janet would rival
Russell in her spanking ability.

They made it out of the hot tub, drying off with the sumptuous, extra-large towels. When Emma reached for a robe, Janet
tugged it out of her hand. "You don't need it here," she said,
then squeezed Emma's cheek. That pressure alone was enough
to make her twitch.

Emma thought about calling Russell on their way back to the
room, but she removed her hand from her phone. She wanted
Janet for herself, wanted to see what it was like to be spanked
by this aggressive, sexy woman, before sharing her with Russell.
The idea of Russell watching was exciting, but she didn't want
to feel like she was putting on a show, the way she sometimes
did at the play parties they attended. She liked showing off, but
only under the right circumstances.

Emma shivered as they walked, noticing the envious stares,
from men as well as women, when Janet put her arm around
her, her hand resting on Emma's hip. Emma's fingers trembled

as she inserted the key in the lock, and she took deep breaths to center herself. "Relax," Janet whispered in her ear. "I'd say I don't want to hurt you but, well...you know. I want to make you happy, though. I want to give you what you need, what you deserve, Emma. Why don't you show me your toys?"

Janet's voice was calm but inviting, almost soothing. Emma pulled out their toy box and showed Janet a fraction of the kinky implements they owned; the ones that offered the most bang for the buck and were easy to travel with. Janet held up a wooden paddle with holes in it as well as a shiny red-leather slapper and the old standby, a solid hairbrush that Emma had never used on her hair. "Do you want to get over my knee?" Janet asked, her tone respectful but, Emma sensed, not for much longer.

"Yes," Emma said, caught somewhere between nerves and confidence. She wasn't scared that she wouldn't be able to take what Janet dished out, or that she wouldn't like it. Her fears were more amorphous, more about opening this Pandora's box.

"It's going to hurt, Emma, and it's going to mark you. You have to be ready for that," Janet said as Emma settled herself across the naked woman's lap, her hair draping down toward the ground, her legs sticking out in the air. "Your safeword is *spa*." Emma committed the word to memory, testing out the start of it, the hissing of the *sp* against her lips, making sure it was nestled somewhere at the back of her mind in case she needed to call it forth. She settled herself until she got comfortable, murmuring a confirmation. And then there was the first blow, rougher than Russell usually started out with, one that startled her into paying full attention. There was no Russell, no concern about what any of the guests would think, not even, except remotely, concern about what she herself would think. Emma's focus was on Janet, on making sure she was good for her.

And that was clearly Janet's focus, too, as she praised her

with "Good girl," before using her right hand to deliver loud, stinging slaps, and then turning to the hairbrush. The blows were brisk and stern; Emma realized quickly that Janet was stronger than she looked. She wasn't tasked with counting, the way Russell often made her, and she sank into the sensation of the spanking, the feel of every blow on her skin, which was still just tender enough from earlier to feel the sensation doubly.

Emma was quiet, her quaking silent and internal, until she couldn't keep it in anymore. "Ow," she cried out, receiving a harder blow next. Her next cries weren't words, merely screams, ones that made the smacks feel even better, helping her get through them in the same way she grunted when lifting a heavy weight at the gym. When Janet cupped her hand again against Emma's hot ass and dug her long, sharp nails briefly into her skin, Emma whimpered. Janet picked up the paddle and smacked her on the border where her upper thigh met her ass. Emma knew she was getting wet, but she was too focused on her ass to care.

The next blows were even fiercer, and Emma felt tears starting to fall as stuttering moans left her lips. "Do you want me to stop, Emma?" Janet asked, pausing in her ministrations to stroke Emma's upper back. "Or should I get something else out of your toy box?"

"Something else," Emma said, her face heating up as she admitted that she wanted more.

Janet lifted Emma and placed her facedown on the bed, then slid her red silk eye mask over her eyes. "You just lie there and wait for me. Actually, spread those legs enough so I can see your pussy." Just as Emma was obeying her, she heard a fumbling at the door. If she hadn't had the blindfold on, she'd have given Janet a stricken look, but Janet simply pushed her head down and said, "Stay there, or your spanking ends. In fact, spread your legs even wider. I think Russell will want to see how pretty your lips look."

Emma sucked in a deep breath and did spread her legs. Janet moved toward the door and she heard only whispers before Janet laughed and said, "Come in, come in, you guys are just in time."

So Paul was still with Russell. "You don't mind waiting until I'm done, do you? Honey, Emma was admiring my ass—very good job, sweetie—and apparently decided she needed to match me. Beautiful, isn't she?" Janet said, and as she did so, Emma felt a blow from the riding crop greet her ass. They'd shifted from the wider heads to this crop, with its smaller, and therefore more stinging tip, one that Janet took full advantage of. The blows were more concentrated, striking one small section of Emma's ass and making her bite her lip before moving on to another equally tender spot. "Don't clench your cheeks, Emma; you won't get to really feel it that way, and I know you like to feel it. Doesn't she, Russell?"

"Oh, yes," he said, and she could hear the grin in his voice. Janet kept on striking her, occasionally making forays to her upper thighs and once or twice tapping at her pussy, which made more of the squeaking whimpers escape Emma's lips. "Want a turn?" Janet asked, handing the crop to one of the men. Emma wasn't sure which, even when the first very strong blow landed. She was too busy sucking the two fingers Janet had inserted into her mouth, pulling them as deep as she could, trying not to bite as the blows got harder and harder, ones she knew were leaving behind reminders on her skin that would be there throughout the trip. Emma sucked harder and harder on Janet's fingers as the crop kept going and going, until finally she felt it ease away from her ass, the leather meandering down one leg, tickling the ball of a foot, then pressing against her pussy in a way that made her throb.

"What do you think, Russell?" Janet asked as she eased her fingers out of Emma's mouth. Emma was grateful for the eye mask, because she wasn't sure she could handle seeing her husband and the man and woman they'd just met that afternoon seeing her in such a state.

"Stunning. My Emma's such a good girl, isn't she? I hope you don't mind, but I think I can take over from here."

"Not at all," Janet said, and Emma wondered if he was going to keep spanking her, and wondered if she could take it.

In moments, he was on top of her, his skin warm from the sun as he whispered in her ear. "You're amazing, do you know that? I had no idea you had that in you. I'm going to reward you now, baby," he said and then just like that, he was sliding his cock inside her. She didn't care that Janet and Paul were watching, not after what they'd just seen. Well, she did care, actually, she found out as she heard them kissing. She cared enough to get even wetter as Russell shifted them so she was on top and he held her asscheeks, pulling them in a way that surely bared her asshole, not to mention made her hot cheeks even hotter. He kissed her fiercely, like they'd been apart for weeks rather than hours. Emma whimpered some more as she came, the intensity hitting her all at once. Russell, who wasn't usually one to make much noise at the moment of climax, let out a roar in Emma's ear. When he went to remove the eye mask, she shook her head, keeping it on as she nestled into him, curling her body toward him as she breathed into the pillow and a few stray tears trickled down her face.

After Emma had some time to recover, they decided to head out for cocktails at the bar. The air was bordering on cool, but still pleasant enough that they could go in their birthday suits, which is precisely what they did. Emma had to resist the urge to keep reaching for her ass, feeling the raised skin, the heat that had stayed with her, stroking her flesh like it was a kinky kind of Braille she could use to read how much of a pain slut she was.

The marks were something she could carry with her, claim utterly and completely as hers. They branded her as a woman who could take a mean spanking, whether she liked it or not. Emma liked that they invited speculation, and now that she'd gotten used to it, she welcomed the stares. It was like having a particularly bold tattoo, or, in her case, five, the kind people can't look away from, yet more powerful. Their eyes, even in such a sensual setting, were drawn her way and instead of the judgment she'd expected, there was desire, admiration, respect and curiosity. She could see the questions as they were being raised on people's faces, and she liked having the power to answer them, or not answer and just let them guess.

Walking hand in hand between Janet and Russell, with Paul on Janet's other side, Emma knew they were attracting attention, all of them nude, the women with matching red bottoms. And this time she stood tall, claiming every marker of who she was, what she wanted. If anything, maybe she could be a kind of spanking ambassador and inspire some other attendees to bend over themselves. Either way, she was looking forward to the rest of the stay, and the marks she'd take with her on her way home.

ABOUT THE AUTHORS

ELIZABETH COLDWELL lives and writes in London. Her spanking-themed stories have appeared in anthologies including *Spanked, Bottoms Up* and *Naughty Spanking 2* and *3*. She can be found at The (Really) Naughty Corner, elizabethcoldwell.wordpress.com.

Called a "legendary erotica heavy-hitter" (by the über-legendary Violet Blue), **ANDREA DALE** (cyvarwydd.com) writes sizzling erotica with a generous dash of romance, which has appeared in the Lambda Literary Award–winning anthology *Lesbian Cowboys* and *Romantic Times* 4.5-star anthology *Fairy Tale Lust*, as well as about one hundred other anthologies from Harlequin Spice, Avon Red and Cleis Press.

KIKI DELOVELY is a queer femme performer/writer whose work has appeared in *Best Lesbian Erotica 2011* and *2012*, *Salacious* magazine, *Gotta Have It: 69 Stories of Sudden Sex*, *Say Please: Lesbian BDSM Erotica* and *Take Me There:*

Transgender and Genderqueer Erotica. Kiki's greatest passions include artichokes, words, alternative baking and taking on research for her writing.

KATE DOMINIC is a former technical writer who now writes about much more interesting ways to put a Tab A into Slot B (or C or D). She is the author of over three hundred short stories and is currently researching hot new settings for stories.

CECILIA DUVALLE is a writer, blogger, knitter and mother. Her work is available at Tinglemedia.com, she writes about sex and writing sexy stuff on her blog and she enjoys steamy electronic role-play. She lives in suburbia near Seattle with her husband and two children.

LUCY FELTHOUSE studied creative writing at university. Whilst there, she was dared to write an erotic story. It went down a storm and she's never looked back. Lucy has had stories published by Cleis Press, Noble Romance, Ravenous Romance, Summerhouse Publishing and Xcite Books. Find out more at lucyfelthouse.co.uk.

DOROTHY FREED is the pseudonym of an artist turned writer who lives near San Francisco with her husband and dog. She writes both memoir and fiction, and is currently working on a collection of erotic stories. Her interest in erotica came about because art imitates life.

SHANNA GERMAIN has a thing for the smell of leather toys, the shine of silver and the heated pink of a well-spanked ass. Her work has appeared in places *like Best American Erotica, Best Bondage Erotica, Best Gay Erotica, Best Erotic Romance,*

Best Lesbian Romance, He's On Top, Please, Sir and more. Visit her online at shannagermain.com.

ISABELLE GRAY's writing appears in numerous anthologies including *Fast Girls, Please, Sir* and *Yes, Ma'am.*

ADELE HAZE writes sexy stories because she doesn't know how not to. When she isn't writing fiction, she tries to educate the world about sex-positive attitudes, female gaze in erotic arts and acceptance of sexual preferences of others. For the rest of the time she models for BDSM erotica. Find her at adelehaze.com.

LUCY HUGHES lives by the Gulf of Mexico, amid the palm trees and pelicans.

JADE MELISANDE is an erotica writer, sex and relationship blogger, and all-around kinky woman living in the Midwest with her two partners. You can find her writings in various anthologies, including *Orgasmic* and *Lesbian Lust,* as well as on the net at piecesofjade.wordpress.com.

EVAN MORA's stories of submission and desire have appeared in places like *Please, Sir: Erotic Stories of Female Submission, Spank!, Best Bondage Erotica 1011, Bound by Lust: Romantic Stories of Submission and Sensuality,* and *The Harder She Comes: Butch Femme Erotica.* She lives in Toronto.

MAGGIE MORTON lives in California with her partner and their Japanese Bobtail. She has been published in *The Girl with the Million Dollar Butt, Sugar and Spice* and she has two stand-alone stories sold by Ravenous Romance, *Julie Repents* and *From Top to Bottom.*

CYNTHIA RAYNE is a multi-published author in many romance, erotica and erotic romance fiction genres including romantic comedy, bondage/discipline, contemporary, fantasy, gay/lesbian and light and dark paranormal. She was nominated for a 2006 Ecatoromance award and a finalist in the 2007 Brava Novella Contest. More information is available at paranormal-passions-romance.blogspot.com.

Eroticist **GISELLE RENARDE** (wix.com/gisellerenarde/erotica) is a queer Canadian, avid volunteer, contributor to more than fifty short-story anthologies and author of dozens of electronic and print books, including *Anonymous, Ondine* and *My Mistress' Thighs.*

TERESA NOELLE ROBERTS's short fiction has appeared in numerous anthologies, including *Best Bondage Erotica 2011, Obsessed: Erotic Romance for Women* and *Kinky Girls.* She also writes erotic romance for several publishers. She writes a lot about spanking and the ocean, but rarely about both at once.

THOMAS S. ROCHE's debut novel, *The Panama Laugh,* is a zombie apocalypse that's been compared to Jim Thompson and Hunter S. Thompson. He is a widely published author of sex-positive erotica and an occasional purveyor of horror and crime-noir short stories, and blogs at ThomasRoche.com and many other blogs.

ELIZABETH SILVER is an erotic romance author, a self-proclaimed Internet junkie, an editor and an international woman of mystery. She can be found writing in diners, libraries and coffee shops, either working happily or blogging polyamorously at various places, including her website at UrbanSilver.net.

J. SINCLAIRE is a Toronto-based writer by profession but erotic by nature. Her work has appeared in anthologies such as *Lips Like Sugar*, *Got a Minute?* and *The Happy Birthday Book of Erotica*. A firm believer that sex and masturbation are both healthy and necessary, she considers it her civic duty to write smut. The rest is up to you.

CRAIG J. SORENSEN used to sneak peeks into his parents' closet when Christmas approached. It took years for him to learn the true joy of anticipation, which he loves to distill into his short stories. His works have appeared in numerous anthologies and periodicals. Visit him at just-craig.blogspot.com.

DONNA GEORGE STOREY is the author of *Amorous Woman*, a steamy novel about an American woman's love affair with Japan. Her short fiction has appeared in numerous journals and anthologies including *Spanked, Bottoms Up, Obsessed, Penthouse* and *Best Women's Erotica*. Read more of her work at www.DonnaGeorgeStorey.com.

ABOUT
THE EDITOR

RACHEL KRAMER BUSSEL (rachelkramerbussel.com) is a New York–based author, editor and blogger. She has edited over forty books of erotica, including *Going Down; Irresistible; Best Bondage Erotica 2011* and *2012; Gotta Have It; Obsessed; Women in Lust; Her Surrender; Orgasmic; Bottoms Up: Spanking Good Stories; Spanked: Red-Cheeked Erotica; Naughty Spanking Stories from A to Z 1* and *2; Fast Girls; Smooth; Passion; The Mile High Club; Do Not Disturb; Going Down; Tasting Him; Tasting Her; Please, Sir; Please, Ma'am; He's on Top; She's on Top; Caught Looking; Hide and Seek; Crossdressing; Rubber Sex; Anything for You* and *Suite Encounters.* She is *Best Sex Writing* series editor, and winner of 6 IPPY (Independent Publisher) Awards. Her work has been published in over one hundred anthologies, including *Best American Erotica 2004* and *2006;* Zane's *Chocolate Flava 2* and *Purple Panties; Everything You Know About Sex Is Wrong; Single State of the Union* and *Desire: Women Write*

About Wanting. She wrote the popular "Lusty Lady" column for the *Village Voice.*

Rachel has written for *AVN, Bust,* Cleansheets.com, *Cosmopolitan, Curve,* The Daily Beast, Fresh Yarn, TheFrisky. com, *Glamour,* Gothamist, Huffington Post, *Inked,* Mediabistro, *Newsday, New York Post, Penthouse, Playgirl, Radar,* The Root, Salon, *San Francisco Chronicle, Time Out New York* and *Zink,* among others. She has appeared on "The Gayle King Show," "The Martha Stewart Show," "The Berman and Berman Show," NY1 and Showtime's "Family Business." She hosted the popular In the Flesh Erotic Reading Series (inthefleshreadingseries.com), featuring readers from Susie Bright to Zane, and speaks at conferences, does readings and teaches erotic writing workshops across the country. She blogs at lustylady.blogspot.com.

More from Rachel Kramer Bussel

Buy 4 books, Get 1 *FREE* *

Do Not Disturb
Hotel Sex Stories
Edited by Rachel Kramer Bussel
A delicious array of hotel hookups where it seems like anything can happen—and quite often does. "If *Do Not Disturb* were a hotel, it would a 5-star hotel with the luxury of 24/7 entertainment available."—Erotica Revealed
978-1-57344-344-9 $14.95

Bottoms Up
Spanking Good Stories
Edited by Rachel Kramer Bussel

As sweet as it is kinky, *Bottoms Up* will propel you to pick up a paddle and share in both pleasure and pain, or perhaps simply turn the other cheek.
ISBN 978-1-57344-362-3 $14.95

Orgasmic
Erotica for Women
Edited by Rachel Kramer Bussel

What gets you off? Let *Orgasmic* count the ways...with 25 stories focused on female orgasm, there is something here for every reader.
ISBN 978-1-57344-402-6 $14.95

Please, Sir
Erotic Stories of Female Submission
Edited by Rachel Kramer Bussel

These 22 kinky stories celebrate the thrill of submission by women who know exactly what they want.
ISBN 978-1-57344-389-0 $14.95

Fast Girls
Erotica for Women
Edited by Rachel Kramer Bussel

Fast Girls celebrates the girl with a reputation, the girl who goes all the way, and the girl who doesn't know how to say "no."
ISBN 978-1-57344-384-5 $14.95

Red Hot Erotic Romance

Obsessed
Erotic Romance for Women
Edited by Rachel Kramer Bussel

These stories sizzle with the kind of obsession that is fueled by our deepest desires, the ones that hold couples togeth-er, the ones that haunt us and don't let go. Whether just-blooming passions, rekindled sparks or reinvented relation-ships, these lovers put the object of their obsession first.
ISBN 978-1-57344-718-8 $14.95

Passion
Erotic Romance for Women
Edited by Rachel Kramer Bussel

Love and sex have always been intimately intertwined—and *Passion* shows just how delicious the possibilities are when they mingle in this sensual collection edited by award-winning author Rachel Kramer Bussel.
ISBN 978-1-57344-415-6 $14.95

Girls Who Bite
Lesbian Vampire Erotica
Edited by Delilah Devlin

Bestselling romance writer Delilah Devlin and her contributors add fresh girl-on-girl blood to the pantheon of the paranormal. The stories in *Girls Who Bite* are varied, un-expected, and soul-scorching.
ISBN 978-1-57344-715-7 $14.95

Irresistible
Erotic Romance for Couples
Edited by Rachel Kramer Bussel

This prolific editor has gathered the most popular fantasies and created a sizzling, no-holds-barred collection of explicit encoun-ters in which couples turn their deepest desires into reality.
978-1-57344-762-1 $14.95

Heat Wave
Hot, Hot, Hot Erotica
Edited by Alison Tyler

What could be sexier or more seductive than bare, sun-warmed skin? Bestselling erotica author Alison Tyler gathers explicit stories of summer sex bursting with the sweet eroticism of swimsuits, sprinklers, and ripe strawberries.
ISBN 978-1-57344-710-2 $15.95

Erotica for Every Kink

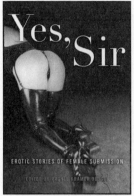

Yes, Sir
Erotic Stories of Female Submission
Edited by Rachel Kramer Bussel

The lucky women in *Yes, Sir* give up control to irresistibly powerful men who understand that dominance is about exulting in power that is freely yielded.
ISBN 978-1-57344-310-4 $15.95

Best Bondage Erotica
Edited by Alison Tyler

Always playful and dangerously explicit, these arresting fantasies grab you, tie you down, and never let you go.
ISBN 978-1-57344-173-5 $15.95

Best Bondage Erotica 2
Edited by Alison Tyler

From start to finish, these stories of women and men in the throes of pleasurable restraint will have you bound to your chair and begging for more!
ISBN 978-1-57344-214-5 $16.95

Spanked
Red Cheeked Erotica
Edited by Rachel Kramer Bussel

"Editrix extraordinaire Rachel Kramer Bussel has rounded up twenty brisk and stinging tales that reveal the many sides of spanking, from playful erotic accent to punishing payback for a long ago wrong."—Clean Sheets
ISBN 978-1-57344-319-7 $14.95

Rubber Sex
Edited by Rachel Kramer Bussel

Rachel Kramer Bussel showcases a world where skin gets slipped on tightly, then polished, stroked, and caressed—while the bodies inside heat up with lust.
ISBN 978-1-57344-313-5 $14.95

Fuel Your Fantasies

Carnal Machines
Steampunk Erotica
Edited by D. L. King

In this decadent fusing of technology and romance, out-standing contemporary erotica writers use the enthrall-ing possibilities of the 19th-century steam age to tease and titillate.
ISBN 978-1-57344-654-9 $14.95

The Sweetest Kiss
Ravishing Vampire Erotica
Edited by D.L. King

These sanguine tales give new meaning to the term "dead sexy" and feature beautiful bloodsuckers whose desires go far beyond blood.
ISBN 978-1-57344-371-5 $15.95

The Handsome Prince
Gay Erotic Romance
Edited by Neil Plakcy

A bawdy collection of bedtime stories brimming with classic fairy tale charac-ters, reimagined and recast for any man who has dreamt of the day his prince will come. These sexy stories fuel fantasies and remind us all of the power of true romance.
ISBN 978-1-57344-659-4 $14.95

Daughters of Darkness
Lesbian Vampire Tales
Edited by Pam Keesey

"A tribute to the sexually aggressive woman and her archetypal roles, from nurturing goddess to dangerous preda-tor."—*The Advocate*
ISBN 978-1-57344-233-6 $14.95

Dark Angels
Lesbian Vampire Erotica
Edited by Pam Keesey

Dark Angels collects tales of lesbian vampires, the quintessential bad girls, archetypes of passion and terror. These tales of desire are so sharply erotic you'll swear you've been bitten!
ISBN 978-1-57344-252-7 $13.95

Best Erotica Series

"Gets racier every year."—*San Francisco Bay Guardian*

Best Women's Erotica 2012
Edited by Violet Blue
ISBN 978-1-57344-755-3 $15.95

Best Women's Erotica 2011
Edited by Violet Blue
ISBN 978-1-57344-423-1 $15.95

Best Women's Erotica 2010
Edited by Violet Blue
ISBN 978-1-57344-373-9 $15.95

Best Bondage Erotica 2012
Edited by Rachel Kramer Bussel
ISBN 978-1-57344-754-6 $15.95

Best Bondage Erotica 2011
Edited by Rachel Kramer Bussel
ISBN 978-1-57344-426-2 $15.95

Best Fetish Erotica
Edited by Cara Bruce
ISBN 978-1-57344-355-5 $15.95

Best Lesbian Erotica 2012
Edited by Kathleen Warnock. Selected and
introduced by Sinclair Sexsmith.
ISBN 978-1-57344-752-2 $15.95

Best Lesbian Erotica 2011
Edited by Kathleen Warnock.
Selected and introduced by Lea DeLaria.
ISBN 978-1-57344-425-5 $15.95

Best Lesbian Erotica 2010
Edited by Kathleen Warnock.
Selected and introduced by BETTY.
ISBN 978-1-57344-375-3 $15.95

Best Gay Erotica 2012
Edited by Richard Labonté. Selected and
introduced by Larry Duplechan.
ISBN 978-1-57344-753-9, $15.95

Best Gay Erotica 2011
Edited by Richard Labonté.
Selected and introduced by Kevin Killian.
ISBN 978-1-57344-424-8 $15.95

Best Gay Erotica 2010
Edited by Richard Labonté. Selected and
introduced by Blair Mastbaum.
ISBN 978-1-57344-374-6 $15.95

In Sleeping Beauty's Bed
Erotic Fairy Tales
By Mitzi Szereto
ISBN 978-1-57344-367-8 $16.95

Can't Help the Way That I Feel
Sultry Stories of African American Love
Edited by Lori Bryant-Woolridge
ISBN 978-1-57344-386-9 $14.95

Making the Hook-Up
Edgy Sex with Soul
Edited by Cole Riley
ISBN 978-1-57344-3838 $14.95

★ **Free book of equal or lesser value. Shipping and applicable sales tax extra.**
Cleis Press • (800) 780-2279 • orders@cleispress.com
www.cleispress.com

Ordering is easy! Call us toll free or fax us to place your MC/VISA order.
You can also mail the order form below with payment to:
Cleis Press, 2246 Sixth St., Berkeley, CA 94710.

Buy 4 books,
Get 1 *FREE**

ORDER FORM

QTY	TITLE	PRICE
_____	_____	_____
_____	_____	_____
_____	_____	_____
_____	_____	_____
_____	_____	_____
_____	_____	_____
_____	_____	_____

SUBTOTAL _____

SHIPPING _____

SALES TAX _____

TOTAL _____

Add $3.95 postage/handling for the first book ordered and $1.00 for each additional
book. Outside North America, please contact us for shipping rates. California residents
add 8.75% sales tax. Payment in U.S. dollars only.

* Free book of equal or lesser value. Shipping and applicable sales tax extra.

Cleis Press • Phone: (800) 780-2279 • Fax: (510) 845-8001
orders@cleispress.com • www.cleispress.com
You'll find more great books on our website

Follow us on Twitter @cleispress • Friend/fan us on Facebook